I0618941

Deceased DORA

A MUST-READ NOVEL IN
THE DEMON DIARIES

CLAIRE CHILTON

First published in Great Britain by Ragz Books 2013

This edition published by Ragz Books 2017

Published in Great Britain by Ragz Books

ISBN-10: 1908822287
ISBN-13: 978-1908822284

Bibliography
Wilde, Oscar. (2000).
The Plays of Oscar Wilde.
Hertfordshire, Wordsworth Editions Limited.

MORE BOOKS

THE DEMON DIARIES
A Hint of Magic
Bewitched by Magic

Demonic Dora
Bewitched in Hell

Deceased Dora
Bewitched in Death

Divine Dora
Bewitched in Heaven

A Hint of Hell
Bewitched by Christmas

DEDICATIONS

I dedicate this book to JJ for being the inspiration for many of the characters, most importantly Lucian. The world really did move!

ACKNOWLEDGEMENTS

I'd like to thank all my wonderful friends for keeping me laughing over the years. Without you, I wouldn't see the world in the same way.

But mostly, I'd like to thank all my amazing fans. Without you, these books would not exist. Thank you for continuing to read my stories, thank you for patiently waiting for the next one, thank you for voting for my books and thank you for making me smile every time you leave a comment or a review.

"Every saint has a past, and every sinner has a future."
 – *A Woman of No Importance*
The Plays of Oscar Wilde
Oscar Wilde (2000) p256..

STAYING ALIVE

Dora Carridine fidgeted in her coffin. She had been staring into the darkness for what seemed like forever. She tried to stretch her legs, but the casket left little room for movement, so she attempted to rub some feeling back into her numb ass instead. She moved her hand towards her hip, and her elbow collided with the side of the coffin causing her to yelp in pain.

Oww! Not the funny bone.

She tried to sit up in a reflexive motion and smacked her forehead against the coffin lid, which caused her to slump back onto the not-so-soft burial pillow.

She lay on her back and stared up into the darkness while exhaling a sigh.

Perfect! What the hell am I supposed to do about this nightmare?

She didn't know how long she'd been in here for, but it seemed like a long time, and it was bloody boring.

She'd tried everything she could think of to deal with

the situation, but there weren't any guidelines for being thrown out of Hell and into a grave.

As a wave of panic washed over her, she banged her fists against the inside of the casket. The air was stale, and it was becoming increasingly difficult to breathe. Surrounded by suffocating darkness and confined in such a small space, she feared she would never get out of here.

She didn't know how long she'd been alone in the darkness, but it felt like a long time. She called for help, but no one had heard her. If they had, they'd ignored it.

She slammed another fist into the wooden lid, trying to break through it.

What happens if I die here? Will I be stuck here forever?

It had only recently dawned on her that being exiled from Hell didn't leave her many options after death.

Is this my punishment for being thrown out of Hell and for choosing to go there in the first place? Am I doomed to die and be stuck in this coffin forever?

"No!" She shouted as she drove her fist into the wood again with as much force as she could muster. The lid finally splintered under the pressure, and moist earth fell through the cracks onto her body.

She rubbed her arms to brush away the dirt, and then frowned. She paused and felt her arms. They were fluffy.

What the hell am I wearing?

It was pitch black inside the coffin. It didn't feel as if anything existed but her.

Her muscles ached after prolonged confinement. She could feel the wooden casket surrounding her, and she could smell the earth surrounding the burial box. However, without being able to see anything, not even her own hand in front of her face, she wondered if she was imagining it all.

One thing was certain, she didn't feel normal. She didn't feel human.

She brushed her fingers down her body to try to work out what she was wearing. It was some kind of silky dress that she didn't recognize. The sound of her fingers rustling the material seemed so loud in the cloying silence, but then all of her senses seemed to be extra alert in the dark.

The soil was still sifting through the splintered wood of the casket lid and landing on the material covering her arms and body. She could feel every grain, and she was sure she could hear them landing on her too.

Is that normal?

She exhaled slowly. The air seemed thinner.

I have to get out of here. I promised Kieron I would find him.

She frowned again. If she was in a coffin, where had Kieron and Pooey been exiled to? Were they suffocating in graves too?

The last thing she remembered before landing here was being sucked into a portal here from the arena in Hell. They had been sucked in with her, but a force had pulled them away from her, and she had landed here alone.

I have to find them. Two demons on Earth are bound to get into trouble.

Visions of Kieron flying across the major cities with his newly found angel wings, and being shot down by local authorities filled her mind.

A demon-angel probably won't fly under the radar here.

With renewed vigor, she clawed at the splinters of

3

wood, ripping them apart and creating a hole in the coffin lid. Mud poured through the gap, rapidly filling the casket.

She tightly closed her mouth and eyes while pushing herself upwards through the broken lid and into the loose soil. She clawed and forced herself through the earth, determined to get up to ground level.

Cold dirt pressed against her face and body, chilling her to the bone. She struggled for air as her last breath slowly escaped her lungs. Using her arms and legs, she punched and kicked her way through the soil, desperately trying to escape her own grave.

If I die like this, I'll be a unique archeological discovery in a few thousand years.

She frowned as she found herself standing in a superhero pose with one fist punching through the soil above her, and her body encased in a muddy cage.

Her lungs ached for air, and her throat burned. She began to panic.

No! Come on, this can't be how I die.

She tensed every muscle in her body and punched up through the earth again, willing her body to rise from her grave.

Theodore Carridine stared at his daughter's grave. He frowned at the wilting roses around the newly laid headstone.

She had been doomed from the start. Even at an early age, she had chosen the wrong path. It had been heartbreaking and a relief at the same time when she had

4

died.

He loved his Dora. Regardless of the path she had chosen in life, she would always be his little girl, but he'd known he couldn't save her.

She had been on life support in Berkville General Hospital for months before they had finally made the decision to disconnect her last week.

The funeral had been respectable. He didn't know what he would have done without the support of his congregation.

He still hadn't come to terms with her death. Watching her body being lowered into the ground had made him question his faith, but he was a man of God.

He raised his chin and stood proud. Above all else, he had his faith, faith that she was in a better place, faith that everything happened for a reason and faith that he had done the right thing by exorcizing out her demons.

He leaned over her grave and laid a single white rose on it for his little girl.

"Rest now, Dora. Nothing can hurt you anymore."

A dirtied hand shot through the earth and gripped his wrist. He stared at the mud-caked nails in horror as the pale, cold fingers tightened around his wrist in an iron grip.

He let out a high-pitched scream, which would have made any little girl proud. He tried to dislodge the hand by pulling away from it, but the grip was solid.

As he backed away in terror, he unwillingly dragged the deathly pale body attached to it with him. First an arm, and then a shoulder until finally a face he knew all too well popped up through the earth and stared at him with her soulful dark eyes.

"Dad, what the fuck? You buried me?" Dora said.

"No!" Dora heard her father shriek. She squinted, trying to make her eyes focus on him as he scrambled backwards.

"Stay back demon!" her father cried.

Her vision was still a bit fuzzy, but she could see him fumble for the crucifix hanging around his neck before he fell backwards over the gravestone behind him in a failed attempt to ward her off.

She shook her head.

My dad, the hero

She struggled to pull herself out of her grave. She clawed at the earth around her and hauled her body out of the muddy hole.

Once free of the earth, she stood up and took a deep breath of fresh air. Her lungs didn't seem to ache for it any more. They didn't seem to do anything at all. She slowly exhaled. Air whooshed out, but she didn't feel the need to inhale again afterwards.

What the hell?

She frowned and stood completely still, not breathing or moving. Something weird was going on. Her lungs should be burning by now, shouldn't they?

She stared around the graveyard and winced. It seemed so bright outside of her grave. It was nighttime. She could tell because the moon was high in the sky.

Why is it so bright?

She covered her eyes with her hands.

What the fuck? Is Dad using floodlights in here now?

6

She rubbed her eyes, and then slowly opened them again, trying to focus on her own feet. It was hazy at first, and then her focus seemed to sharpen. She could see a pair of cute white slippers on her feet. They were made of silk, but tarnished with streaks of mud. On her legs, she wore white pantyhose that were ripped and muddy after her escape from her final resting place.

She groaned as she peered at her dress. A white high-necked dress ended at her knees. It would have been the perfect outfit for a little girl.

She plucked some of the skirt material between her fingers and stared at it in distaste.

"You've gotta be fucking kidding me."

Then she stared at her wrist and nearly flipped out when she saw a pearl bracelet hanging around it, and worse—the sleeve of a fluffy white cardigan!

"Back demon!"

She glanced up to see her father standing before her. He was trembling and cowering behind his crucifix.

"Pearls?" She angrily shook her wrist at him, "A fucking cardigan and pearls! What did you do to me? I swear to Sata—" She paused as she felt something brush against her face.

"Oh no, you didn't." She cautiously ran her fingers over her hair, encountering an array of ringlets and bows. "Fucking ringlets!" she shouted while pulling bows out of her hair.

"Agh! B-back, get back d-demon." Her father backed away from her, his body trembling.

She purposefully strode towards him. She was fuming with anger. It was bad enough being buried alive, but being dressed like a China doll in her final hours—that was the limit.

"No." He squeaked as she neared him, and he stumbled backwards.

"Demon!" he cried before he turned and fled.

"Yeah, so what?" she shouted as she ran after him.

He stumbled and fell as he ran from her, quickly scrambling to his feet before taking off running again.

For some reason the more he ran, the more she wanted to chase him.

"Rawrrr!" she cried and raised her hands in the air as she ran after him.

He flung himself over the perimeter fence and fell face-forward into the adjoining field, which unfortunately for him was farmland that smelled as if it had been recently fertilized with manure.

"Brainssss!" she cried. She didn't really want his brains. She just wanted to make him shit his pants.

"Ohmigod!" She heard her father cry out in panic when he glanced back and realized she was still chasing him. He turned and sprinted across the field.

She finally stopped following her father and bent over laughing as he scrambled through horse shit to get away from her. When the laughter subsided, she wiped a stray tear from her eye.

That was just great!

Once her father was gone, her laughter subsided. She sat on the fence that bordered the graveyard, staring up at the moon and trying to figure out what to do next.

As she scanned the rows of gravestones and the ancient family crypts behind them, she realized that Kieron and

Pooey could be anywhere, but this was as good a place as any to start looking.

She eyed the graves.

How am I going to find Kieron and Pooey if they are buried here?

2

THE PEASANTS ARE REVOLTING

"**G**rave robber!" Dora heard someone shout behind her, and she paused trying to dig up the grave.

Shit!

She glanced back, overcome with a strange feeling of déjà vu when she saw a group of angry townsfolk glaring at her. Some were carrying torches, others halogen lanterns. Most were wearing their nightwear. A small cluster from the rambler's club were kitted out in outdoor wear, breathable jackets and fleeces

She released the clump of mud she held in her hands.

"I can explain this." She told them.

"Zombie!" one woman cried, and she waved her Maglite in outrage.

"Are you calling me brain dead?" Dora scowled at her.

"Kill the vampire bitch." An angry farmer shook his pitchfork at her.

"Do I look fucking sparkly to you?" she snapped. She knew she looked a mess. She'd been wandering around the graveyard for hours trying to figure out if Kieron or Pooey were there. She'd called their names over and over again and even listened to the ground to try and hear them. But in the end, the only option had been to start digging up graves.

She'd only managed to start on one and hadn't gotten very far by using her hands to dig it up.

I'm sure I heard a sound coming from this one though.

"Only the good and sexy vampires are sparkly." A pre-pubescent girl interrupted her thoughts.

"And they call me a bitch," Dora muttered.

"Kill the vampire!" The group of ramblers cried in unison.

"I'm not a bloody vampire."

"Bloodless fiend!" She recognized the old lady who had shouted that. It was Alice Wainwright from her mother's sewing circle.

"Hey Alice, have you seen my mom?"

"Out damn demon!"

Dora groaned as she recognized her father's voice. "I'm not a fucki—"

Someone threw a Molotov cocktail into the hole she was standing in, and she stared down are the burning bottle.

"What the he—" The material wick burned into the bottle of gasoline, and then the bottle exploded in a burst of fire. Hot air whooshed past her face, and she panicked before she realized she couldn't feel anything burning.

She shrugged and climbed out of the fiery hole, untouched by the flames and brushing soil off her dress.

"What the hell was that for?"

"Oh my God, she won't burn!" one of the ramblers cried. He dropped his torch and spun on his heel before fleeing towards the gates of the graveyard.

She wondered why she hadn't burned, but it didn't seem as important as dealing with the angry mob in front of her, so she put the thought to the back of her mind.

"Cut her head off," a voice cried.

She blinked.

They wouldn't really try to cut my head off would they?

But given her past experiences with the stupidity of the townspeople of Berkville, she realized that they probably would try cutting her head off.

She held up her hands as two men rushed towards her, both carrying axes.

"Wait!"

They paused and stared at her with blank expressions.

Okay, stupid I can handle. This is good.

"Have those been certified?" She nodded at the axes.

"Huh?" One of them managed, displaying a blank expression.

"Well, what I mean to say is that cutting something's head off is listed as inhumane under the farming regulations isn't it?"

The first man, who was a farmer judging by his rather unattractive dungarees and the straw hat he was wearing, peered at his ax in contemplation.

"Yes, ma'am." He nodded.

"So has that ax been certified as a humane culling implement?" She knew she was spewing out bullshit, but whatever kept her head attached to her neck was good in

12

her book.

"Er?" The farmer blankly stared at the ax again, appearing to contemplate the question.

"Well Doug, has it been certified?" She heard Police Chief Dawson ask.

Doug shook his head. "No, Sir. We have to shoot the pigs with a stunner for them there humane laws."

He turned to face Dora. "Although I think the pigs don't much give a shit. Dead is dead, right?" he said in a confidential tone.

She nodded with as much fake sympathy as she could muster towards Doug. "It's a shame everything is so regulated these days."

"I know, right?" he replied. "If you want happy pigs, don't kill 'em. I dunno why everything has to be so complicated."

"I totally agree with you, Doug. Just save yourself the hassle and don't kill any pigs," she said.

"But then who's going to bring home the bacon?" he asked.

She shrugged. "You ever tried Quorn?"

Doug seemed to consider her suggestion before nodding. "You know, you might be right. I'll look into having one of them there Quorn farms, instead."

"I'm sure the pigs will be much happier if you do." She smiled at him.

"Let's shoot her then." Police Chief Dawson suggested as he pulled his gun out of the holster at his hip.

Aww shit.

"I'll have to go get my bolt gun, Chief. You can't just shoot her with any old gun. It's in the regulations," Doug said before he turned to Dora with a sympathetic smile. "You won't feel a thing, honey."

She smiled brightly and nodded at him.

Too fucking right I won't. I won't be here when you get back, Idiot!

She watched Doug sprint off towards the gates of the graveyard to get his bolt gun while she considered her options.

Who else was stupid enough to go and get something? If she could thin the group, she could probably make a run for it.

While thinking about graveyard regulations, she heard a weird noise coming from the nearby grave.

"What's that noise?" Chief Dawson asked.

"You can hear it too?" She glanced down at the grave.

"Yeah, it's like ..." He paused as he holstered his gun, and then scratched his head. "Is that singing?"

She listened closely and realized he was right. It was muffled and grossly out of tune, but it was singing, and it was coming from the grave.

"Kieron!" she cried. It must be Kieron. Who else would be singing in a grave?

She leapt into the hole and began digging with her hands again.

"Hey, stop doing that!" The chief cried.

She glanced over her shoulder to see him drawing his gun again.

"No, listen. There's someone in here."

The police chief holstered the weapon and drummed his fingers on the handle of it, appearing deep in thought. After a few minutes of contemplation, he turned to the crowd of townspeople.

"She's right. There is someone singing in there. Hal, go fetch some spades. We need to dig this guy out of here."

Hal turned out to be the overweight groundskeeper of the graveyard. He nodded before dashing towards his hut behind the family crypts.

"Step out of there, little lady. We'll sort this out." The chief told her, offering her his hand and stepping towards the grave.

"Don't go running off anywhere though. We still need to shoot you in the head," he added sternly.

She took the offered hand, allowing the chief pull her out of the pit. She stood near the edge of it, nodding in awe of ridiculousness of the situation.

These people are fucking idiots.

Hal came back panting, and both he and the chief jumped down into the pit, brandishing spades. The chief took off his jacket, rolling his sleeves up his muscular arms before beginning to dig up the singing coffin below them.

She peered around. Everyone was staring into the pit.

I could just make a run for it, but what if it is Kieron inside the coffin.

She realized she would have to wait to find out, shaking her head at her own stupidity.

The deeper the two men dug, the clearer it became that the singer was not Kieron. The voice was high-pitched.

"Come into the garden, Maud." The voice trilled. It sounded like an old music hall song.

Even Kieron isn't that old.

After several minutes, the unearthed grave revealed an ancient-looking coffin. The casket was made of smooth dark wood, which had begun to rot. A symbol of a fang was

15

carved into the top of it.

"I don't think you should open that," Dora said.

"Don't be foolish, girl. There's a man trapped in there." The chief snapped at her before turning and calling out to the occupant of the coffin. "Don't worry. We're here to help."

"Oh, that'd be lovely." A cheerful British accent called out from within the coffin.

She knew she should take this opportunity to escape, but she couldn't. She really wanted to know what was in the coffin. Also, her father was here. If the coffin held what she thought it did, someone had to save his dumb ass.

The police chief used his spade to smash through the lid of the coffin. He and Hal ripped it open to reveal a pale man wearing a Victorian-style velvet suit.

The man sat up and languidly stretched.

"Oh, that's so much better. It's a tight fit in there."

Dora studied him. His skin was pale even in the dimly lit graveyard. His ebony hair was slicked back, and his lips were blood red.

The chief offered him a hand to help him out of the coffin.

"Don't!" She shouted on instinct.

The man's head snapped scarily fast in her direction, and his black eyes glittered over her for a moment before his glare softened with surprise.

"Mon amour, mon désir, ma Carissa!" he cried.

"What?" She glanced behind her to try to find the person the coffin-guy was talking to.

The old man standing behind her in a flannel bathrobe shrugged at her. "I think he means you."

She turned back towards the coffin as the pale man stood up in it.

"My love, my desire, my Carissa. Sweetie, I knew you'd wait for me." He repeated his words in English to her.

He clambered out of the grave, heading towards her with a glint of love in his eyes and his arms outstretched.

"Oh fuck!" She backed up and bumped into the man behind her, trying to avoid the imminent hug.

The man in the velvet suit tightly hugged her against him.

"It's Terrance. Don't you remember me? It's been so long, my love, but I'd recognize those glossy ringlets anywhere, my sweet, sweet passion."

"Oh fuck, get off me!" She struggled to push Terrance away from her.

"My name is Dora, not Carissa."

He released her as quickly as he'd embraced her, and he stepped back with a bow.

"Of course. Forgive me, my dear. I forgot myself in a moment of tumultuous passion. Please forgive my deviant behavior. I did not mean to defile you with my touch so soon." He stared at her for a moment, but then a glint of amusement lit up his dark eyes. "Ah ha! You play with my emotions as always, my virginal vixen. For what would Paris have been without your dark passionate embrace? You don't fool me, my snookums. We'll be so happy together in this new world, daring to go beyond villainous kisses and to break in new horizons." He hugged her to his chest, and she smelled something musty and old.

She scowled before kicking him in the shins as hard as she could.

"Okay, Pepe Le Pew, back the fuck off before I break you."

He backed off a little, but judging by the dopey grin on his face, it was clear he wasn't listening to a word she said.

"You know I love it when you break me, my little love bug." He winked at her, nervously placing an arm around her waist.

She tried to remove the arm, but it was like trying to bend iron. His grip was scarily solid and immovable.

"Isn't he a dream?" The pre-pubescent girl breathed, staring at Terrance with adoration.

"More like a nightmare." Dora tried to push him away from her and struggled to escape his iron grip, but he didn't appear to notice as he turned to face the group of townspeople.

"My good friends, I am so grateful to you. You have not only freed me on this night, but you have brought my love back to me too. A debt I may never be able to repay, but for which I offer my hand of friendship for a lifetime, perhaps even two," he declared, beaming happily at the crowd.

"No, she's not your love. She's a putrid, skanky, vampire whore." One of the ramblers pointed out.

"Ah, she is both, and so much more." Terrence smiled. "Farewell, my new-found friends." He bowed at the group, and then snapped his fingers.

The graveyard spun around her, and all she could feel was Terrence's hand around her waist. After some sickening spinning, the world blurred and reformed before her eyes.

She was no longer in a graveyard. They had been transported inside of what appeared to be a stately mansion.

She blinked several times to gain some focus before shoving Terrance away from her, which only worked because he was releasing his grip on her anyway.

"What the fuck just happened?"

"I brought you home, my love. After all, no matter how long I have slept for, time will never change the fact that the peasants are always revolting in some way or another. The view is much more pleasant here."

"Where are we?" She scanned the room. It was a large parlor decorated with Victorian chic, including a grand piano and chaise longue.

"This is my townhouse, my love." He attempted to stroke her hair, and she slapped his hand away as she backed up.

She studied him. He stood almost to attention under her gaze, one hand resting on a grand piano and the other smoothing back his dark hair. He appeared to be around twenty years old, but she was certain he was much older.

He winked at her, and she rolled her eyes in reply before glancing around the room and pausing at the large bay window.

She ran to the window, thinking only of escaping. She sighed with relief when she recognized the streets outside.

For a while there, she thought he'd transported her back in time. She breathed easy when she saw Main Street through the window. They were still in modern Berkville, in one of the older gothic houses on the outskirts of town by the looks of it.

"Do you care to take a turn around the gardens, my dear?" he asked her.

She turned to face him, thinking only of escape. "Sure, why not?"

3
DEAD THINGS AND JUNK

D ora shot a sideways glance at Terrence. He was smiling while gazing across his vast garden. He appeared completely oblivious to the fact that the garden was a barren landscape of dead weeds and rubbish.

"Beautiful isn't it?" he asked, turning to face her.

She grimaced as she stared at the twisted old oak tree, which was a hollow husk now and quite dead. "Yeah, if you like dead things …"

He let out a loud laugh, and then kissed her on the forehead. "You know I do, my love."

She rubbed the Terrance-spit off her forehead while scowling at him.

"Did you just call me dead?"

"Oh, don't be so coy. Dead, undead or whatever term you use nowadays. I know I'm behind the times, but there's no need to be sensitive, my dear." He condescendingly patted her on the head before turning on his heel and walking over to the dried-out pond in the middle of the garden.

She frowned as she watched him cross the overgrown lawn.

Am I fucking dead?

In some ways, it made sense. She didn't breathe normally, and her senses were super-sensitive now. She'd begun to notice improved hearing, eyesight and ugh—a stronger sense of smell.

I'm not a fucking vampire. I just can't be!

"Are you coming, dear?" He called out behind him as he paused at a dead rose bush.

She reluctantly walked over to him. She needed information, and unfortunately, he was the only available source she had right now.

"We need to talk," she said when she reached his side.

"Of course, my love."

"Let's start with that. Who do you think I am?"

"My Carissa." He beamed at her, and she scowled back.

His smile faltered for a moment. "My Dora?"

Her scowl deepened.

"Just Dora?" He tried again.

She smiled at him. "Good. Now tell me who Carissa is."

"You are," he said. "I like this game."

She punched him in the shoulder. "No, dumbass! I'm not. I'm just Dora."

"You look like Carissa." He leaned over her, and his hot breath warmed her neck. He inhaled deeply. "You smell like her."

She idly wondered what she smelled like.

Mud and hell-dust?

She shook her head and pushed him away again.

21

"Look, it doesn't matter what I smell like. I'm not Carissa."

"You have her hair." He played with one of her ringlets, and she slapped his hand away. "So does orphan Annie."

"Who?"

"Never mind." She sighed. "Lots of people have ringlets."

"Lots of people aren't creatures of the night with ringlets." He tried to play with her hair again, but she was onto his moves by now and swiftly smacked his hand away.

"I'm not undead!" she snapped, shaking her head.

"Well you're dead and still walking around," he said. "You have supernatural powers, and …" He sniffed her hair again. "You smell as if you've danced with a demon."

"I'm not dead! What powers? And the demon thing—well, that's because I'm sort of dating one."

His eyes widened as a look of pure horror appeared on his face.

"Tragedy befalls my blackened heart. Woe is me for loving such a devious temptress. Betrayed!" he wailed as his face fell in anguish. "Betrayed by my eternal love. I must end this pain, and take thy final kiss as my final breath." He reached for her in a dramatic stance while ripping a branch off a nearby tree and holding it to his chest like a stake.

Oh great, a suicidal vampire. That's just perfect.

She kicked him in the balls with all her strength. There was a loud clanging sound, and he didn't react.

"What the hell was that?"

"What?" He pulled an innocent expression.

"That clinking noise in your er, pants."

22

"You mean my bond with my maker?" he asked.

"If your bond with your maker clinks in your pants, then yes," she said.

"Well yes, it does on occasion." He appeared uncomfortable talking about it.

"Could you describe your bond with your maker?" she persisted.

"It's um, made of silver, and it protects my maker's claim on me," he evasively replied.

"In what way does it protect their claim?"

"Oh you know. Honor, loyalty, ahem-tity." He coughed out the last word.

"What?" she asked.

"Chastity," he muttered.

She burst out laughing.

"It's not funny!"

"It so is, man. You've got a silver chastity belt on your—" She burst out laughing again at the idea.

"I assure you, it's quite a terrible punishment. For one thing, it chafes." He appeared appalled by her reaction.

"Sorry, it's just … bahahahaha!" She fought to control the laughter, eventually managing to gain control of herself.

"Just take it off, and it won't chafe."

"If only I could," he said. "I can't touch silver. It burns."

"Doesn't it burn your er, bits?" She tried not to imagine burning vampire junk and failed.

"No it's silk lined," he said. "I wonder if perhaps one of those nice peasants would assist me?"

"Just don't ask them when I'm around." She laughed again.

"Once it is removed, I can seduce my devious temptress once more." He lunged at her, and she punched him in the face on instinct. He reeled backwards and fell onto his ass.

"Woe is me! Bound to a heartless maker and punished by my love." He held the stick up to his chest.

"Dude! I'm not your devious temptress. I don't even know who she is. And if you're going to stake yourself, can you fucking do it after we've figured out why you think I'm dead?"

"My heart cannot endure this." He sobbed while peering down at the ground. "Why would love abandon me with such vicious intent?"

"Maybe she got tired of hearing you whine and cry like a wet blanket?"

He peered up at her "Do you think so? Because I could resolve that and be the man she wants. But then, what if it is not enough? Perhaps I should end it now, once and for all. Perhaps I should remove myself from this world, so that my love can find a man worthy of her daunting beauty. Into the dark night I should go, bravely forward into the abyss of—"

"Bullshit." She interrupted his tirade of suicidal glorifying. "How did you end up in that coffin?"

"Oh, her evil mother tore us apart and had me exiled there, and I vowed to wait there until my love came for me," he said. "It was a cruel exile, but I would suffer it until she came. She was supposed to come find me when she had forgiven me. She was supposed to set me free when her heart was ripe with forgiveness, and we could love again."

"Did she know you were in the coffin?"

"I sent her a note."

"A note, you mean a flimsy piece of paper? Are you

24

sure she even got the note?"

"Of course, why wouldn't she? There's no postal service more reliable than the Royal Mail. With a Penny Red on my letter, it's certain to have found my love." He declared while twirling the stake between his fingers.

"What the fuck is a Penny Red?" She wondered if it was a fish of some kind. It sounded like one.

Please tell me he didn't send a fish to Carissa with a love letter.

"It's a stamp. Surely, you still have postage stamps in this year?"

"Yes, we have stamps and pennies still, but we also have dead letter offices. What if the letter got lost in the post?"

He frowned for a moment. "No, but—" He stood up and dropped the stick from his hands. "But if she didn't get the letter, then my years of exile were for nothing. If she didn't get this note, does that mean she didn't get the others either?"

"How many notes did you send?"

"One for every time I took my life in her name. She always came back for me, but not this time. I waited, but when she still did not come to me, I chose eternal exile."

"And how many times did you kill yourself over a girl you haven't even had sex with?"

"Only a few hundred times, I'm not that desperate a soul." He shook his head and laughed.

She stared at him in disbelief.

"It's not desperate!" He defended his actions with a pout on his rosy lips. "Only a few hundred is nothing in all my years."

"How old are you?"

"What year is it?" he asked.

"What year was it when you went into that coffin?"

"Eighteen sixty-five."

"And what year were you born?" she asked.

"That's not relevant." He shook his head.

She just stared at him.

"Fine! I'll tell you if it will satisfy thy accusing eyes. I was born in eighteen forty-five."

"When did you become undead?" She realized that twenty years since birth didn't give him much time to be a vampire.

If that's even what he is.

"My journey into the dark realm of the undead began in the year eighteen sixty-three. I was but a young man of eighteen years when the dark kiss was bestowed upon me."

"And you killed yourself over a hundred times in two years?" She blinked. "What the fuck, man."

"There are three-hundred and sixty-five days in a year," he said, appearing offended by her accusation as he turned away from her.

"So, what happened? You woke up every morning and said; *I feel like killing myself today. It must be Tuesday.*"

"You clearly have no concept of the darkness within." He shook his head at her.

"You clearly have no concept of overdoing it," she muttered.

"So it's probable that when Carissa didn't get your notes, you exiled yourself in a coffin because you're a total emo?"

"Well, yes. No wait, it was for love! What's an emo?"

"Was it worth missing a hundred and forty plus years of

living? And *you* are an emo!"

"Um, I dunno? What did I miss?" He peered around the garden. "It seems the world is a far more barren place now."

She grinned as an idea came to her. "How I about I show you the world?"

"Oh, that sounds lovely. Should we pack for a journey?"

"No need," she said. "The mall is just down the street."

ANGELS AND DEMONS

K ieron Lascher silently watched the three men through the holes in his dark cage. He'd woken in darkness with his body encased in some kind of cold stone. He couldn t move an inch or make a sound, and his eyes were pinned open. He was only able to see through two small holes in his suit of rock. He found himself staring out into a shadowy room lit only by the glow of the moon from an open balcony.

The sound of people whispering around him had awoken him, but when he tried to move, he realized that he couldn't even close his eyes.

What the hell is going on?

Looking through the holes, he could just make out that he was in some kind of palace adorned with golden statues and red velvet upholstery. It seemed familiar to him. But with just one angle of view, all he could make out was some ornate furniture and a window that led to a balcony. Standing in front of the balcony were three men in odd costumes.

Two of the men had giant pointy hats on their heads, which to Kieron looked like elongated cardboard crowns. The shortest man wore a long pointy crown, which was brightly colored in red, gold and white with gems embedded in it. The second tallest man wore a simple black tower on his head.

What the fuck, did I land on an alien spaceship?

He had never seen anything like this before. Both men wore robes that matched their hats and appeared to have ballerina slippers on their feet.

Kieron wasn't a master of fashion, but he was pretty sure these were the stupidest costumes he'd ever seen.

He examined the third man. He wore a stylish black suit and sunglasses. He looked like a bodyguard of some kind.

Is this the hotel room of a rock star?

Barring the height of the silly looking hats, the two men in dresses were quite short and appeared to be very old.

Grandpa rock?

He would have shaken his head if he could move it.

He tried to hear their words as the two men whispered to each other while the bodyguard stood resolute and silent beside them. The big hats banged against each other a couple of times when both men nodded, and then the men turned to leave the room. All three men made their way past him, none glancing in his direction.

"Bishop, this is quite concerning," the more colorfully dressed man said to his somber dressed companion.

"I agree, Stuart. We should send in PISS," the man named Bishop replied.

Send in what? Eww!

Images of a guy pissing in a post box jumped into Kieron's mind.

Stuart sighed while adjusting his sparkling cardboard crown.

"I suppose we must. If this is going to be an issue, then I'll leave it in your capable hands." He turned to the larger man in the suit. "And Johnson's, of course."

"Thank you, Stuart You won't regret it," Bishop replied, and Kieron noticed an evil smile spread across his face after Stuart turned and left the room.

"Do you wish me to organize PISS, sir?" Johnson asked Bishop.

Bishop's sharp beady eyes narrowed at Johnson. "I will organize PISS. You will follow my commands." He snapped at the younger man.

"Yes, Black Bishop." Johnson cast his eyes downwards in shame.

Bishop's scowl deepened, then he turned away from the man and followed Stuart out of the room.

Kieron heard Johnson sigh before he too followed the others out of the room.

The Black Bishop am I in some kind of messed up chess game?

After they had gone, he helplessly peered around the empty room.

What am I supposed to do now?

After a few moments, he felt an itch on his left ass cheek and tried to scratch it against the plaster. He stopped wriggling and froze when he noticed shadows moving across the room.

Oh fuck, what now?

The shadows swiftly moved from the dark corners of the room. As they passed through the beam of moonlight from the open window, they became visible as people dressed in black. They moved stealthily and quickly slipped past his line of vision.

Ninjas, is this a fancy dress party?

His heart jumped into his throat as a strange face, mostly covered by a black mask, appeared directly in front of his and menacingly stared at him.

Oh, fuck.

The man's wolfish eyes frowned at him from beneath the black mask.

"Jerry, what the fuck are you doing?" Kieron heard a woman hiss.

"This one's freaky." The gravelly voice of the wolfish man replied. "Its eyes follow you," he added, moving his head left and right in front of Kieron as if testing the theory.

"Fucking amateurs." The woman let out a loud sigh.

"No really, look into his eyes! I swear they move."

Kieron crossed his eyes in an attempt to try to communicate with the man.

"Agh!" Jerry fell backwards onto his ass and stared at him in horror.

Jerry was a heavy-set man, who was wearing black sweats, a mask over his face and leather gloves on his large hands.

"Jesus fucking Christ, Jerry! You'll wake up the whole city. What the fuck do you think you're doing?" The female voice snapped.

"It crossed its fucking eyes. I swear it did!"

"Just for that, we're taking this one," the woman said. "Because Jerry, if you don't get your shit sorted out soon, you're out. Do you understand me?"

Jerry nodded, refusing to look at Kieron again as he pushed himself up off the floor.

Kieron felt disappointed that he'd failed in communicating with Jerry and began to worry that he'd be stuck here forever. He realized that was about to change as it became clear that these thieves were intent on stealing him.

"Pick it up," the woman commanded.

He stared at the woman as she walked past him. For a moment, he thought it was Dora, and his instinct was to call her name. The stone around his mouth made it impossible to move his lips, and he only managed to expel a low moan.

She frowned and glanced at him, and then shook her head.

After closer inspection, he realized it wasn't Dora. The same long ebony hair flowed down her back in glossy curls. Her slim figure, which was clad in skin-tight black jeans and a t-shirt, was similar to Dora's, but she didn't move the same way as Dora. She was more fluid, like a panther. Even with the black mask over her eyes, her face didn't seem the right shape. It was more angular.

"It's too heavy." Jerry moaned close to Kieron's ear.

"I'm not dicking around, Jerry. Pick up the fucking statue. You were only hired for your strength. If you botch this job, you'll never work with us again," the woman snapped.

Jerry growled. "Fine, but don't blame me if you have claw marks up your back later."

"You wish." The woman shook her head and rolled her eyes. "Chris, help him before he wolfs out and wakes up the old man."

Wolfs out, what the fuck does that mean?

Kieron realized he was being lifted when his stomach dropped to somewhere near his knees. Gravity flattened his face against the cold stone as his encasing tipped forwards, and the rough plaster rubbed against his skin when he was jolted around inside it.

He realized he was helpless in this cage when the view changed from being that of a hot cat burglar, to seeing some guy's groin that was clad in a pair of black jeans.

Great, I'm staring at Chris's junk.

"Okay, move it," the woman said. "We've got five minutes before the guard change. We need to get this into the van, and then out of here before that happens."

"His wings will never fit through that doorway." Kieron heard a second male voice. It was a higher pitch than the other guy, so he assumed it was Chris.

"Yes they will if you turn it as you go through," the woman muttered.

The stone encasing Kieron shook. His head bounced off it a few times while his body spun around with the stone.

What happens if I throw up in here?

He tried not to think about being stuck in here with his own sick, but his stomach churned at the thought anyway.

The spinning finally stopped with a jolt, and he was suspended face down. He could see the floor through the holes in his suit of plaster. The area was unlit, but from what he could make out, the floor was made of decorative marble and ceramic tiles. As he was carried through the building, he

33

noticed that some areas were carpeted in red and others had golden rugs.

Where the hell am I?

He was jolted several times and banged against things by the incompetent thieves. Each time he hit something, cracks appeared around the holes, and he could see a little more.

"Don't dent the fucking statue!" the woman hissed.

Is that what I'm stuck in, a fucking statue?

After some jostling and a lot of bitching from the thieves, he realized they had taken him out of the building. He felt fresh air blowing through the cracks, and inhaled with a sigh. It was a relief to breathe fresh air.

His stomach dropped to his feet again as he was turned upwards, but he could finally see the front of the building he'd been stored in. It had an ornate stone entrance, and there was a sign carved above it. He tried to read the sign:

MVSEI VATICANI

The Vatican, where have I heard that word before?

"Stop messing around, and put it in the fucking van." The woman's voice interrupted his thoughts.

The crack in the thick stone splintered downwards as he was thrown into the back of a dark van. He tried to flex his way out of the statue, but it didn't budge.

"Don't fucking break it," the woman said. "Idiots!" she muttered, and then he heard the van doors slam shut. The vehicle shook for a moment, and he assumed the thieves had got into it.

He heard the van's engine purr, and then it began

moving over what felt like a bumpy road.

He rolled around inside the van, banging against the walls as the vehicle turned sharp corners. He realized that the more things he hit, the longer the cracks in the statue around him grew.

He started rolling into the jolts, trying to make the statue bang harder against the vehicle's interior.

More cracks appeared in the plaster, and he began to feel an inkling of hope.

I might escape this nightmare after all.

He flexed his muscles, trying to expand inside the statue to break out of it. More cracks were appearing, and he could hear splintering noises coming from the stone.

Come on, come on, I'm nearly there.

The van came to an abrupt halt, and he slammed into the doors of it. They must have been unlocked because upon impact, the doors flew open, and he shot out of the van like a rocket before crashing into something solid.

He moved his arms, feeling a rush of relief when he discovered they were free. He could feel his toes moving too and his wings.

I still have wings?

"What the fuck?" He heard the woman shout.

He sat up and lifted the broken statue's head off his own.

Glancing around, he noticed an underground garage surrounding him with only a few parked cars inside it. On the floor around him were broken pieces of statue.

He turned to face the woman. Her heart-shaped face was framed by long dark hair, and her bright green eyes glittered at him with interest.

She must have removed her mask during the journey. She was quite beautiful.

"You appear to have freed me," he said. He wasn't entirely sure what he'd gotten himself into, but it was better than being trapped inside a statue.

"I should have fucking known it wasn't real gold." The woman kicked a piece of broken statue, and he noticed that the plaster had been painted gold. "I bet the real one isn't even on display."

"Sorry," he said. "I'm glad to be out of it though."

The woman glanced at him, and then did a double take. Her eyes widened in horror.

"You're an angel!"

"I am not." He narrowed his eyes at her.

"You've got wings."

"And horns," he replied, checking with his hands that his horns were still in place. He sighed with relief when he felt the small, pointy spikes on his head.

The woman leaned closer. "Oh yeah, they're so small, I didn't notice them."

He scowled. "They're of average size for a demon my age."

The woman laughed. "Well, whatever you are, you're lucky we found you before the Vatican did."

He glanced back at his massive white wings and flexed them, causing the peppered black and white feathers to stretch out.

"I suppose I'm going to have to find some way to hide these things. Would it be too much trouble to ask for your assistance? I need to find my friends, and I appear to be in a bit of trouble."

The woman studied him and appeared to be contemplating his request. After a moment, she offered him her hand.

"Okay, I'll help you, but only because I've never seen something like you before."

"My name is Kieron, nice to meet you," he said as he took her hand, and she pulled him up off the ground.

"Nice to meet you, Kieron. My name is Carissa, and I'm a bit different too." She flashed a pair of fangs at him, and her eyes glowed yellow.

"Where are your friends?"

He pondered the question. He didn't know where Dora and Pooey were, but he knew where Dora used to live.

"Have you ever been to Berkville?" he asked.

5

CAUGHT RED HANDED

"Does it suit me?" Terrance posed in front of Dora while wearing a gold lamé suit.

She sighed. Of all the stores in the mall, it was the costume shop that had appealed to him the most.

She'd ended up sitting on a stool in the Elvis section, eyeing up a packet of fake sideburns with a sense of foreboding.

"Um, yeah?" She didn't really know what else to say. It looked awful. He just wasn't built for the Elvis-look. He was pale and somber in appearance with a vibe that screamed 'People Are Strange', rather than 'Viva Las Vegas'.

"I wonder if it comes in red." He peered down at the jacket, running his fingers over the glittery material.

"Oh, shopkeeper." He called out to the bored-looking shop assistant, who was busy filing her long purple fingernails.

The girl scowled at him.

"What kind of silk is this lining?"

"The cheap plastic kind," the girl replied.

"Plastic? I have not heard of this before. It is quite wondrous." He stroked the lapel of his jacket in awe. "You say it isn't costly. How many shillings per yard is it?"

The girl rolled her eyes and pointed to the back of the store. "The Steampunk section is in the back."

He frowned, and then turned to face Dora. "Does she not understand the Queen's English?"

"Er, no. There is more than one kind of English nowadays," Dora said while trying to work out how to explain modern slang to a Victorian.

He laughed. "You mock me again, witty girl. More than one English, hah! Did the French bastardize it again?"

"Something like that," she muttered. "This is the Americas, so they speak differently."

"Strange. You may have to translate this new world for me. What material is Steampunk?"

She pondered the question for a moment. "It's not material. It is people from my era, dressing like people from your era and obsessing over machinery."

"How very odd," he muttered, and then he stared at himself in the mirror for some time. "I look quite dashing in this, don't I?"

She eyed him up and down. "Er, sure ..." Her mind was busy going over her conversation with him earlier.

What supernatural powers?

"Perhaps I need a hat? A nice top hat or—"

"What supernatural powers?" She interrupted.

"Pardon?"

"You said I had supernatural powers earlier. What

kind?" She still wasn't convinced that she was the same as Terrance, or undead for that matter. She needed to work it all out before she went to find Kieron. The last thing she wanted to do was bite her boyfriend when she found him.

"Mind-reading, necromancy and some sorcery abilities, although not as many as a witch may be endowed with," he said while trying on different hats. "Oh, and of course, supernatural strength and immortality."

"So, if I'm like you, I should be able to read your mind?" she asked.

"No, no. I'm far too powerful. You're early in your youth. At best, you'll be able to read the shopkeeper's mind. Try it."

She eyed the shop girl, who was staring in a hand mirror with her mouth wide open. She appeared to be trying to stick a gem onto her front tooth.

Dora heard Terrance let out an appalled gasp behind her, which she suspected was his reaction to a woman baring her naked tonsils in public.

She shook her head and stared at the girl, trying to concentrate on reading her mind. The girl continued poking a gem onto her right canine with some tweezers.

Dora frowned and tried again. She stared at the girl and willed something to happen. When nothing changed, she let out a frustrated sign and wondered if the girl simply didn't have many thoughts.

Come on! Her mind can't be that blank.

She focused all her energy on the shop assistant and felt something shift inside her. The girl's hair changed from purple to white.

Terrance dropped the hat he was holding. "How did

you do that?"

"I dunno. You told me to do it." She attempted to restore the purple hair, but it remained white.

Crap!

"You shouldn't be able to do that," he said. "What powers have the demons imbued upon you?"

"I dunno, but we should get outta here," she muttered She glanced down at her fingers and noticed they were glowing red. It was as if someone had shone a light through her skin. She quickly pulled down her sleeves to hide her hands. "We need to get out of here now."

"At least restore her hair."

"I can't. I tried! Get back into your clothes, and let's go somewhere else."

She could see a faint glow of red through her jacket sleeve.

What the hell is this?

Her fingers were tingling. It wasn't an unpleasant sensation, but it was strange.

"What about my new suit?" He glanced at it with sadness in his expression.

"We'll get it online." She pushed him into the changing room. "Hurry up!"

"On a washing line, isn't that stealing?"

"Just get changed, and I'll explain later." She tried not to panic over her new found powers and glowing hands, but it took all of her restraint not to freak out. She glanced down at her hand.

What the fuck is that?

"Really dear, there's no need to rush." Terrance tried to pull his arm out of Dora's grasp as she dragged him through the crowds of people in the main food court of the Berkville Mall.

"We're probably on the security cameras. It's only a matter of time until that girl flips out over her sudden change in hair color," she said.

"Cameras, you mean there was a photographer in there? Don't be silly. There wasn't room for his equipment." He paused as he stared around the food court with wide eyes.

"I'd like to try a Dunkin' Doughnut before we leave, and what is a Panda Express? Does it have fast Pandas in it? Is it like horse racing, but with Pandas?"

"No it's a take away."

"What does it take away?"

"Your waistline," she muttered.

"Why would you go to a place like that?" He stopped to watch a family with small children enter the restaurant.

"Because it's fast food." She tugged on his arm to try to make him keep moving.

"Why does everything need to be so rushed?" He kept his ground, refusing to keep moving. "Even us."

"It's just normal." She eyed the exit. They were so close to it, and she really didn't want to get caught here by any of her father's congregation. It was Saturday, so some of them were bound to be in the mall.

"Come on. Let's just get out of here."

"I need to explore this world." He folded his arms and

refused to budge. "You may go, but I would like to stay."

She groaned, trying to think of a good reason that would persuade him to leave. She knew she couldn't leave him here alone. It would be a disaster.

She glanced down at her fingers. The red glow had now spread across her entire hand. She knew if she didn't get out of here soon, everyone would notice it.

"Fuck it. Terrance, if you want to stay, you're on your own." She let go of his arm and rushed towards the exit, leaving him behind.

Why am I glowing? What the fuck is this?

Her pulse raced so quickly that she worried her heart might stop.

She glanced back to see Terrance turn in the opposite direction and head towards the statue of Ronald MacDonald that stood outside the restaurant.

He'll be fine.

She tried to convince herself that he would be, but a nagging sense of guilt refused to let her believe that. Also, the fact that he appeared to be trying to hold a conversation with Ronald was a tad worrying.

She stepped out into the mall parking lot and scowled.

She was trying to decide whether to go back and get him when someone grabbed her from behind. She opened her mouth to scream, but a rag was stuffed into it, and then a dark hood was pulled over her eyes.

She struggled to escape, but it felt as if several hands were holding her.

She was pushed forward, and then forced to bend forward before being shoved into a vehicle of some kind.

She smelled whiskey and cheap aftershave as people got

into the back seat of the vehicle and hemmed her between them.

"Time to die, demon." A dark voice echoed close to her ear.

She shivered. These people seemed way creepier than her father's congregation did.

HOME SWEET HOME

Kieron trudged along the side of the road with his head down as the scorching sunshine beamed down onto him. The roadside was dusty with sparse patches of dry grass.

He let out a sigh of relief as a large sign came into view.

WELCOME TO BERKVILLE
POPULATION: 54,245

He wiped sweat off his brow. The sun burning down on him was unbearably hot, especially since he wore a long coat to hide his wings. For the first time in his existence, he felt irritable and uncomfortable.

He turned to face Carissa. "Thank Satan, this is nearly over."

"We've only been walking for a mile. You act like you've never walked before." Carissa looked cool in her jeans and loose shirt. Her wavy hair was tied up in a neat ponytail, and she didn't even look warm, let alone sweaty.

He groaned and tried to stretch the muscles in his wings under the raincoat, which didn't budge as they were tied to his torso to keep them down.

"You try walking while covered in feathers."

"Be thankful the truck driver let us hitch this far," she said.

"There has to be an easier way to get around in this world."

"If your wings were more than decorative, there would be. What kind of angel are you? You can't even fly."

"I'm not an angel!" he snapped. He was getting really tired of her calling him an angel. Couldn't she tell the difference between an angel and a demon?

She put her hand on his arm, turning him to face her in the process.

"Look, I know you don't want to hear this, but whatever you are, it isn't a demon lord. I know that much."

"How would you know the intricacies of Hell? I lived there, you haven't even been there." He brushed her hand away from him and stormed down the road ahead of her.

"I may not have been there, but I've studied Hell more than anyone else on Earth." She caught up with him easily. "And there's one thing that's certain, nothing keeps its own soul in Hell."

He knew she was right, but he didn't want her to be. If he wasn't a demon, why did he have horns? How had he lived in Hell for so long unnoticed?

What am I?

"Dora kept her soul in Hell," he said. He refused to admit he wasn't a demon. He'd always been a demon and didn't know how to be anything else.

"Then maybe she can help us find out what you really are."

She brushed a wisp of hair out of her face and stared down the road. "Look, there's a building ahead. If it's a gas station, maybe we can hitch a ride to near her house. What's her address?"

"Huh?" he asked.

"You said you've been to her house, so you should know her address."

"I was summoned there. Can't we just use a location spell?"

"Unless you have some powers I haven't seen yet, spells won't work. I don't know about you, but I'm not a witch."

He studied her. She wasn't human, he knew that much, but he still didn't know what she was.

"What are you?"

"That's none of your business." She avoided the question. "What about her surname?"

"What's a surname?"

"Oh you've gotta be fucking kidding me. You don't even know her second name? What do you call her besides Dora?"

He thought about the question for a moment. "Dora-minx."

"Have you ever called her anything else?" She appeared frustrated, and her eyes began to glow golden again as a growl entered her voice.

"Minx-witch."

"Dude, you've gotta give me more to work with than that." She appeared to be battling with her frustration and

47

losing as her front canines elongated into fangs.

"Are you a vampire? No wait, they don't have gold eyes. What the fuck are you?"

"Give me Dora's full name, and I'll tell you." She snarled as she emitted a low growl.

He pondered all the names he'd heard people call Dora and began listing them. ' Dora, minx, whore, bitch, witch, demon … Dora-demon?"

Carissa shook her head.

"Human, Carridine, wicked—"

"Wait, go back one. Carridine, that must be it."

"Really? I thought it was a human word for prisoner," he said. "Earth is so confusing, full of meaningless names and addresses."

She squinted at the building ahead. "I think you're about to find more of those very soon."

"What do you mean?"

"That's not a gas station. It's the sorting office for the postal service." She pointed ahead.

"Will we be able to hitch a ride there?" He stared at the rather dull-looking building.

"I don't know, but we'll be able to find Dora's address in their database," she said with a wink.

"Databases, wait I've heard of those. They are torture devices for office workers." He slowed his steps. "I don't want to go near a database. I've suffered enough."

"Don't be such a chicken." She growled, and her eyes flashed gold again.

"I'm not taking one more step until you tell me what you are." He stubbornly folded his arms across his chest.

She scowled at him.

"We made a deal," he added.

"Fine!" she snapped. "If you really want to know, then I'll show you."

"Yeah, yeah, I'm sure you will." He turned his back to her and stared at the postal office, warily checking for Hell portals or demons carrying databases.

He heard a growl behind him a few seconds before something heavy launched at him, and he was knocked off the roadside into the thick forest beside it.

Hot breath heated the back of his neck, and sharp teeth grazed his skin.

He rolled over with a yelp, peering up at a giant wolf with golden eyes and totally fucked-up teeth. The fangs were too long in the tooth, and the claws weren't long enough to be a werewolf. The wolf was still wearing Carissa's loose shirt, but the jeans were nowhere to be seen.

"Carissa, what the fuck? Get off me!" he cried, but it was clear that Carissa wasn't in control as her fetid breath whooshed in his face. Her wolf tongue lolled out of the side of her mouth, and a menacing growl rumbled through her body.

He didn't wait to find out what she planned to do with her teeth. He ripped off his coat and untied the ropes around his chest, freeing his wings.

The second the wings were free, he stretched them out and used them to push his body off the ground, jerkily throwing the Carissa-wolf off him.

She smashed against the trunk of a tree and slid down it with a whimper.

"Good doggy, stay down."

She growled and shook her shaggy head before jumping

up onto all fours and launching herself at him again.

Instinctively, he flapped his wings and leapt into the air, rising on the power of his massive wing-span. The wolf couldn't jump that high and landed on the forest floor below, panting instead. She woofed up at him and repeatedly tried to jump at him, but he was hovering in the air, a safe distance from her.

"Will you calm down, please?" He called down to her.

Judging by the expression on her wolf face, her inner animal was fighting with her conscious mind to be in control.

She peered down and sniffed the forest floor. He watched in awe as her furry legs became bare human ones.

"Is it safe to come down yet?" he asked.

"Shit, where are my jeans?" He heard the now human-looking Carissa grumble.

He descended back towards to ground and stood behind her. "Want me to look for them?"

She crouched on the ground covering as much of herself with the shirt as she could. "No, just give me your coat for now."

He grudgingly picked up the beige coat from the ground and handed it to her before glancing around the dense forest.

"What will I hide my wings with?"

She put on the raincoat and tightly wrapped it around her slender form as she stood up. She tied a knot at the waist before glancing up at him. Her eyes widened in horror.

"What wings?"

He quickly reached back to feel his shoulders, and then let out a loud sigh. "Thank all that is unholy," he muttered.

"Where did they go?" She appeared terrified. "Did flying make you human?"

"No, I don't know. I think when you tried to kill me, it made me access whatever powers they have. I can fly and conceal them now. Well, maybe? Thank you for trying to kill me, Carissa," he politely added.

That's how it worked in Hell. It must be what happened.

"Yeah, er, sorry about that. I just meant to scare you. I didn't expect to lose control." She grimaced.

"So you're a werewolf?" he asked.

"Half of me is." She admitted while pulling a twig out of her hair.

"What's the other half of you?"

"That's where things get kinda complicated." She shrugged off the question.

"Let's get into the post office and see what we can find out. We've wasted enough time."

"Okay." He nodded in agreement while rubbing his bare arms and feeling naked. "Maybe they have a shirt I can borrow."

"Chill dude. This is Berkville. A topless guy in jeans is normal around here," she said as they made their way through the rough forest to reach the back of the postal depot.

"This is it!" Kieron cried, and then quickly glanced up from the computer terminal and around the empty sorting room to ensure no one outside of it had heard him.

Way to be stealthy.

"Carissa?" he hissed, but there was no reply. He quickly jotted down the address before scanning the vast room for her.

Where the hell is she?

He stood up from the administration desk and switched off the computer. He walked down the long aisle between the sorting machines and various industrial machines that filled the room.

"Carissa, where are you?" The room was silent. He searched the dark room for movement until he finally found her reading a stack of letters at a counter on the left. Above her was a sign for:

THE DEAD LETTERS OFFICE

"Hey," he whispered. She didn't turn around.

"Carissa, what are you doing?" he hissed again.

They'd broken in, and he'd finally found Dora's address. The last thing he wanted was to get caught now.

"I've found it. You can stop looking now," he whispered.

"Carissa!" He eventually snapped in a louder voice.

She jumped and dropped the letter she was reading on the counter, and then spun around to face him.

"What? Don't make so much noise."

"What are you doing? I found Dora's address in the evil database. We can go now. Come on."

"Fine, I mean good." She gathered up the pile of letters and stuffed them into the pocket of her coat. "But we need to make a stop along the way."

"What? Why?"

"I need to pay a visit to an old friend," she said.

He frowned. "You have an old friend in Berkville, where?"

"The graveyard," she muttered.

THE JEEZEBIT ORDER

Dora was floating at the bottom of the Berkville Park Lake. It was kind of peaceful, all things considered. She'd been down here for a while now, watching the fish swim past her.

She glanced down at the giant boulder she was chained to. She tried to remove the chains again, but the padlock wasn't making it easy for her.

She sighed and sat down on the boulder, dropping her shoulders in defeat.

Maybe I should stay down here. It's nice and peaceful.

By the time she'd been dropped into the lake by a group of angry townsfolk, she hadn't much cared about what happened to her. She'd already been shot, hung, burned and exorcized.

Decapitation hadn't worked on her—the axes had just shattered. The bolt gun had exploded in Doug's hands when he tried to use it on her head.

For some reason even after fifteen attempts, nothing the citizens of Berkville did could kill her, so they'd bound her to a rock and pushed her into the lake in a final act of desperation.

She had panicked at first while gasping for air. But after a few minutes, she'd calmed down and realized that she didn't even need oxygen.

What the hell am I?

A giant tropical goldfish shimmied past her face, completely oblivious to her being there.

She smiled at it.

The goldfish must have felt the vibration of her movement because it quickly swam away.

One thing about being under the water was that she had time to think, something that she hadn't been able to do since she escaped her coffin.

With no interruptions, she'd gone over the events that had led to this point, from Hell and back.

She'd been losing her soul in Hell and had cast all kinds of spells upon herself to kill Kieron in the final arena. Fire, ice, earth and the final spell had been stone-based—it had been about making her strong.

Was that why I came back to Earth impervious to everything?

You didn't cast air, but you don't need to breathe to survive.

She shook her head.

No, it didn't make sense. Neither did the glowing hand. None of this was from Hell.

She peered down at her hand. Her skin appeared to be totally normal again. The red glow had never spread past her wrist, and had begun to fade when she was kidnapped from the mall.

What's with the whiskey smelling kidnappers, anyway, did the congregation turn into alcoholics?

Even her father smelled as if he was hitting the bottle.

But he never drinks.

She shrugged. With a heavy heart, she realized that no one was looking for her. Whatever happened next was her problem. She was on her own.

I should have stuck with Terrance. At least he just wanted to woo me, not kill me.

She peered up towards the surface of the lake, which was about eight-feet above her. She could make out the blurry shapes of a mob of people standing around the edges, looking down. She had hoped that if she looked dead enough, they would go away, but it seemed they were waiting for something to happen.

Well, I can't sit here forever, she thought, although it was a tempting idea.

She waved to the people above.

Hello idiots, I'm still here.

Several figures jumped into the lake and began swimming towards her. Rough hands grabbed her, and she felt the chains loosen as the police chief and his subordinates unlocked her and dragged her up from the depths of the lake.

Her head broke the surface of the water, and she inhaled deeply, out of habit.

She glanced sideways to see the chief bobbing next to her in the lake.

He pulled her arms behind her back and tightly bound them in handcuffs.

"It didn't work. Any other ideas?" He shouted to her father.

56

She glanced at her father. His white hair was in disarray, and he looked as if he hadn't slept for a week.

Mom would never let him leave the house looking like that.

She searched the crowd for her mother's face, but couldn't find it.

Where is mom?

"There's only one other option," her father said with a sigh. "We need to call PISS."

Who the fuck are PISS?

Dora scanned the interrogation room. She was sitting in an uncomfortable plastic chair, facing a desk and a two-way mirror.

She stared into the mirror and scowled. She knew there were people behind it, but all she saw was her own reflection, and it wasn't pretty.

Her hair was hanging over her shoulders in messy wet strands, her black eye-makeup had gathered under her eyes in big black streaks and her skin was even paler than normal.

"Can I at least get a towel?" she asked the two-way mirror while her hair dripped lake-water onto the desk.

"Silence, demon." A metallic voice commanded through the intercom.

"I'm not a fucking demon," she muttered.

Loud footsteps echoed down the hallway outside the room.

She turned her head to hear what was happening outside. There were some hushed whispers, and then a sharp

57

voice clearly ordered for the door to be opened.

She reclined back in the chair and studied the door.

I guess PISS have arrived.

The door swung open, and two men wearing black suits entered the room. Both wore dark glasses and carried matching briefcases.

"Agent Smith, I presume," she said.

"Do not speak. We shall not answer to you," one of the men said.

"Er, you just did, and we're in an interrogation room, which is usually intended for talking in." She shook her head at them.

"What are you then? What is PISS? Is it like that British phrase—taking of the piss?"

"Isn't it, 'taking the piss'?" The second man corrected, but he stopped talking when the first agent glared at him.

"Since you won't benefit by knowing any of this information, I will introduce us. Although bear in mind that you have no rights because you are a heretic and you have no right to live because you are a woman," the first agent said.

"Er Jeff, that's the wrong way round," the second agent said.

"Speak again, Agent Orange, and I will report you to the Black Bishop." The first agent snapped at his partner.

Agent Orange bowed his head and nodded in silence.

"Good," the first agent said as he took a seat opposite her.

She examined her interrogator. He was a small, thin man with a gray pallor to his skin. His lips were a narrow line that had a purple tint to them. There were gray streaks in his dark hair and deep lines beneath his eyes.

"You don't like women very much, do you?" she asked.

"My name is Agent Ochre—"

"Wait." She interrupted. "Isn't that a diarrhea yellow color? How come he gets orange and you get diarrhea?"

Agent Orange covered his mouth with his hand as a smile broke out across his face.

Agent Ochre's frown deepened so much it disappeared behind his dark glasses "In our division of the P.I.S.S—"

"The higher the rank, the more shitty the codename?" She butted in again.

Agent Ochre growled. "Silence, woman!"

"Or what, you'll kill me again? Good luck with that."

Agent Ochre angrily exhaled, and his nostrils flared. "The Pope's Intelligence Service Subdivision is often referred to as P.I.S.S. It is a subdivision of the—"

"Jeezebit Order." Doug interrupted as he walked into the room carrying two cups of coffee.

"For fucksake! Can you rednecks stop fucking interrupting me!" Agent Ochre exploded.

Doug visibly blanched and placed the drinks on the table in front of the agents. Then he gave Dora a sympathetic smile before he turned and left the room.

"So you work for the Pope?" Dora raised an eyebrow. This guy was so much fun to fuck with. "Do you polish the Pope's pallium?"

Agent Ochre scowled at her. "Amongst other things, PISS has been responsible for erecting monoliths in every major city on Earth in honor of the—"

"Well I suppose you have to find some way to display

your massive erections." She interrupted again. "It's not like you can use them in any other way since you hate women and gay people."

"We don't hate women," Agent Orange said. "We're just not allowed to be near them."

"Why not?" she asked.

"They can seduce us from our holy mission," Agent Orange replied.

"Ah, so you fear women."

"What? No, we don't fear anything!" Agent Ochre snapped.

"Except women and gay people, who have you cowering in your chastity belts. I get it." She nodded with understanding.

"Agents of PISS fear nothing." Agent Ochre stood up and slammed his fists into the desk.

"Get that idiot redneck back in here, and tell him to bring my knife." He turned and shouted at the two-way mirror.

"What do you need a knife for?" she asked. "You can't kill me."

Agent Ochre said nothing and turned towards the door as Doug opened it and came into the room carrying a knife in a sheath.

Agent Ochre took the knife from him and showed it to Dora.

"This is a very special knife." He told her as he pulled the intricately carved shiv out of its sleeve. It was gold with silver swirls and copper lines running down the blade. Red gems were incrusted into the hilt. The blade glinted as he waved it near her face.

"Why is it self-sharpening?" she asked, trying to appear as bored as she possibly could.

"It was blessed by the Pope himself, and cursed by the Black Bishop." Agent Ochre flashed an evil grin.

"I've seen bigger. What exactly are you planning on doing with it?" she asked.

She tried to ignore the feeling, but an instinctive shudder of fear ran through her.

"Eventually, I'm going to run it through your black heart." Agent Ochre smiled at her again. "But first, Agent Orange is going to cut off your fingers. The crease between them looks too much like a vagina."

"Eww!" she cried.

Meanwhile, Doug examined his own hands and began opening and closing his fingers with a confused expression on his face.

"Agent Orange, come here and—" Agent Ochre began.

"Wait." Doug interrupted. "I think you need to do me first. These look just like Daisey Mae's—"

"Doug! Please don't finish that sentence." Dora jumped up from her seat.

Doug was dumb as shit, but she didn't want to see him get his fingers cut off.

"And you two." She pointed to Agent Orange and Agent Ochre. "You both need to give up the forty-year old virgin lifestyle and get laid."

"Sacrilege!" Agent Ochre cried, but Agent Orange appeared to be considering her suggestion.

"What's Daisey Mae like?" Agent Orange asked Doug.

"She's got a great personality," Doug replied. "And a

wonderful pair of—"

"Doug! Too much info." Dora quickly interrupted.

"Monster!" Agent Ochre clearly wasn't happy with Agent Orange's defection over curiosity about Daisey Mae. He ran at Dora holding the knife high above him.

She jumped back towards the wall and looked for an escape route, but there wasn't one.

I guess I'm about to find out if that thing will pierce my heart or not.

Fortunately for her, the blade never reached her. The two-way mirror smashed behind them all, sending glass flying in all directions and causing everyone in the room except Dora to cower.

Agent Ochre let out a high-pitched yelp of fear before scurrying under the desk.

Terrance leapt through the broken window and calmly strolled into the room. Behind him, several other people, who were possibly Goths or vampires, also climbed through the broken window to enter the room.

"Have no fear, fair Dora. I have come to rescue you." Terrance declared.

She contemplated her answer and her options. Agent Ochre was cowering under the desk and rocking back and forth while chanting some kind of prayer. Doug and Agent Orange were huddled near the door, hugging each other.

She turned back to Terrance and smiled. "My hero."

What the hell, it beats being killed again.

FURRY FIENDS

As Kieron stared at the gravestone, a numb feeling engulfed his whole body. He could no longer feel the breeze, see the trees or hear the birds. An ongoing scream roared through his head, and his eyes were glued to the name carved into the marble headstone:

DORA CARRIDINE
1997—2013
REST IN PEACE

Dora was dead. Nothing else seemed to matter.

He clenched his hands in to fists. "No!"

He'd bring her back. He'd go back to Hell and find her.

Electricity tingled through his limbs, and he felt his wings burst out of his back, flashing with anger.

"Portelus!" he cried, trying to open a portal to Hell. When nothing happened, he sank to his knees and began drawing a circle around him in the Earth.

If basic magic didn't work, he would carve a hole through the ether to get into Hell and bring her back.

He began chanting Latin, and then started to bite his own hand to make it bleed.

"Kieron, stop! What are you doing?" Carissa knelt beside him and pulled his hand away from his mouth.

"You can't use blood magic here, of all places."

"Why not? I'm going to bring back Dora, and damn the consequences!"

"Even if the consequences are these bodies all rising from their graves? Stop, this is not the answer."

"I won't leave her there!" He ripped his hand from Carissa's grip. He was consumed with anger. All he could think about was saving Dora.

Damn this world and the consequences of his spells. He couldn't lose her.

"You don't even know where she is." Carissa snapped as she tried to stop him completing his spell.

He let his hands drop to his sides, staring at the headstone while he shook his head. "There's only one place she can be. They'd never let her into Heaven."

"That's not what I meant," Carissa said. "Look at her grave."

He frowned and examined the grave, gasping when he realized the earth had been dug up, and only the remnants of a shattered coffin remained inside it. "Someone desecrated her grave and stole her body!"

"No, I don't think so." Carissa stood up and scanned the hole in the ground.

"What do you mean?"

"Look at the scratch marks. Someone or something dug

its way out of that grave."

He stared at the splintered lid. She was right. Dora must have clawed her way out of her own grave.

"How is this possible? How could she survive? No human could survive being buried alive."

Carissa nodded in agreement. "No human could."

She turned on her heel and slowly scanned the graveyard.

"What do you mean? Dora didn't come back as Dora?" He got to his feet and glanced in the direction Carissa was staring. There was a second grave that had been dug up.

"I don't know, but you didn't come back the same did you?" She glanced at him.

He made his wings retract. He was embarrassed of what he was. He really didn't want to tell her that he'd been just as messed up in Hell.

"Me? No, I was a scary demon lord, one of the worst." He lied.

"Well then, it stands to reason that Dora may have been changed too when she was rejected from Hell."

He wondered what had happened to Dora as he followed Carissa to the second unearthed grave.

This one was older, much older. The headstone was dull gray stone, and the words carved into it had been worn by time. Moss grew in the cracks and pieces of the stone had chipped away.

"Terrance," Carissa whispered the name that was barely legible on the headstone.

"This one's been dug up too, but it looks like someone used a spade," Kieron said.

"Yes, it does." She wasn't saying much. She was just

staring at the headstone.

"Did you know him?" he asked.

"It's not important at the moment." She flashed him a sad smile and shook her head.

"But—"

"We need to find Dora, right?" She interrupted.

"Yes." He had the feeling she was hiding something, but Dora was his priority, so he ignored the nagging feeling in his gut.

"Let's go to her house. Maybe she went there after she got out of her grave."

He didn't entirely trust Carissa. She was acting very strange right now, but he desperately wanted to find Dora, so he nodded and followed Carissa towards the gates of the graveyard.

It took a few moments for him to realize they were being followed. He heard footsteps crunching behind them first and glanced back to see a group of squirrels, who appeared to be rushing to keep up with them.

When the squirrels noticed him watching, they stopped abruptly and began sniffing the grass or innocently looking around.

He shook his head.

I must be going crazy. They're just squirrels.

He continued walking and caught up with Carissa.

A few seconds later, he heard the crunching of leaves behind them again. He frowned and quickly spun around to see what was following them.

The group of squirrels froze mid-run, and then quickly scattered before taking on woodland poses. One perched on top of a headstone sniffing it, and another climbed halfway up a tree and froze in position. A big gray one picked up an acorn and studied it with interest.

"What?" Carissa asked as she turned around to see what he was looking it.

He scowled at the sunlit graveyard. It seemed like a tranquil, natural scene. There were birds flying from tree to tree, and vibrant green grass spread across landscape beneath clear blue skies.

The squirrels appeared perfectly harmless in the scene.

"What?" she repeated.

"You'll think I'm crazy," he said. "It's nothing. I must be imagining it. Come on let's keep going."

She scanned the graveyard before shrugging at him and nodding. "Okay."

They turned and began walking towards the exit again. A few seconds later, he heard the crunching steps behind them again.

"What the fuck?" he cried as he spun around, finding the big gray squirrel only a couple of feet behind him.

It froze and stared up at him with big, soulful black eyes. The other squirrels also froze. They were following in a large group several feet behind them.

Carissa spun around too and glanced down. "What is it this time?"

"The same fucking thing," he said as he watched the big gray squirrel pluck an acorn out of the grass and hold it in its hands.

"The squirrels are following us." He had to force the words out because they were insane.

She stared at the squirrel for a moment, and then looked at him with worry on her face. "Did I damage your head when I attacked you?"

"No." He sighed. "I swear I'm not imagining it."

Disbelief crossed her face, followed by an expression of sympathy.

"I'm not crazy! The fucking squirrels are following us."

"It's just a hungry squirrel," she said. "Look at it."

He stared at the big gray squirrel. A wicked grin appeared on its face, and its eyes glowed yellow.

He blinked and shook his head. When he looked again, the big gray squirrel looked cute and innocent again.

Maybe I am nuts?

"Did you see that?" she asked. Her eyes had widened, and she was staring at the squirrel in pure horror.

"You mean its eyes?" he asked.

"Yeah, what the fuck?" She began warily backing away from it.

He yelped and jumped backwards when the squirrel grinned, and its little fangs glinted in the sunlight.

"Oh no, they wouldn't ..." She held her hand to her mouth in shock.

"Who wouldn't what?" he asked.

"I think they're hybrids, I think ..." She paused with a look of pure horror growing on her face. "I think they're were-squirrels!"

"That's the stupidest thing I've ever heard o—" He didn't finish the sentence as the squirrels stopped acting innocent and grouped together into a large pack.

They stalked towards them, and he could hear a high-pitched growl coming from them.

"Eeeeeeeeee." The squirrels growled as they drew closer.

"What exactly can were-squirrels do to us?" he asked.

A shiver of fear shot up his spine as one of the rodents extended its sharp claws and grinned at him.

"Let's not find out."

One squirrel launched itself at his face. He tried to smack it away from him, but it clung to his arm and tried to bite him.

He panicked and tried to dislodge the fluffy critter. He violently swung his arm, and the squirrel lost its grip and flew into the air with a 'wheeee' sound. He heard a thud in the distance as it landed in a copse of trees.

"Don't let them bite you. You don't want to be a were-squirrel-angel." Carissa cried as she dodged an attack from the big gray squirrel.

"We need to get out of here!" he cried as a vicious squirrel shot past his face, just missing him.

He tensed all his muscles, and then felt his wings pop out of his back. He turned to face the squirrels and flashed his wings at them.

They abated for a moment, backing away from his massive wingspan, which flapped menacingly in their direction.

He wrapped an arm around Carissa. "Hold on," he said as he flapped his wings with as much power as he could muster.

The squirrels that tried to attack were blown backwards as the gust of wind from his wings hit them.

The hardier squirrels attempted to roar at him in defiance, making angry squeaking noises before they too were blown away.

He noticed some of them were coming back for more,

so he pushed off the ground and flew into the skies with Carissa tightly holding onto him.

"You said, *'oh, no they wouldn't'* earlier. Who wouldn't? What kind of lunatic would do that to squirrels?" he asked as he headed towards Dora's house.

She sighed. "There's only one person I can think of who would take something adorable and try to make it deadly."

"Who?"

"My mother," she ground out.

9

THE ISLAND OF DOCTOR MORON

Pooey slipped into the dark room and silently closed the door behind him. His new bulky form made being a ninja difficult, but not impossible. He flexed his muscled arms and grinned. Being a were-bear wasn't all bad. He felt big and strong.

Stop dicking around.

He shook himself out of it. This was no time for admiring his beastly body. He needed to get the hell out of here.

For all his new strength, he had not arrived on Earth in a good place. He'd been discovered in the woods by a supernatural matriarch and become her prisoner. She was an even more massive beast than he was. After capturing him, she had made him into her bitch.

I'm no one's bitch!

He had tried to escape a few times, but this time it was going to work. It'd taken him a while to become acclimatized to his new position on Earth.

Earth had changed a lot since his time here, but it didn't

take him long to realize that his ninja skills were always there, no matter what hellhole he was dropped into.

So with some schematics of the building and a small torch, he was going to finally get the fuck out of here.

And after all this shit, those Hell judges are going to pay!

He flipped on the torch and scanned the room. It was a large room filled with packing crates and boxes with tarps over them.

He silently rushed down the aisle to get to the end, glancing at a small laboratory as he passed it. It was home to bubbling vials and computers.

I wonder what kind of shit they experiment on in here?

He shook his head. He didn't care as long as he got to the elevator shaft and escaped this place, once and for all.

He continued down the aisle, but paused when he heard a croak followed by a squeak coming from one of the boxes.

He turned to face the box and frowned.

One look can't hurt, right?

He lifted the tarp and inhaled sharply when he saw a pair of kitten eyes blinking at him from the body of a toad.

What the fuck?

The kitten-toad mewled from inside a glass cage.

He almost felt sorry for it until a ridiculously long tongue with teeth on it shot out of its mouth and stuck to the glass.

The kitten-toad hissed as its eyes glowed yellow.

He stumbled away from it and fell backwards in shock, grabbing onto the tarp behind him to stop himself falling over.

The tarp slipped off all the boxes behind him to reveal hundreds of cages with creatures inside them.

The sudden light from the torch must have woken the creatures up because they all started making noises. An array of chirps, barks, roars and growls filled the room.

He hit the floor with the tarpaulin.

Shit!

Using the storage rack to pull himself up from the floor, his eyes connected with creatures in glass cages as he rose.

In the first cage, a creature that looked like a fluffy ball with an asshole and a mouth walked around in circles, eating and shitting.

He watched it in awe as it ate a piece of carrot, and then crapped it out, looking exactly the same, a few seconds later.

What the fuck is that?

He read the label on the front of the box:

AMOEBALUS PRIME:
DEVOID OF DIGESTIVE SYSTEM.

No shit!

He watched a piece of sweetcorn drop out of its fluffy backside.

Shaking his head, he pulled himself up further and encountered the next cage.

A cute white mouse blinked its big sad eyes at him.

"Hey little fella," he whispered. "What are you doing in here with all the freaks?"

The mouse roared like a lion and vicious spikes shot up all over its body, including out of its ass. It turned it's ass to the glass and sprayed some kind of green liquid that sizzled in his direction.

"Urgh!" Pooey jumped back into the tarp-covered boxes behind him, and the tarp fell away to reveal more boxes.

He came face-to-face with a pair of scary glowing eyes.

He shone the torch on the cage to see a giant spider that had the cute head of a bush baby attached to its fat arachnid body.

"Agh!"

With his heart hammering, he made a run for it, bouncing off one cage to another as he tumbled down the remainder of the aisle.

Where the fuck am I, The Island of Dr Moron? What idiot would make a fluffy fucking amoeba?

He nearly defecated in his pants when a giant lion-looking beast with a missing tail came into view at the end of the aisle.

It stealthily turned in its cage to face him and opened its massive jaws to roar, but all that came out was a girly squeak.

Pooey widened his eyes in terror when he saw it eat a peanut that was the size of a melon. The peanut was a monstrous creation all by itself, but it was the fact that the lion's head puffed up like a hamster's when storing food that shocked him the most.

He read the label on the cage:

HAMSTEROUS LIONESS: VEGETARIAN.

A shiver of fear ran down his spine.

Was this what his evil mistress had planned for him—to have spikes coming out of his ass, or to be made into a squeaking vegetarian?

Well, she does keep making me wear dresses. Could it be any worse? Yes, fuck this!

He turned and fled. All his carefully laid plans for escape were now a muddled mess in his mind.

He couldn't hide in an elevator shaft until morning. He

couldn't stay here one more minute.

He spun around looking for a way out. His pulse was racing, and he feared he'd never get away until he saw a vent in the wall.

He ran over to it and sniffed.

Fresh air!

This would do. He pulled the cover off the grate and clambered into it as fast as he could.

He was escaping tonight, right now. He pushed himself through the grate, struggling to fit his shoulders through the small gap and into the dark shaft.

He heard the tweets and roars of the crazy animals behind him and pushed himself deeper through the opening.

I'm not going to make it.

He panicked.

Emitting a low growl, he used all his strength to push himself through the small hole in the wall, feeling the edges of the vent cutting into his sides.

After struggling for some time to get his ass through the hole, he realized he wasn't going to escape this way. His body was too big.

He tried to back up and find another way of escaping, but there was a problem. He was now stuck in the vent, with his ass hanging out of the front of it.

Noooo!

He struggled and clawed at the vent, trying to either get in or get out, but his body was wedged half in and half out of it.

Fuck!

A few minutes later, he heard a noise that chilled him to the bone.

"Oh, Snookums!" He heard his mistresses call. "Where are youuu?"

He stopped struggling, and his head flopped onto the cold vent in defeat.

I'm doomed...

FULL MOON

D ora shifted uncomfortably in the inflatable pool chair. It protested with a loud and elongated squeak.

She glanced around the deserted corridor, feeling out of place.

Terrance had been dragged away by the other vampires for some kind of ritual. They told Dora to wait here for an audience with the Ancient One.

Whoever the hell that is.

She felt uncomfortable. The vampires weren't exactly a welcoming bunch.

She peered down the hallway of the gothic mansion. It was lined with inflatable plastic chairs and pool furniture, which seemed terribly bright and garish in such an austere setting.

A giant of a man walked into the corridor with a vampire that she recognized as the Ancient One's secretary.

The man wore a velvet smoking jacket and glared at her

with steely gray eyes.

Is that the Ancient One?

"Please take a seat. You'll be called when he is ready to see you." The secretary told the man before she turned with a flip of her red hair and clattered out of the hallway on her six-inch heels.

I guess not.

The man in the velvet jacket glanced around him, looking for a chair. He frowned when his eyes settled on the pink inflatable chair behind him.

He tried to sit down in it. But because it was so low to the ground, he ended up squatting over it.

Dora watched him in silence as he struggled into the chair. He ended up stuck in it, facing her with his arms and legs hanging out of it in an uncomfortable slouched position.

His eyes connected with hers in moment of silent anguish as he fought to sit up straight and regain a shred of dignity. His chair made random farting noises every time he moved.

She did her very best to not laugh as the elegant man was reduced to a wriggling suit in a pink bubble.

He tried to pull something out of his jacket pocket and the chair made a long, slow farting noise.

A gasp of laughter escaped her lips.

Incensed by her laughter, the man shot her a steely glance with anger flashing in his eyes.

He pulled out a cigar and popped it in his mouth. The chair erupted into several long squeaks and farts as he searched for his lighter. Eventually, after some struggling he pulled out a Zippo and lit the cigar.

He took a slow drag of it and stared at her with distain.

He attempted to appear regal as he raised his chin and rested his smoking hand on arm of the chair.

The chair let out a long, loud fart.

She felt tears of laughter brimming in her eyes and fought to contain the urge to burst out laughing. Her resolve cracked when a burning ember of ash fell off the cigar and onto the chair.

The chair popped like a balloon, and she exploded with laughter as the chair deflated, and the man flopped into and ungainly heap on the floor.

He glared up at her from his slumped position.

She was about to apologize when the doors to the Ancient One's sanctum opened.

A waifish girl with spikey green hair stepped out of the room.

"He'll see you now." She nodded at Dora. "Come with me."

Dora stood up and gave the man a wink before she followed the girl into the room.

There was haunting music playing in the room as she stepped over the threshold. Behind an ornate mahogany desk was a plush, leather chair that was turned away from them.

"You may leave us, Janet." A hollow voice echoed from the direction of the desk.

Spikey-haired Janet silently exited through a side door into another room, leaving Dora alone with the Ancient One.

Dora attempted to control the urge to continue laughing as she heard a random farting noise come from the hallway outside.

I guess he found a new chair.

She forced herself to focus on the brown leather back of the chair. She could see the left arm of the Ancient One and not much else.

"Er, hello?" she said.

"You are brave to speak so freely in my presence," the Ancient One replied.

"Why is speaking against the rules?" she asked while glancing around for something that would indicate a vow of silence.

"Ha!" The Ancient One exploded with a deep laugh. "Such arrogance in one so young." His voice boomed around the room.

She wondered what Terrance had got her into with this coven of vampires.

He'd come to her rescue with several members of the coven, who he'd told her he'd met in the mall. But the other vampires all seemed a bit creepy, and they called him 'The Savior', whatever that was supposed to mean.

"I haven't been arrogant, yet," she said. "How old are you anyway?"

"You toy with my patience, child. When you've lived as long as I hav—"

"And how long is that exactly?" She interrupted.

The chair spun around, and a man in his forties with a gray goatee leapt out of it.

"You dare to question me about my age, of all things?" His eyes glowed red.

"Doesn't everyone?" She eyed him with curiosity.

He wore a black biker jacket, worn jeans and several chains around his neck. A tattoo of some kind ended at his throat, but the tip could be seen over the collar of his Kiss t-shirt.

"Yes, actually." He lowered his voice.

"It's not a surprise, really," she said while her eyes wandered over his desk, noticing a battered laptop and some files resting upon it.

"Why, because I don't wear a fucking cape and haunt married women?" He scowled. "Don't you know it's rude to ask a vampire their age?" His fangs popped out, and he hissed at her.

"Dude, you're called *The Ancient One*. Who wouldn't wonder how old you are?"

His fangs disappeared as his eyes widened with realization.

"So how old are you?" she asked again.

"I have seen more of this world than you will ever know, foolish child. I am the oldest vampire in this province, and the most powerful," he muttered ominously.

"And how many years has that been for?" She persisted.

He rumbled with a growl that was filled with threat. "I have survived some of this world's greatest disasters."

"Oh, which ones?" she asked with interest.

"The great stock market crash," he said.

"The one in the nineteen-twenties?"

"No, the one in two-thousand and ten," he mumbled.

She rolled her eyes. "Just fess up how old you are."

"Do not speak to me with such disrespect. I am a creature of the dark, an ancient one!" he cried.

"So what, I lived in Hell for a while. Get over it already."

"Really?" He perked up with interest.

"Yeah, it wasn't how they describe it in the movies,"

she said as memories of Kieron standing beside her in Hell's arena flooded into her mind.

She felt a moment of longing for her demon-friend.

Where is he now? I hope he's okay.

"How was it?" the Ancient One asked.

"How old are you?" She countered.

The Ancient One dramatically flopped into his leather chair and sighed.

"Fine, it has been seven-hundred and eighty moons since I arrived on this Earth. And for three-hundred of those, I have been seated on the dark throne of the undead."

It took a moment for her to do the math, but when she did, she scowled at him.

"Dude, you're only sixty-five years old! My grandfather is older than that, and he's still alive!

"Can your grandfather do this?" His eyes glowed red, and then he hissed while his fangs popped out.

"Yes! He hisses when his dentures come out all the time. Also, he had a bad case of pink eye this one time and—"

"Enough!" The Ancient One snapped. "I have seen more terrible things than you can possibly imagine."

"Like what?"

"Rick Astley in concert."

"Fair point."

"You should bow in my superior presence."

"You should kiss my as—wait a minute! The oldest vampire in this province is sixty-five. How old are all the other ones?"

"They vary from very young to close to my age. The older ones are my lieutenants."

"Lieutenants, are you at war?" she asked.

"That we are." He slyly eyed her. "Perhaps I shall send you out into the trenches as punishment for your disobedience."

"There aren't any trenches in Berkville." She corrected him.

Dora stood behind a roughly dug trench in the middle of the Berkville Forest and sighed.

How do I get myself into these situations?

She glanced at the three young vampires beside her. They were so young that they'd only been undead for a few months.

She eyed the leader. He was a geeky boy with slicked back hair who called himself Fredward. He wore a dark suit and some kind of glittery make up.

"Dude, you look like a plank." She told him.

"Hush, you'll give away our position, and we'll lose." A painfully thin girl with dark circles under her dark eyes whined.

"Why the fuck are you all wearing glitter if you're supposed to be hiding?" Dora asked.

The reflection off their faces was glowing in the dark.

"It reflects the sun," a small blonde girl called Melanie whispered.

"It's midnight. There is no sun," Dora said.

"Quiet!" Fredward ordered. "I sense a beast approaching."

"Ooh, I hope it's Carob. He's so hot." Melanie

squealed.

"He's a disgusting werewolf. They are never hot!" The dark-haired girl snapped before then peering up at Fredward for approval.

He nodded at her with an endearing smile on his face.

"Correct, Stella. We only wage war with werewolves."

Melanie sighed. "You guys should just make out already, and then the rest of us could enjoy some hot wolf ass."

Fredward gripped Melanie by the shoulders and shook her. "Don't be a fool! You know it will kill you."

Then he hugged her to his chest and stroked her hair. "Silly Melanie, don't let your big, vampire heart lead you into destruction."

"Or your overactive vampire hormones," Stella added. Her dark eyes flared with jealousy as she stared at the other two vampires. She glanced around as if looking for a target for her frustration. Her eyes settled upon Dora.

"You! What are you doing?" Stella snarled at Dora.

Dora glanced up from the rock she was sitting on and paused filing her nails.

"Watching a Twilight fan-fiction and getting bored," she said.

Fredward gasped He released Melanie as his eyes widened in shock. "She used the sacred name."

Melanie held her hand to her mouth and trembled.

"What, Twilight?" Dora asked.

Stella paled in terror, which was hard to notice given how pale she already was.

"Ah ha!" A young man interrupted as he jumped out from behind a bush wearing only some jeans.

"Now you die, vampire scum."

"Carob!" Melanie cried, and then stopped herself.
"I mean. What brings you to our territory, deceptively hot wolfscum?"

Carob brushed back his auburn hair and stared at Melanie with longing. "Run, Melanie. You can't be part of this."

Fredward shot a dramatic stare at Melanie. "Traitor!" he cried.

Melanie glanced around panic-stricken before she turned and fled into the forest.

"Find me, my love," she cried in the distance.

Dora shook her head and carried on filing her nails. They were a mess after climbing out of her grave.

"For that wolf, you shall die." Fredward threatened Carob and bared his fangs.

"You first," Carob replied. "Burn under the blaze of a full moon," he said as he spun around, dropped his trousers and flashed his ass at the vampires.

Fredward and Stella both shrank back in fear, hissing at the glowing white ass of the werewolf.

They seemed to glow too as their glitter makeup sparkled in the light.

"It burns, my love!" Stella cried, clinging to Fredward.

Dora glanced at them and frowned when she noticed that there was smoke coming off both vampires.

Fredward scooped Stella into his arms before leaping out of the trench and fleeing into the forest.

"Are you shitting me?" Dora asked, feeling no effect from Carob's naked ass other than a mild discomfort from staring at it for so long.

85

Carob straightened up and pulled up his pants. He turned to face her while fastening them.

"What are you?" he asked her.

"I dunno," she said with a shrug.

"If you're with the vampires, then you are an enemy of mine," he said. His shiny chest muscles rippled as he tensed them.

"Yeah? I'm not with anyone, I don't think. So, you're a werewolf?" she asked.

"Yes."

"And your special power is flashing your ass at people?"

"Have you never heard that werewolves are most powerful during a full moon?" he asked her.

"I didn't think it meant their ass."

He shrugged. "It's open to interpretation."

"What your ass is?" She shook her head as the idea of a talking ass jumped into her mind.

"Some people cannot handle the true nature of what it is to be supernatural." He scowled at her.

"I wish my power was unseeing your ass," she said.

"What do you mean? I have a nice ass." He glanced back at his pert backside.

"Dude, it's seriously hairy!"

"I'm not waxing my ass." He pouted. "Real men have hair!"

"Real men don't scamper around the woods and flash their asses at strangers."

"I didn't know you were here." He flushed with embarrassment.

After a moment, he glanced up and studied her. "Why are you here?"

"The vampires think I'm a vampire, and I guess this is their initiation or something." She didn't really know why she was here. She'd come to find out more about the supernatural world, but so far all she'd discovered was that there were a lot of supernatural creatures, and most of them appeared to be a bit fucked in the head.

"You're not a vampire. You'd have burned up if you'd been exposed to a full moon for that long."

"I wonder what I am then."

"I dunno." He shook his head. "Do you want to come with me on a spirit ride to find out?"

"A what?"

He sniffed the air, and then glanced at her. "No time for stupid questions, yes or no?"

She considered her options. The vampires were pissing her off, and this guy might know something she didn't. She needed to find out what she was, then she could use whatever dumbass powers she had to find Kieron.

"Yes."

"Come with me." He offered his hand.

She took it and stood beside him.

"The vampires are coming back." He pulled her after him as they ran through the forest. "I'll see if I can help you while we hide from them."

"Thanks, I think?" She gasped as her pulled her into a dark cave.

11

DIVINE INTERRUPTION

Kieron paused outside the gates of the gothic church that had once been Dora's home. The old stone was chipped and dirty with moss growing in the cracks. He could see holes in the roof where broken tiles had fallen away.

He stared up at the window in the spire, which had once been the window to Dora's room. The glass was dusty and dark, and one of the wooden shutters was broken and hanging off.

They've really let this place go since I was last here.

He glanced at Carissa. She was staring down the road and appeared deep in thought. She'd been distracted since the dead letter office, and still hadn't explained who her mother was.

He contemplated the gates again, considering his options.

If I want to find Dora, this is the best place to start looking. But last time I was here, we got attacked by a deranged holy man.

"What are we waiting for?" Carissa interrupted his thoughts.

"I'm not sure the people we find here will be very friendly," he said.

She shrugged. "We're not looking for friends. We just need information."

He nodded.

What's the worst that could happen?

He pushed open the gate, gritting his teeth at the menacing creak it made. He walked up the path towards the double doors of the church. The wooden doors were old and cracked with rusty handles. A pale, beam of light shone through the opening.

He silently pushed the door open wide, staring into the silent chapel. In the dim candlelight, he could just make out the rows of empty pews down the deserted aisle.

He intended to call out a greeting, but the gloomy feeling of the place silenced him. He glanced at Carissa and placed a finger to his lips, gesturing for her to be quiet. Something felt very wrong.

Peering down at the worn welcome mat of the church, he shuddered. He knew that as a demon, he was not supposed to enter a church, but he was also aware that he'd been in this place before with no problems.

With a sense of foreboding, he crossed the threshold and stepped into the gloomy building. Instinctively, he waited a moment for lightning to strike. When nothing happened, he continued walking down the aisle towards the pulpit.

Shadows moved around the chapel as the breeze caused

the candle flames to shiver. His footsteps echoed around the room as he walked on the cold stone.

His senses were on full alert. There was a feeling of impending doom in the old church and something wholly rotten here.

How has it become run down so quickly?

He paused when he heard a small sob. It was faint. He wouldn't have heard it at all if the room hadn't been so quiet. He turned his head to the left. The sound appeared to be coming from inside the confessional boxes.

He glanced at Carissa. She looked paler than usual. He motioned towards the confessional box that he had heard the sound coming from. She nodded in understanding. She must have heard it too.

They silently walked towards the curtained entrance, standing on either side of it. Another tiny sob echoed through the curtain.

Someone is in there crying.

He shot a look Carissa, and she nodded while she unsheathed her knife.

The air was alive with dark tension. Whatever was inside this booth was not good. There was a dark, ominous feeling radiating from it.

His hand hovered over the curtain for a moment. He dreaded what he would find inside this box. Even hell spawn didn't freak him out this much. There was a stench in the chapel that he couldn't place, but it reminded him of something dark. Being from Hell, he'd seen a lot of darkness in his time.

He shook off the feeling as he ripped open the curtain to see what was contained within the wooden box, freezing in shock as his eyes drank in the visage before him.

The sobbing abruptly ceased, and he heard Carissa gasp beside him.

Slumped inside the box was a drunk and sobbing Theodore Carridine. Several days' growth of dark stubble marred his whiskey face. Food stains and sweat marks dirtied his once white undershirt that bulged out where his potbelly poked against it. His white hair stuck out at crazy angles, and his eyes shone with tears of sadness.

Kieron watched his hand as he raised the bottle of whiskey he nursed to his lips and took long a swig.

"Er, Mr. Carridine?" Kieron asked. He wasn't even sure it was the same man. This guy was a wreck.

"Thas Reverent Carridine to yous." The drunk snapped in response. "I's a reverent."

"Sure you are," Carissa muttered while she sheathed her knife.

Theodore peered at Carissa. He jerked back in his seat and dropped the bottle of whiskey onto the floor. His eyes widened in terror.

"A ghost." He gasped. "No! Make her go away." He rocked back and forth while holding his head. "No more ghosts, no more haunting. I can't vanquish anymore demons. Oh God, please save me. Forgive me for my sins …"

Kieron frowned.

Does he think she's Dora?

"What the fuck?" Carissa peered at Kieron. "Is everyone in this town insane?"

He shrugged. In his experience of Berkville, the only answer he had to that was 'yes'. Although, this situation was new. Dora's father appeared to be suffering from guilt and remorse.

About bloody time.

He frowned.

But why now?

What had made him fall now when he'd been happily burning his daughter alive not so long ago?

Vanquish demons ..

He felt a shiver of fear shoot down his spine. Had Theodore found Dora when she came back from Hell? Had he vanquished her?

"Where is Dora?" He demanded as sparks of anger shot through his body.

If he's hurt her...

Theodore peeked through the fingers he held over his eyes.

"What are you dense? She's there!" He removed one hand and pointed at Carissa. "Back from the dead again, and again ... always haunting me. Why Lord, why?" Theodore cried.

Kieron felt anger burn in his throat as it became clear that they'd hurt his Dora again.

He growled, feeling his demon form fight its way to the surface. His wings flashed out of his back and flapped at Theodore, threatening retribution.

"Where is Dora?" His voice seemed deeper, even to him, as he coldly stared at the broken preacher.

Theodore must have heard the threat in his voice because he looked up at him. His eyes widened even more.

The preacher slid off the pew and fell to his knees before him with awe in his expression. "Thank you Lord, thank you!" He bowed his head to him. "Save me angel."

Kieron frowned.

What the hell? He isn't supposed to like this.

"Where is Dora?" Kieron repeated.

"Dude, you're glowing," Carissa said.

He glanced around the church, which was illuminated by a holy light emitting from his wings as if the church itself had juiced him up.

That's kinda weird.

"She's been taken. I t-t-tried to save her, but the demons have her. Command me angel, and let me serve you." Theodore begged.

He realized that Theodore thought he was an angel, which was kind of amusing. He worried because it sounded as if Dora was in danger. He needed to find her.

"You need to take me to Dora, pathetic human," he said. "And er, have a shower and some coffee before we go to her.

"Yes! Theodore got to his feet. "I'll cleanse my body and soul."

"Yep, and put on a clean shirt because you stink, dude," he added for good measure.

"Oh, right. Sorry about that." Theodore glanced down at his shirt. "After Josie left, I had some problems with the washing machine."

"And lay off the whiskey," he said.

"The devil's drug!" Theodore kicked the bottle in agreement.

"Actually I hear he's more into bee—"

A shot rang out, interrupting him, and a bullet whizzed past his face.

He spun around to see two men wearing dark suits and sunglasses. They were shooting at him from the far end of the chapel.

He grabbed Carissa and launched into the air, on instinct, flying up high to avoid being shot.

"No! Wait." Theodore shouted at the men. "He's an angel of the Lord. Stop shooting. The Vatican will want him alive."

"The Vatican, again?" Kieron heard Carissa mutter.

"Wait, Great Angelic Being. What do you want from me?" Theodore shouted up to Kieron as he rose towards the roof of the church.

Kieron darted left and right to avoid the flying bullets.

"Find Dora, and save her!" he shouted back. "You must save Dora." On that final command, he quickly ascended, bursting through the roof of the church and taking Carissa into the sky with him. He kept going until the men below were just dots beneath them.

"What do we do now?" Carissa asked.

"I dunno. Follow him, I guess? He knows where Dora is."

"If they think she's a demon, he might not be the only one who knows where she is," she said.

"What do you mean?"

"Berkville has a lot of supernatural creatures in it, or it used to. If there was a new demon in town, they would know."

"How would you know that?"

"I've been here before." She shrugged. "It was a very long time ago."

"With your mother?"

She nodded. "It's a long story."

He glanced down at the men who were now outside the church. They were handcuffing Theodore and taking him away.

"It doesn't look like I'll be following him for a while. Okay, let's try it your way. Where to?"

"Head for the brightest neon lights you can find," she said.

He raised a questioning eyebrow.

"Eighties bars attract the freaks," she muttered.

SPIRIT RIDES

Dora tried to push away the sweaty werewolf she was crushed against.

"Dude, get the fuck off me!"

"Shh," Carob said as he covered her mouth with his hand. "They might hear us."

She bit his hand, and he yelped. "There's no one here," She narrowed her eyes at him while trying to get past him in the narrow passage of the cave.

"We might have been followed." He brushed back his auburn bangs and narrowed his eyes at her.

She pushed him back against the rough stone of the cave before stepping back and brushing herself off.

"Eww, do you oil your chest?" She glanced down at her black jacket, which was now shiny with either sweat or oil.

"It's for protection against the cold." He appeared embarrassed.

"Very manly," she muttered.

"My skin chaps easily!"

She shook her head. "Great, a metrosexual werewolf."

He leaned over her. "I'm all man, and I like my women silent," he said with a growl.

"I thought you were half wolf?"

"I am!" He proudly beat his chest. "But I still like women."

"Clearly not if you like them silent. Great, a misogynist," she said with a shake of her head.

"I'm not whatever that is, and I'm not gay!" he cried.

"Metrosexual, not homosexual, you idiot."

"I'm not any sexual!" He folded his arms, and his biceps bulged angrily at her.

"Asexual?" she asked with a grin. It was kind of fun seeing the confused expression appear on his face.

Are all werewolves this stupid?

"Do you want my help or not?" He growled.

"Only if you promise not to rub your baby oil all over me again, and no humping my leg either."

He narrowed his eyes and snarled at her.

She hissed back like an angry kitten. It seemed appropriate.

A confused expression crossed his face again. "You're a weird girl," he said.

"It has been mentioned before." She nodded. "So, which way to the spirit ride thing?"

He paused, appearing deep in thought for a moment.

"Fine, but I'm starting to wonder if this is a bad idea," he muttered. "Follow me." He walked past her, down the narrow passage inside the cave.

She followed him, unable to see much as they went

deeper into the cave. She stumbled on the uneven floor a few times before reaching for the rough, stone wall to steady herself. Her fingers brushed against spongy moss and cold granite.

"I can't see shit," she hissed.

"You will soon. We're nearly there." He called out over his shoulder.

"What is a spirit ride anyway?"

"What do you think it is?"

She considered the words for a moment. "Is it some kind of soul ritual?"

"Some people say it is a spiritual experience."

"Have you done it?"

"Not yet." He shook his head.

She was about to ask more when she noticed a light shining ahead.

The passageway opened up into a wide cavern. In the center was a large pool of water. When she looked up, she saw the moon in the sky above them, lighting up the cave through a hole in the top of the cavern. The opening in the ceiling looked as if it had been worn away by time.

"What happens now?" She sat down on a large rock and peered down into the pool.

"We call the spirit," he said.

"Okay .. " She was beginning to get a bad feeling about this.

What spirit, whose spirit?

He walked to the pool and knelt over the edge. The only sound in the cavern was the hollow drip of water trickling down the side of the walls. The pool glowed white because of the moon's reflection, and the waters were clear all the way down to the rocky ground at the bottom.

He knelt over the pool on all fours and closed his eyes as if in a trance. He let out a low humming sound that vibrated through the cave.

She watched him in silence, holding her breath in anticipation. He slowly inhaled, and she couldn't help but notice his bulging muscles tense. Then he dunked his head in the water in a quick spasmodic movement.

She raised an eyebrow. It had looked kind of cool until he did that.

He pulled his head back out of the water and got to his feet.

"Is that it? Because that was just lam—" She began.

Wind rushed round the cave in a swirling force that shoved hard against her and knocked her into the pool.

She fought to get to the surface, but something grabbed her feet and yanked her down into the watery depths.

She thought she heard Carob say, "Enjoy the ride," before she was sucked down into a deeper part of the caves.

Dora landed with a wet flop onto cold stone. She groaned and rolled over onto her back.

Above her was the pond. It appeared to be levitating in the air above her head.

She sat up and rubbed her back.

Okay, that sucked.

She warily glanced around the stone chamber. It was

dimly lit by candles, and unoccupied. There was a swirling white mist in the far corner that was twisting around in constant movement, shaping and reshaping.

She squinted at it. It seemed to be coming towards her.

What the fuck is that?

She tried to stand as the mist drew closer to her, but her legs wouldn't move. She shook her head trying to clear it and glanced down at her legs. Thick vines were tightly wrapped around them.

Oh, shit.

She glanced back at the mist to find that it had moved rapidly. It was now hovering next to her.

Oh, double shit!

She struggled against the thick vines around her legs, but they refused to budge.

"Help!" she shouted up to Carob, but he didn't seem to be able to see or hear her. He was making his pectorals dance in the reflection of the pool instead.

What a poser.

The mist began to take form. It swirled into the shape of a young man.

She paused struggling as the face reshaped into a familiar one.

"Kieron?"

A completely white and slightly transparent Kieron stood beside her.

She frowned.

Is it him? Is it really him?

"Kieron, is that you?"

"Of course, Dora." His voice sounded wrong.

She shook her head. It didn't feel like Kieron.

"You don't sound like Kieron," she said while trying to tug the vines off her legs.

The mist coughed and lowered his voice. "It has been a long day, Dora." He echoed in a dodgy, southern accent.

She narrowed her eyes. "Wrong accent, and Kieron rarely calls me Dora."

"Snookums?" the mist said in a very odd Russian accent.

"Not even close."

"Ahh fuck it," the Kieron-mist replied in a whiny, male voice. "You are bound to me, and now we must ride."

"Ride what?" She had a sinking suspicion she wasn't going to like the answer, and she struggled to untangle the vines around her legs.

"Each other." The Kieron-mist grinned.

"Well, at least you got that part of his personality right," she muttered as she searched her jeans pocket for her trusty zippo.

"You know, most people fall for the mind-fuck," the Kieron-mist said.

"Yeah, I hear that happens to a lot of people," she said as she pulled the lighter out of her pocket.

The Kieron-mist leaned over her, and his form solidified as his face drew closer to hers.

She cringed inside when it became clear that he intended to kiss her.

Narrowing her eyes, she flicked open the zippo, hoping the dip in the pool hadn't soaked it too much for it to light.

She ducked as his lips neared hers and tried to light the zippo. It lit on the third grind of the wheel. She held it under the vines, trying to burn through them.

"Oww, fuck!" The mist recoiled, and so did the vines, freeing her legs.

She leapt to her feet and pointed the lighter at the misty shape. He was now shifting from Kieron to random people in her life.

"Get the fuck out of my head."

"Or else?" The mist flashed an evil smile.

"Or else I'll ..." She trailed off.

How do I harm mist?

The mist grinned. "Just stop fighting, and enjoy the ride." It floated towards her again.

"Never gonna happen," she muttered. "This might hurt a bit," she said as she conjured up an image of her grandmother naked in her mind.

"Oh, eww!" The mist cringed. "Agh! Make it stop."

"The only way to make it stop is to send me back up there." She pointed to the pond.

"Aww, come on. It's lonely down here." The mist reformed into a sad teenager who was wearing geeky glasses.

"You tell me what I want to know, and I'll hang out with you for a while, but no groping, kissing or going into my head uninvited, or else." She extinguished the zippo and dropped it back in her pocket. "Deal?"

The mist-boy nodded. "Okay, what do you want to know?" he said with a sigh.

"What are you?" she asked.

"I am the last spirit wolf to roam the Earth."

"And, what's a spirit wolf?"

"It's the spirit of a werewolf."

"So, a ghost?"

"Not just a run of the mill ghost! I'm a mystical being

with the power to control nature. I can cont—"

"A pervert is what you are." She interrupted.

"Most people enjoy it." The spirit shrugged.

"People or supernatural creatures that are fucked in the head?"

"Fair point."

"Okay, so what am I?" she asked.

"What do you mean?"

"What kind of messed up supernatural being am I?"

The spirit sniffed the air. "You're not. No wait." He sniffed again, and his eyes widened. "That's just … weird."

"What's weird?"

"You smell human, but there's some kind of demon thing going on in there." He waved his hand over her body. "It's like a strawberry milkshake with barbecue chicken in it—kinda nasty."

"But, what is it?"

"Fucked if I know." The spirit shrugged.

"I thought you were supposed to know all the answers?" She scowled.

"Only the answers on Earth. You're not from here, are you?"

"Yes I am!"

"Well then, you're something new."

She digested the information.

Something new that smells like strawberry chicken, great!

"Wonderful."

"Anything else?" the spirit asked.

"How do you know all the answers?" She wasn't in the mood to trust his vague answers.

"Oh, I was one of the first creatures on Earth. I've always been here watching."

She shot him a look of disbelief as she eyed his Star Wars t-shirt. "You look like you grew up in the eighties."

"It gets boring down here," he grumbled. "Eighties movies are a wonderful way to spend endless time."

"What happens when you run out of eighties movies?"

"Darkness will fall." The spirit ominously intoned. "I'll have to start on the nineties TV show box sets."

"Red Dwarf's a good one."

"Seen it," the spirit said. "Smeghead."

She snorted, and the spirit wiggled his eyebrows at her.

"Okay, what's going on with the vampires and werewolves here? Why are they at war?"

"Ooh, I like that question! Prepare yourself for the story of their dark past."

"Okay." She glanced around wondering how you prepare yourself in a small, dark cave.

"When the first demons walked upon the Eart—" the spirit began.

"Skip the intro." She interrupted.

"It's the best part."

She scowled.

"Okay, okay. Fast forward, buuzzzzz. For a time, the vampires and werewolves were allied and living in harmony. They shared the night, and er, everyone was happy. The great matriarch of the werewolves was young and very beautiful when she inherited the throne from her father. Her reign was prophesized to be the beginning of a great new nation on Earth. She was to marry Prince Devereaux of the vampire clan, a union to bring the fangs together."

"Bring the fangs together, really?" She laughed.

"What? It works with the story. Shut up, and let me finish it." The spirit complained.

"Okay, but no more tacky, movie lines."

"Can't make any promises about that," the spirit said. "Okay, so where was I? Oh yeah, an unholy union ... The marriage was a huge success, and for the first few years, the soon to be king of the vampires and mother of all werewolves lived in wedded bliss. It wasn't long before a child was born, a beautiful girl with both her parent's powers. Word traveled through the supernatural lands about this immortal werewolf, this gifted child, but tragedy was soon to strike."

"In the dark corners of the human world, the Black Bishop heard of this child and wanted her for his own nefarious plans, but she was protected by both the vampires and the werewolves, taking her would not be easy. He set in motion an event that would break the alliance between the species to get his hands on the child."

"What kind of event?" Dora asked.

"He screwed the mother of werewolves. A cheap bottle of wine and the right words, and she was easy."

"Skanky." She wrinkled her nose.

The spirit nodded in agreement. "That's what the king of the vampires thought, so they got a divorce, and he left the realm, never to be seen again."

"The realm?"

"You call it Berkville."

"Oh, okay. What happened next?"

"The mother of the werewolves went insane with grief. She began to believe her husband had cheated on her and

105

waged bloody battles against vampire-kind, which she still does to this day."

"Wait a minute. She inherited her throne, right? How is she still alive now?" she asked.

"Fucked if I know, but she is." The spirit shrugged.

She frowned. There were a lot of things that the spirit didn't know. She was beginning to question his wisdom. Well, she hadn't thought he had much to begin with, but even his memory seemed a bit vague.

"Fast forward again, buuzzzzz. The matriarch's daughter was now fully grown and at a loss in her werewolf world, for she was both vampire and werewolf—a were-pire, if you like, or is it a vamp-wolf?" The spirit paused for a moment, looking confused.

"Anyway." He continued with a shake of his head. "She met a vampire and fell in love. This vampire was honorable and brave He vowed to rescue her from her evil mother and restore the peace between the species, but the matriarch was stronger and killed him before he could fulfill his promise. The were-pire princess was heartbroken and defeated. She ran away never to be seen again. No one knows what happened to her."

"The matriarch still wages war and is winning as the vampire population dwindles. New vampires rise and fall. They pray for a savior, a vampire powerful enough to end this war, but time runs short for them as the wolves advance."

"What is the savior supposed to do, exactly?" she asked while thinking about Terrance.

Isn't that what the vampires called him, 'The Savior'?

"Through his bloodline, the ancient matriarch will be

defeated. His power will bring peace to both species."

She tried to imagine Terrance siring an army of warriors and facing down a beastly matriarch with a stamp collection in one hand and a Dunkin' Doughnut in the other.

"Yeah, or he'll get himself killed," she muttered. She pondered Terrance's options and realized that she needed to get back to him and warn him.

"What about the king of vampires or the were-pire woman? Can't they defeat the werewolf mother?"

"Not so far. Anyway, they're gone now. Probably died out years ago," the spirit said. "Over the years, the matriarch has wielded more power—her immortality for one thing. It's said that nothing can defeat her."

"What happened to the Black Bishop?" she asked. "He started this, didn't he? What about his plans?"

The spirit waved his hand, appearing bored. "Oh, he was just a human. He died long ago."

"Then how come his agents tried to arrest me a few days ago?" She narrowed her eyes.

"It isn't the same guy. Human logic—one dies, and they make another one who's just as lame."

"So, the Black Bishop is a title, like a job? Doing what?"

The spirit pondered the question for a moment. "Last time I checked, they do some accounting, scheming and a bit of spying."

"For who?" She frowned. As a human, she'd never heard of the Black Bishop.

"The Po-pe," the spirit said with a yawn. "You know it's been fun and all, but I'm kind of tired."

"That yawn was beyond fake. Are you blowing me off?" She scowled.

"No, really! I'm soooo sleepy right now."

"Uh, huh?" She rolled her eyes.

"Honest!"

"What's that in your hand?" She noticed an X-box controller had appeared in his left hand.

"This? Oh, nothing. It's a ritual summo—"

"Cut the crap. I'm done anyway. Send me back to Carob, and enjoy your epic game of Gears of War."

"I beat that ages ago."

"I feel a minus-one registering on my care-o-meter." She flipped him off.

"So immature," the spirit muttered as he waved his arms. She felt her body being pulled upwards as she was instantly sucked into the pool above.

She broke the surface and gasped for air before swimming over to Carob and pulling herself out.

"Did you enjoy the ride?" he asked with a wink.

"I didn't go on one."

"What did you do?" He appeared confused.

"I chatted with the spirit instead."

His eyes widened. "B-bu-but he rarely speaks in his own image."

"Yeah? Well, geeks rarely do. Anyway, I need to get going now, but er, thanks for the help."

"Why do you need to go?" He frowned. "What did the spirit tell you?"

"I need to save the Savior and find the Black Bishop," she said with determination.

I need to save Terrance's dumb ass.

13

THE BLACK BISHOP

The Black Bishop took a soothing sip of his fruit tea and reclined back in the Iron Throne. It wasn't really an iron throne. It was the executive chair in the Black Pope's office, known in the ranks as the Iron Throne.

To the Black Bishop, it felt like a throne. For the last five weeks, he had ruled from here while the Black Pope was on vacation.

He slowly exhaled and stared down at his minions, who were working hard in the brightly lit offices below.

The headquarters were quite cheerful even though the office was buried beneath the Vatican.

I could get used to this.

He felt a smile spread across his face as a peaceful serenity washed over him.

In the past four weeks of the Black Pope's absence, he'd averted a gay rights protest in Vatican City, stopped two reports about bestiality in the church going public and captured a demon in Berkville. Life was looking up.

If he kept up his achievement rate for one more week, he'd be able to permanently oust the Black Pope out of his throne.

Black Bishops had been kept out of power for too long. This was his destiny. He just needed everything to go perfect in the Black Pope's absence.

"Hole-eee, hole-eee ..." The phone blared out.

He jumped in his chair with fright and dropped the boiling hot, fruity tea on his crotch.

"Yahh! I hate that fucking phone!" He snarled while brushing hot tea off his groin. He snatched up the handset and held it to his ear.

"Yes?"

"Agent Ochre reporting from Berkville, sir," the voice on the other end said.

"What is it, Ochre? Your report isn't due until next week," he replied.

PISS. I should have known. Who else would have that idiot ring tone?

"I know, sir, but a situation has developed here."

"What situation, the demon?" the Black Bishop asked. He needed that demon. They better not have screwed this up.

"She escaped, sir. But there's more ... er, she was rescued by a group of demons. We think the town is infested."

The Black Bishop didn't reply. His mind was swimming with ideas on how he could use this information. Capturing one real demon was a winning ticket, but a gang of them would be so much more. Hell, he'd probably be the next Pope if he pulled that off. No one had seen a demon since the Dark Ages, capturing several would make him into a hero.

"Sir?" Agent Ochre asked.

"Yes, yes. I'm here. You said more demons. Do you know what kind?"

"Er, evil ones?"

He rolled his eyes. Didn't anyone read Vatican lore anymore? He could swear these agents got dumber every single day.

"What did they look like? You fool!"

"Ohh gothic, they definitely had a gothic vibe."

The Black Bishop slapped his forehead and then sighed. *This man is an imbecile.*

"Did they all look the same?"

"Yes, sir! Well, except the one we saw in the church."

"Which church? What did that demon look like?"

"We saw it at the Berkville Trinity Church. It was kind of weird really," Agent Ochre said.

"How so?"

"We went to the church as it was the last place the first demon …" The Black Bishop heard a rustling of paper when the agent paused. "Dora Carridine is the name she goes by. Anyway, the church was where she lived as a child. Her father is the reverend there, so we dropped by on the off-chance she'd tried to hide there."

The Black Bishop shook his head.

What kind of idiot would try to find devil spawn inside a church?

"She wasn't there." Agent Ochre continued.

Big surprise.

The Black Bishop sighed at how stupid his minions were. PISS were the worst. The Pope's Intelligence Service Subdivision, what a joke. He knew vegetables with more intelligence.

"But we saw this guy with wings there and determined that it was a different demon. Unfortunately, even when we shot at it, it got away."

A guy with wings?

"What did it look like?" He felt a sudden sinking feeling in the pit of his stomach

"Well, the guy was quite young and—Hey Agent Orange, did you think that guy with the wings was attractive?" Agent Ochre shouted down the phone.

The Black Bishop held the phone away from his ear and scowled at it.

"No, you can't go meet Daisey Mae for pie in the diner, fucking idiot! Just answer the question."

There was a muffled agreement in the background before Agent Ochre spoke again.

"Sorry about that, sir. I can confirm that he was a young, attractive man with big white wings. He also was glowing. We checked for radiation, but have yet to decipher the cause of the glow."

"So," the Black Bishop said in a slow and calm voice. "What you are trying to tell me is that while you were inside a church, you saw an attractive man with white wings, who emitted a glow—is it fair to call it a holy glow?"

"Yes, sir. I'd call it a holy glow." Agent Ochre agreed.

"Okay." The Black Bishop continued, and his voice rose in volume. "So upon seeing what the average person may consider to be an angel inside a church, you, in your infinite wisdom, felt the best course of action was to shoot at it?"

"I-I—er ..." Agent Ochre stammered down the phone.

"You fucking idiot! You shot at an angel of the Lord!"

"W-well he didn't identify himself ..." Agent Ochre trailed off.

"They don't carry photo ID with them, you bloody moron!" The Black Bishop slammed his fist into his desk.

"I'm sorry. We'll go find him an—"

"You'll do no such thing!" the Black Bishop said as an idea crossed his mind. "I want surveillance only on this. Look but don't touch."

"B-but why? Shouldn't we try to speak to it?"

"You won't do anything. You've already proven you're incompetent. No, I want surveillance reports only. There is only one person capable of dealing with this."

"Who?"

"Me," he said. "Make arrangements for my arrival. I'm coming to Berkville." He smiled at his reflection in the polished desk.

I'll be the new Black Pope before the end of the week if I kill some demons and discover an angel.

MEEBLE ZIP

Dora stood outside the tall, iron gates of the vampire's nest. She stared at the somber exterior of the gloomy mansion house and shook her head.

They might as well put up a sign outside it saying, 'Vampire's Nest Here'.

The dark gothic building loomed high in the sky, standing out in startling contrast to the cozy suburban houses surrounding it, which all had perfect lawns and warm and inviting façades. It looked as if it belonged in a horror movie.

"Morning!" A cheerful voice called out behind her. She spun around to see a man in an argyle sweater across the street, picking up his newspaper off his driveway.

"Hi," she said to the smiling man.

"Just moved in?" He nodded at the haunting mansion.

"Thinking about it," she said while she plastered a pleasant smile on her face and wondered what the neighbors thought about the vampire nest.

"They're a lovely bunch." The man encouraged. "At

first I was worried. You know, rock stars like that moving in, but they've been a real addition to the neighborhood. They joined the neighborhood watch and helped out at the local school bake sale."

She nodded still smiling.

Vampires at a bake sale. That could only happen in the fucking burbs.

"Well, nice to meet you." The man smiled again and then turned to walk back to his house while swinging his paper in time to his jaunty whistle.

She turned back to the mansion and shrugged as she rang the doorbell. She peered up at the six-foot gates and waited. After a few moments, an electronic voice burred out of the intercom to her left.

"State your purpose."

"Um, what?" she said to the box.

"State your purpose." The intercom repeated in an electronic voice.

She stared at the box. "Do you mean my purpose for visiting here?"

"Meeble-zip." The intercom buzzed.

"What?" She shouted at it.

"Mmmnnzzzz-state your purpose. Presszzzz the fricken button. No mimezzz here." The intercom screeched.

She scowled at the intercom. There were no buttons on it, just a speaker. "There's no fucking button to press!" She pointed at it while getting frustrated by the stupid thing.

"No mimezzz allowed. Pleazzze go away, buzz." The machine blared.

"I'm not a mime! Just open the fucking gates," she snapped.

115

"Please state your purposezz-zip." The intercom repeated.

"I'm here to kill you," she said as she glanced up to the top of the fence, contemplating breaking in instead.

She spotted a CCTV camera mounted at the top of the stone gatepost, which was pointing down at her.

"Pleazzzzzzzzzzzzzzzze   prezzzzzzzzz   the buttonzzzzzzz. No mimezzzz here," the intercom replied.

She scowled and flipped off the CCTV camera.

"Welcome to the Devereaux House," the intercom said in a crisp voice.

There was a loud creak as the iron gates opened. She stormed through the gates, intent on murdering the person behind the intercom. "Thank you and have a nice day. Meeble-zip." She heard the intercom behind her as she rushed up the driveway.

She stomped her way up the long hill that led to the entrance of the house, and her cheeks burned with anger. Whoever had been fucking with her over the intercom was going to get a gigantic slap.

She burst through the front doors and frowned. The hallway was deserted, as was every room she passed.

Okay, it was daytime now, but last time she was here every room had been milling with glittery vampires. Hell, they'd had a pool party and a barbecue.

She shook her head. All that mattered was finding the person on the intercom and slapping the meeble-zip right out of them.

She headed for the main hall, expecting to find a few sniggering vampires hanging around the intercom, but it too was deserted.

Where the hell is everyone?

Something felt very wrong.

Terrance!

She raced down the wood-paneled halls to the sweeping staircase that led up to his rooms. She paused at the foot of the stairs when she heard chanting.

She stood still for a moment and listened. It was coming from a door beneath the staircase.

She noticed the door was ajar, and there was a faint light emitting through the gap. She peered through the gap and gasped.

Inside the room were hundreds of vampires seated in dark wooden pews that surrounded a circular stage. The vampires all wore blood-red robes and were chanting.

The Ancient One stood on the stage, leading the chant. He wore a black robe and held a golden staff in his left hand.

He banged the staff onto the stage, and the chanting ceased.

"My fellow rulers of the dark, the time of prophecy is upon us. Now, we shall wreak our vengeance upon those who wish to harm us. Now, we shall shower in the blood of our enemies!"

The crowds of vampires cheered loudly, some standing and applauding.

"But to do this, my immortal allies …" He continued as the cheering abated. "We must embrace our enemy."

Some vampires booed while others unenthusiastically clapped.

"And so it is written," The Ancient One roared. "The Savior shall smite our enemy with the power of his blood, and we shall rule over all until his last drop. Only his blood can convert them to our clan." The Ancient One held up a vial of blood and stepped aside to reveal a werewolf chained to a table.

Dora frowned.

What the fuck are they doing?

The Ancient One forced open the growling wolf's mouth and poured the vial of blood into it. The wolf howled as his body began to convulse.

The vampires in the crowds all gasped in awe as wolf fur fell off its body. Its snout shrank, and its eyes glowed red.

The howling became a scream as its body jolted and shuddered, and it transformed into the body of a pale man.

The Ancient One unfastened the chains around the man and handed him a robe. "Welcome to our clan." He smiled at the man.

"I'm hungry." The man's vampire fangs popped out.

The crowds applauded in a standing ovation.

"But how many can the Savior create?" Someone shouted over the din.

"At least a few thousand until we've bled him dry." The Ancient One stroked his beard as a crazy glint appeared in his eyes.

Dora felt a shiver of fear.

Terrance, they mean to bleed him dry!

She turned and raced up the stairs to his room, worry knotting in her stomach.

I need to get him out of here, right now!

She burst into Terrance's room to find him lying on a plush bed. He had cucumber slices over his eyes and cotton wool balls between his toes, which were wiggling in time to the lame music that was playing from an old record player.

"Terrance, what the fuck are you doing?" she cried.

"What?" He jolted off the bed, and the cucumber slices splatted onto the marble floor.

"Oh Dora, my lov—er, companion," he said with a smile. "Isn't this new world wonderful?"

"No, it sucks ass. Come on. We need to get out of here."

"But why? I just had my first spa day. A spa! It's wonderful. You must try it."

She grabbed his arm and tried to pull him out of the room. "We don't have time for this shit. They're coming for you!"

"Coming for me, who? Not the angry townsfolk again?" He hobbled after her while trying to pluck the cotton wool out from between his toes.

"No, it's worse. This time it's the vampires," she said.

"Don't be silly. I am their Savior. They'd never hurt me."

"Did they take some of your blood?" she asked.

"I had a blood test." He nodded. "But that's normal isn't it?"

"It wasn't a blood test. They plan to bleed you dry!"

He pulled back and smiled at her while shaking his head. "Silly Dora, you'd need more than one vial to bleed a vampire dry."

"Terrance, I swear, if you don't move your ass right now, I am going to slap you."

"Oh, how kinky. Okay, I'll try that." He winked.

She growled and raised her hand to slap him for real, but vampires burst into the room behind her, surrounding them both.

An iron grip clamped around her wrists and tugged her arms behind her back.

"What are you doing?" Terrance cried. "Release my Dora!"

"I'm sorry it had to come to this," the Ancient One said.

"Come to what?" Terrance asked.

A doe-eyed female vampire patted Terrance on the shoulder. He turned around, and she injected something into his neck. He swooned and fell unconscious into the girl's arms.

"Your imprisonment," the Ancient One said.

"What did you do to him?" Dora cried while struggling against the hands holding her wrists and shoulders.

"Shall I do her too?" the doe-eyed vampire asked.

"No, she won't be any trouble." The Ancient One shook his head. "She's just a pathetic human. Put them in the dungeons."

Dora scowled at him as she was led out of the room. Behind her, she heard the doe-eyed vampire say, "Meeble-zip," before laughing.

15

THE FALLEN ONE

Carissa came to an abrupt halt on the busy high street, and Kieron paused beside her.

"What?" he asked.

"I think we're being followed," she said, glancing at their reflection in a store window.

"Don't be ridiculous. There are hundreds of people here." He scanned the busy shopping area and only saw masses of humans spending their hard-earned money on bits of crap that they didn't need.

He was about to turn around when she stopped him. "Don't! I don't want them to know we've spotted them," she hissed.

"Who?" He scanned the reflection in the glass too. He saw humans of all shapes and sizes bustling down the busy street behind them.

"Everyone is following us because of the direction of the street," he said, watching an old lady shuffle out of a store, which sold slot machines judging by the window display.

Why would an old lady want to buy a slot machine? He wondered as she turned in their direction and headed towards them.

"Pension thieving bastards," she muttered as she walked by.

"You see the two men in dark suits standing beside the trash cans?" Carissa interrupted his thoughts.

He spotted them straight away because unlike everyone else, they weren't moving. They were standing to attention beside each other, staring directly at him and Carissa.

"Okay, they are acting a bit strange," he admitted.

"Come on." She grabbed his arm. "Let's see if they continue following us."

He nodded as he and Carissa made their way down the bustling shopping street, keeping their eyes on the reflections of the men in the shop windows.

His heart beat faster when he noticed the men were following them. The suited strangers kept a steady pace behind them.

"Shit, we need to lose them," she said. "They can't come into the Demon District with us."

"We could try making a run for it."

"No, it won't work. I tried that earlier when I raced you across the street."

His pulse raced. He knew he couldn't take to the air in these crowds, and so far, his powers on Earth were lacking in anything other than the ability to fly.

"Buy a shirt, you cheap bastard!" A vendor from a market stall shouted out to him.

Kieron glanced at the stall owner who was waving his

wares at him. It wasn't the best marketing pitch he'd ever heard. It wasn't the worst one either.

He glanced down at his naked chest and realized he was defenseless in many ways. Along with not owning a shirt, he also didn't know if his spells would work here.

He turned to Carissa as the people around them seemed to close in on him, and panic bubbled in his throat. "What are we going to do?"

She grinned at the market stall vendor. "That just gave me a great idea. When I say freeze, I want you to stand completely still. No matter what, don't move, okay?"

He frowned. It sounded like the stupidest idea ever, but he nodded. "Okay."

They walked past large window of a store called J. C. Penney. In the window was an array of models in a various poses. The window stretched from floor to ceiling and seemed to go on forever.

He watched the men's reflections in the glass when a bus drove by, blocking his view.

Carissa slammed him sideways against the window, so he was facing her.

"Freeze," she hissed while placing her finger on her chin in a thoughtful pose and freezing in position.

He froze in position with a frown on his face. He could see the men across the street. They were rushing by in a panic and shouting at each other.

He couldn't hear their comments, but they appeared to be bickering when one slapped the other one across the face.

He watched in awe as they ran straight past him and Carissa and past a crossroads into the next section of the shopping area.

"Okay, you can move now," Carissa said.

"Were those the stupidest spies ever or something?" he asked.

"I've actually seen worse, but they were pretty close. Come on. Let's lose them before they come back. We're nearly there!"

He peeled himself off the store window and ran after her as she led him down a side street.

"What is the Demon District anyway?"

"You'll see." She wiggled her eyebrows at him, leading him into a dark alley.

The walls were slimy with moss, and drainpipes continually dripped water down the cracked bricks. The alley was a narrow space between two tall buildings that was confined and dimly lit.

He followed her, carefully trying not to touch the walls with his bare arms.

I really should have bought a shirt.

There was a red glow at the end of the alley. It reminded him of Hell for a moment. He could almost smell the burnt air of his abandoned home.

He sighed. He hadn't signed up for this. When he left Hell, it was to be with Dora, not to be trapped on Earth on an endless quest to find her. The longer he was apart from her, the more he worried he would never find her.

And then what? Will I get an Ikea-furnished condo and a job in marketing just so I can kiss Satan's ball-sack every morning?

He shivered. He couldn't think of a worse fate.

As they neared the end of the dark tunnel, his hopes lifted when he finally saw something in this world that felt familiar.

He stared in awe at the neon lights, people fighting in the streets, burly guards in doorways, and hundreds of unusual looking creatures milling down the busy strip.

Some were humans in costume, and others were demonic creatures blending into the crowds. The red neon sign for 'The Demon District' made his heart glow. It was home, it was Hell on Earth and it was a place he could belong.

"Welcome to the Demon District." Carissa flashed him a knowing smile.

"What is this place?" He stared in awe at the werewolf dancing with the human girl in a red cape.

Three loud Vikings were brawling with a sloth demon outside of a bar called 'Rawr'. Hundreds of people and things mingled together on the street, some entering bars or nightclubs and others leaving them.

"For human's, it's fun, and for supernatural creatures, it's a place they call home," she said. "It's changed a lot since I was last here, but—oh good, it's still here. She pointed to a dimly lit bar called 'Devlin's Place'.

He followed her through the milling crowds to the entrance of the dark saloon. In comparison to the neon-lit busier bars, this one seemed to melt into the background with no patrons going in or out of it. "Are you sure it's open?" he asked.

"Yeah, it never closes," she said. "If the world exploded tomorrow, Devlin's Place would still hover in the ether. I need you to wait in here for me. I need to visit my old crew."

"Why can't I come with you?"

"They're wary around strangers." She refused to meet his eyes.

"I'm not that strange.'

"It's just easier this way."

"Fine, if you don't want me to meet your friends, I'll wait here."

"It's nothing like that." She finally glanced in his direction.

"What is it then?"

"They don't like angels," she admitted.

"I'm not a fucki—"

"I know!" She interrupted. "But they don't. Just trust me on this. It's easier if you wait here."

"Fine, but I'm not happy about it." He folded his arms and scowled at her.

"Just go in the bar and brood over a beer. I won't be long," she said before she turned and disappeared into the crowds, leaving him behind.

He shook his head in disappointment. "Dora would never have abandoned me outside a bar," he muttered as he pushed his way through the grimy saloon doors and stepped into a dark room.

It was a quiet bar. Only the low music of the jukebox could be heard over the muttering from the various patrons. The lighting was dim with only a few wall lights lighting each booth.

He glanced at the bar, which stretched the length of the room. An old barman was talking to two customers who were slouched on wooden bar stools. The booths adjacent to the bar were all full of customers, who were drinking or speaking in hushed tones.

At the far end of the room, several more booths stood empty, barring one.

He walked towards the bar, studying the lone patron in the booth at the end.

The man appeared to be human. Well, what Kieron could see of him did.

Dark shadows were cast over his eyes. From this angle, all Kieron could see was his leather-clad arm, his stubbled jaw and a glint of a dagger at his hip.

He sipped his drink in silence, and Kieron felt a shiver run up his spine. There was something deadly about him.

Kieron climbed onto a bar stool and continued studying the lone drinker as he waited for the barman.

"Looking over there will bring you nothing but trouble, son," a gruff voice said.

Kieron turned towards the bar and looked up at the gray-bearded barman. He was old and grisly looking. He wore a creased gray shirt and a green apron.

"Why, who is he?" Kieron asked, glancing back at the stranger.

The stranger almost melded into the shadows with his dark presence.

"Some questions are better not asked. Best not rile him the wrong way. The last man who stared at the Fallen One didn't make it out of here in one piece," the barman muttered in an ominous tone. "What can I get ya?"

"A beer would be fine," Kieron said before staring back at the dark man. There was something intriguing about him.

The barman slammed a frothy pint on the counter. "Take my word for it. Some people are best left alone," he muttered before he swept up the coins Kieron had dropped on the bar into his palm and wandered off.

Kieron watched the dark stranger lift the beer to his mouth and realized after a moment that he wasn't the only one watching.

Several patrons were transfixed on the Fallen One, many shooting shifty glances in his direction with fearful eyes.

He felt a shiver of fear as the man tipped his glass, but the feeling evaporated when the stranger missed his mouth and poured the drink down his chest instead.

"Fuck!"

Kieron strained to hear the low whisper of his deep voice as he calmly brushed the beer away.

Behind him, Kieron heard a high-pitched giggle from one of the patrons.

He watched the Fallen One shoot a deadly sideways glare at the patron, and in a smooth and rapid movement fling his glass at the giggling man's head.

Kieron spun on his stool just in time to see the glass hit the patron's forehead with a loud thunk before he slumped to the floor in an unconscious heap.

The Fallen One stepped out of the booth to reveal a tall and muscular man in his mid-twenties. Wisps of short brown hair were visible under his dark hood, which ended just above his deep brown eyes.

There was a spark of danger in the dark pools of his eyes, which were appealingly framed by dark lashes. His cloak flowed to the floor behind him, and his shirt was a tunic made of animal hide. His worn leather pants ended at his hip where his belt hung low because of his sword and dagger attached to it.

He stepped away from the booth, slinging a crossbow over his shoulder. The room was silent, and all eyes were watching him.

Kieron felt a tremble of fear as the Fallen One took a step towards him.

The Fallen One stumbled, and the meaning of his name became clear when he tripped over fresh air and fell face-first onto the floor.

No one in the bar made a sound, but Kieron frowned.

What the fuck did he fall over?

The Fallen One jumped up off the floor and righted himself, brushing dust off his knees.

"The floor fucking moved, I swear it!" he cried.

No one disagreed with him.

He strolled over to the bar and took a seat beside Kieron.

"Another beer." He called out to the barman in a deep and masculine voice.

Kieron stared at the Fallen One. After a moment, the Fallen One turned to face him and stared back with a dangerous glint in his eyes.

"Can I help you?"

"Maybe," Kieron said. "What are you?"

The Fallen One laughed. "I have been many things, most recently, the head warlock of this province. And what the fuck are you?" His eyes scanned over Kieron, and a frown furrowed his brow.

"I'm er, Kieron." He introduced himself.

"I bet you are," the Fallen One said with narrowed eyes. "But that's not what you really are, is it, little one?"

"What do you mean?" He frowned.

Does he know I'm a demon?

"You're totally fucked, dude. That's what you are."

Kieron had the horrible feeling this was not going to end well.

16

FLY MY PRETTIES, FLY

K ieron stared at the Fallen One. "What the hell is that supposed to mean?"

The Fallen One took a sip of his beer. "I know what you are. I could smell it the second you walked in here."

Kieron shivered. Was his demon essence so strong here that people could smell it?

He rubbed his arms. "I don't know what you mean." He glanced around the bar, ensuring no one else was listening.

Several patrons shot him shifty glances.

The Fallen One smoothed the goatee, which curled under his chin. "You may fool them, but you don't fool me. I know what you really are. Your angelic essence smells like rancid ass to my nostrils."

"What did you just call me?" Anger burned in his belly.

Did he just say I smelt like a fucking angel?

"You're an angel," the Fallen One said as he sniffed

him. "A totally fucked up one."

Kieron leapt off his stool and felt his wings shoot out of his back as rage filled his body. "Take that back! I'm not a fucking angel!"

The Fallen One pointed to his massive wings, which were wildly flapping and blowing items off the bar. "Then what the fuck are those?"

"Demon wings."

The Fallen One laughed. "I love it. You're a disillusioned angel. What, you thought those pathetic nubs on your forehead were horns? I've seen bigger spikes on a hedgehog."

Kieron's wings rose above him and flashed in anger at the robed stranger.

How dare he mock my horns.

"At least I have horns!" Kieron narrowed his eyes at him. "I'm not some gravity-confused twat who likes to wear leather."

After the words left his mouth, Kieron felt a shiver of fear.

The Fallen One turned to face him with narrowed dark eyes, and his nostrils flared.

He climbed off his stool and rolled up the sleeves of his cape. "Bitch, imma 'bout to fuck you up."

Kieron heard chairs scraping behind him. Through the mirror behind the bar, he saw the patrons all scramble out of their seats and flee.

He clenched his teeth and tensed his muscles, ignoring his fear and facing the Fallen One instead. "I'm not afraid of you."

"You will be" The Fallen One raised his arms, and

electricity crackled in the air around him. A ball of dark energy swirled between his hands while black and purple mist gathered in the air behind him.

His eyes glittered with dark magic, and his muscles rippled beneath the leathers.

Kieron backed away, fearing what that kind of energy could do to him.

"What the fuck are you, man?"

"I'm the warlock that's about to fuck your angel ass up, boy." The Fallen One shot a ball of dark energy at him, and Kieron yelped and dived sideways into a table to avoid it hitting him.

"Man, I love messing with you guys," the Fallen One said as he shot another burst of dark energy at Kieron, this time hitting him squarely in the chest and sending him shooting back through the saloon doors.

Kieron gasped in pain as dark matter clawed into his chest. He felt some kind of power inside him rear up in protest, and his hand glowed golden.

He touched the swirling dark mass hovering above his chest, and the golden glow and dark energy collided in a small explosion, blowing each other away.

Okay, this angel bullshit is weird.

He heard heavy footsteps coming from inside the saloon and decided not to wait to find out what else was in store for him.

He launched into the air and flew several feet above the ground.

The Fallen One stepped through the saloon doors and scowled up at him.

"Screw you!" Kieron shouted down to the warlock,

and then feigned left as another ball of dark energy shot into the sky. He easily dodged several more balls of dark pain.

"Get some glasses, old timer." He jeered down at the Fallen One. He yelped again when he saw the Fallen One's eyes narrow, and his lips pinch with vengeful intent.

Purple lightning shot from the skies in a million spikes of dark electricity, singeing Kieron's wings as he darted in the air trying to avoid being hit.

Fucknuts!

He panicked and flew higher in the sky to avoid the majority of the spikes shooting through the air.

"Where the fuck do you think you're going?" He heard the Fallen One shout.

Kieron continued to rise until he was hidden behind the clouds. He breathed a sigh and rested for a moment. This was a nightmare.

Where is Carissa? Where is Dora?

His heart ached for a moment. Dora would have one-shotted that warlock fool with a single comment.

"I said … where the fuck do you think you're going?" The Fallen One's voice echoed in his mind, and he nearly fell out of the sky in shock.

"Get out of my head!" he snapped.

"Make me. You're mine now, bitch." The Fallen One laughed. The laugh seemed to extend to outside of Kieron's mind when it became a sharp cackle.

He frowned. That wasn't the Fallen One's deep, husky tone. It was a woman.

He spun in the air towards the direction of the cackle and saw several witches flying at him on what appeared to be flying motorbikes. The biker-looking witches on hogs and choppers shot through the air towards him, cackling while their long tendrils of hair swirled behind them as they raced through the clouds.

Oh, you've gotta be fucking kidding me!

He yelped and turned to flee as the Fallen One's words echoed through his mind.

"Fly, my pretties, fly!"

Kieron flapped his wings as hard as he could, hoping to put some distance between him and the cackling witches.

He headed towards Dora's home. It was the only place he knew in Berkville, and it was a church. If there were such things as sanctuaries on Earth, he knew that would be where he found his.

He swooped through the clouds, feeling cold air rush across his cheeks as his giant wings flapped through the sky in rhythmic repetition, boosting him forward with every flap.

The roar of engines seemed to fade away, and he glanced back to see the distance between the hellish bikers growing. He breathed easy for a moment.

I'm going to make it.

He stared ahead as the spires of Dora's church came into view. His heart almost stopped as his throat closed in fear.

Seven witches on motorbikes hovered in the air in front of him, beckoning him to come closer with their hands.

He pulled back in panic and veered left, heading for the forest. He heard the kick-start of the bikes as the witches followed.

His wings were aching as he fought his way through the sky. He realized he was losing altitude as the treetops of the forest came into view.

Sweat beaded his brow, and his muscles ached with every flap of his wings.

Come on. Don't give up on me now!

Adrenaline flooded through him as a cackle behind him felt close to his ear.

He glanced back to see a red-haired witch directly behind him. She reached out, trying to grab his ankle, and he pointed downwards into the forest to avoid her.

He shot down through the woods, trying to avoid the oncoming trees. Darting as hundreds of trees sped by his face and branches scratched at his bare skin.

Exhaustion and fear took over when he hit a tree and bounced off it. Spinning out of control, he banged into trees and bounced on to other ones.

He cried out in pain as the woodland bitch-slapped him around until he crashed into the leafy forest floor and grazed across it to a painful stop.

A cackle filled the air above him, and he tried to raise himself off the ground on battered and shaking arms.

His muscles trembled with exertion as he tried to get up and escape. His head was unclear and hazy, and his body felt weak. He felt hot breath on his cheek when a witch laughed in his ear.

The last thing he saw was the Fallen One's boots walking towards him before welcoming darkness shrouded his view.

17

WEAPONS OF TINY DESTRUCTION

Dora paced her cell, trying to think of ways to get out of it, but paused when she heard Terrance sigh.

She turned to peer through the bars into his adjoining cell as he threw himself onto the rickety, metal bed at the far end of it.

"Terrance, don't just sit there. Do something!" she cried. The guy could teleport. What was he sitting on his ass for?

"What are you doing?"

He glanced up at her through the bars. "I'm afraid there is little I can do, fair Dora."

"Get off your ass and teleport us out of here, or something."

"I tried. It doesn't work."

She frowned. She hadn't seen him try much of anything so far.

"What do you mean?"

"There is something blocking my powers." He waved

his arms as if to demonstrate the problem, and nothing happened.

"I think it is something to do with these markings in my abode."

She peeked inside his dungeon. Sure enough, there was an array of strange symbols and sigils decorating the walls and ceiling.

She glanced back into her own cell to compare her blank walls to Terrance's marked and engraved ones.

It must be some kind of special vampire cage.

He dropped his shoulders in defeat and sighed. "This is not how I intended to spend my immortality. Why did you have them put us in the dungeons?"

"I didn't ask them to put you in here," she said. "Terrance, you do realize that they plan to kill you, don't you?"

He shrugged. "So? I have died many times now."

"No, they were really going to kill you by draining you dry."

"Don't be silly, Dora. I am their savior. It's prophesized that I shall bring about a new era for vampire-kind." He stood up from his bed and raised his hand to his chest as if to salute vampire-kind.

"And so, the great house of Devereaux shall be restored to its rightful place in the—"

"You're a walking blood bank." She cut in. "A vending machine for special blood. They plan to consume you."

He stared at her with an expression of abject horror. "But, they worship me …" He trailed off.

"Marketing," she said. "All marketing panders to the ego."

Realization seemed to pass over his face, echoing a range of emotions. "Those treacherous monsters!"

He held his hand to his throat. "Betrayed," he wailed. "Betrayed and sentenced to an unworthy end! How could such a fate befall me? How could such misery be fated to one as innocent as I? I shall fight fire with fire," he cried, leaping onto his bed. "I shall take my life before they can have it!"

"No, Terrance don—" She didn't finish her sentence before he gripped his head in his hands.

A wild gleam glittered in his eyes. "Take this you devious fools!" he cried as he twisted his head. There was an audible crack when he broke his own neck.

"You fucking idiot!" She tightly gripped the bars as he fell face-first onto the floor, and his head rolled to the side, staring at her with empty eyes.

Even though the scene was a little upsetting, she knew he'd wake up with no permanent side effects in a few hours.

"Bloody moron!" She told his corpse.

What the hell did he do that for?

She shook her head at the absolute stupidity of his actions. Now she would be stuck here waiting for him to wake up.

"You fucking emo idiot. I swear that when you wake up, I'm going to kill you!"

"Now, now, there's no need to threaten our savior," a familiar voice said behind her.

She spun around to face the Ancient One, who was studying her through the bars of her door.

"Screw you too," she said, narrowing her eyes at the master vampire.

Terrance had totally pissed her off by ruining any escape

plans that she might have had.

Since she was already trapped in a cell, there wasn't any reason to be nice to this wanker.

"You are finally going to reap the rewards of your disrespect," the Ancient One said. "Until now, you have been under the protection of the Savior, but there is no such protection for you anymore, worthless human."

"I'm a human?" She wondered aloud. "Since when?"

"We have studied you and determined that you are nothing more than a human."

"Then, how come I can't die?"

"Just because a group of mentally deficient rednecks can't kill you, it doesn't mean I can't." The Ancient One shot her a devilish smile before turning to the vampire guards behind him. "Open her cell, and bring her to the courtroom."

Dora stared at the massive executioner, who was standing in front of her. He wielded a shiny ax and wore a wicked smile.

She shivered and scanned the pit around her. There was only one exit, which the ax-happy vampire was blocking with his bulging form.

"This is bullshit, man. You call this a trial?" She called out to the Ancient One and his council of five middle-aged vampires.

"If you win the trial, you shall be rewarded with your freedom." The Ancient One called down to her. "All you have to do is walk through the door."

She glanced back at the burly vampire, who was standing in her way. He wore leather pants and a black leather mask.

"Wonderful," she muttered. "You're a fan of Fifty Shades, aren't you?" she asked.

The executioner rolled his eyes. "Just because I like leather, it does not make me a sadist," he said in a squeaky voice.

"No, but the ax is a dead giveaway," she muttered under her breath.

She eyed the sharp ax, focusing on the sigils engraved down the side of it.

If they can trap Terrance with those things, will they be able to kill me with them?

Her pulse raced as the executioner moved towards her. She backed up against the wall of the pit, fighting to ignore her fear.

She took a deep breath and narrowed her eyes, accessing her anger and refusing to crumble. She clenched her hands into fists and tried to call upon the demon powers she once had.

Come on! This screwed up existence has to have some benefits. Hell powers, kick in already!

She concentrated hard on summoning something that would assist her.

She stared at her hands in awe as they glowed red, first her fingers, then her palms. She shook her head. It wasn't enough. She needed more power.

Digging her fingernails into her palms, she willed demonic power to flow through her.

The glow spread up to her wrists while a searing pain

ripped across her chest. She bit back a scream of agony as pain blossomed through her entire body. She closed her eyes in concentration and clenched her jaw, forcing herself to summon a weapon.

After only seconds, she felt something lightweight appear in her left hand. She expelled a sigh of relief before glancing down at it.

Finally, something I can fight back wit—she widened her eyes as she stared down at the miniature crossbow in her hands.

It was golden and shiny with a tiny, toothpick-sized wooden arrow in it.

Are you shitting me? I ask for a vampire weapon and get Tom Thumb's fucking crossbow!

She raised her hand to eyelevel and stared at the tiny contraption. There were holes in it where her fingers should go, so it would fit on her hand like a glove.

Only one arrow! What the hell am I supposed to do with that?

She heard coughing and glanced up to see the executioner waving red smoke out of his face.

Did I make the red smoke too?

Shrugging, she ducked down and slipped the tiny crossbow onto her hand. Using the smoke for stealth, she aimed her gloved hand at the executioner.

Maybe a toothpick can annoy him enough, so I can get past him.

She pulled back her index finger, which activated the triggering mechanism. The tiny arrow shot out of the bow. She watched it fall short of the executioner's chest and embed in his knee instead.

"Fuck! Oww," the executioner cried. "My adventuring days are over now I've taken an arrow in the knee." He whined as he pulled it out. "I'll end up as an NPC in Skyrim." He held the tiny projectile in his massive hands. "Did you just fucking shoot me with a toothpick?"

He stared at the tiny stick with a blank expression. "Did I just take a toothpick in the knee?" He growled while lifting his ax and heading towards her with a mean look in his eyes.

Shit!

She panicked and scanned the small pit for an escape route, but it was too small, and he was too close to her.

Stupid fucking crossbow.

She glanced down at it and paused. It was loaded with a second arrow.

She grinned.

It's self-loading.

She aimed it at the executioner, higher this time, so it hit his chest. Then she pulled back her fingers into a fist.

The arrow shot out of the bow with such force that it slammed her back against the rough wall of the pit.

She barely saw it as it smashed into the vampire's chest and knocked him off his feet. He arched in agony and screamed. Flesh fell away from his bones, and he crumbled to dust on the floor.

She heard gasps coming from the council above, as their head executioner became a giant pile of dust.

She pushed herself off the wall and narrowed her eyes at the vampire council before walking towards the open doorway and climbing the stone steps up to the courtroom.

The elder vampires backed away from her when she raised her hand towards them, but the Ancient One held his ground.

"I'm not afraid of a toothpick, girl." His fangs popped out, and he launched at her.

She feigned left, so he flopped into the pit and landed face-first in the pile of dust with an 'eww' sound. She turned on her heel and raced out of the room towards the door that led to the dungeons.

Her pulse was racing as she ran down the hall, shooting random toothpicks at vampires when she passed them.

She glanced back and gulped when she saw the large group of roaring vampires chasing after her.

Dodging the clawed hands that reached for her, she darted into the cellblock, tugging on the release lever as she dashed past it.

All the cell doors swung open in unison.

Terrance, please don't still be dead, or we're both fucked!

Terrance stepped out of his cell ahead of her and scratched his head, looking around him with a confused expression.

"Terrance!" she cried, and he spun to face her. "Get us the hell out of here!"

"What happened?" he asked as she pumped her arms, hearing the sounds of an army of angry vampires chasing her.

"No time." She gasped as she felt sharp teeth graze the back of her neck. "Teleport." She leapt away from the teeth and into his arms.

Terrance clicked his fingers, and the dungeon full of angry vampires faded away as they swirled into the ether.

THE SPY WHO SQUEAKED

Pooey rested his head on the bars of his cell and sighed.

What if it doesn't work?

For a moment, he felt the urge to give up and just stay here, but some part of him refused to give up.

Ever since he had met Dora, he had realized that there was nothing you couldn't defeat.

He gripped the bars with his paws and let out a loud roar. No, he wouldn't give in to depression, not this time! There weren't any Häagen Daz or cheesy puffs around for him to binge on anyway.

He glanced back and grimaced at the bowl of kibble in the corner.

Fucking rabbit food!

He eyed his fur-lined cell and crossed the room with determination, scowling when he walked over the dark-brown paw print in the center of the floor.

The decorator should be shot.

He pulled his bed aside and reached under the mattress for a small bag that he had hidden beneath it. He stared into the contents of the plastic bag with a grim smile.

Bitch candy, he thought as he pushed the bed back into place with his knee.

He strode back towards the circular door of his cell and peered through the bars, still gripping the bag.

The giant, gray-furred guard was standing down the hall, its fluffy tail standing to attention behind it. It was about the same size as him and wore a red bandana around its neck.

Pooey plucked some bitch candy out of the bag and stared at it. The giant acorn shone as it rested in his hands.

Here boy, come get your treats.

He rolled the acorn through the bars, and it thumped across the tiled floor of the hallway.

He moved back after taking a fleeting glance through the bars. He saw the squirrel guard's flinty eyes follow the noise and then widen when it saw the acorn.

Its tongue lolled out of the side of its mouth, and it began to move towards the acorn.

That's right, dumbass. Follow the food.

He dropped a trail of acorns across the floor of his cell towards his bed. They didn't make a sound as they landed on the soft fur floor. He dropped the full bag beside his bed and then jumped on the mattress and lay down, feigning sleep while peering at the cell door with one eye half open.

The giant squirrel came into view as it picked up the acorn and popped it into its mouth. Pooey saw the creature's cheek puff out as it stored the nut inside, making it have a lopsided face. The guard spun around scanning the ground for more.

Come on, come on, go for the prize.

His heart raced. This was his only chance of getting that door open and finding a way out of here.

The guard's eyes widened when he saw the trail of acorns, and he hopped from paw to paw outside the door while staring at them with hungry eyes.

Pooey was counting on the critter's animal instincts overpowering any obligations of duty. He wanted to jump for joy when the guard unlocked the prison door, but he didn't. He remained completely still, only daring to breath.

He needed the creature to come within grabbing distance, so it couldn't raise the alarms. More than that, he needed information. He didn't plan on blindly running out into the halls—not this time.

The guard checked the hallway was clear before inclining his furry head around the door. He sniffed at the first acorn, which lay on the floor in front of him. After scanning the room, his beady eyes settled on the acorn again.

He scampered after it, leaving the door ajar behind him. He picked up the acorn in both of his paws and studied it with interest.

Pooey's ass twitched. The squirrel's head darted in his direction. Pooey's pulse raced, but he tried to keep his body as relaxed as possible. The guard stared for a moment before popping the acorn into his mouth and scampering forward to the next one.

He watched the squirrel go from one acorn to the next while pondering how stupid the guard was. When the greedy little sod got the bag, Pooey tensed for an attack.

The squirrel didn't see him coming as he launched himself at the large gray animal and pinned it to the floor.

Its sharp claws dug into his bear fur, but he didn't feel it. He had a thick hide these days.

He pinned the guard down with his body and raised a bear paw over it. He grinned as his giant claws popped out and sharply glinted in the bright light.

"Time for you and I to have a little chat." He told the guard as he lowered his claws to the squirrel's neck.

The guard's dark eyes widened when he cut off the red bandana with one swipe.

"Talk!"

The squirrel opened its mouth and an acorn shot out of it and bonked Pooey on the forehead.

He growled and gripped the squirrel's neck. Four more acorns popped out, each one aimed at his face.

He sighed when the last one slapped across the side of his cheek. "Are you done?"

The squirrel shrugged.

"Got any more?"

The squirrel shook his head.

"Right, I want information, and I want it now." He flashed his teeth at the trembling critter and growled again.

An acorn bounced off his forehead.

He narrowed his eyes and squeezed the guard's neck. "Talk or die!"

The squirrel shuddered beneath him and gasped out a squeak. It stared at him with wide, solemn eyes.

"What?" he asked.

The guard squeaked several times.

"Are you fucking shitting me? All you can do is squeak?"

The squirrel squeaked again, and its beady little eyes

shone with fear.

He shook his head and sighed before glancing around the room for something to tie it up with.

"How did I get caught by critters as stupid as you?" he asked it.

An evil gleam appeared in the guard's eyes, and its pointy fangs popped over its bottom lip when it grinned.

Pooey frowned.

What's he looking pleased about?

Several rough hands grabbed him from behind and pushed him against the wall, face-first. He growled while struggling against multiple clawed paws.

He extended his bear claws and ripped into the fluffy beige wall while trying to push away from it as he tried to turn to face his captors, but it was no use. They were too strong and too many.

He turned his head to see the room behind him. The guard was standing up and squeaking at the other guards who had filled the room. He was pointing to the bag of acorns. Several of the squirrels leapt onto it and popped acorns into their mouths. Others squeaked back in some kind of high-pitched communication.

The little fucker was crying for help when he was squeaking!

Pooey sighed and rested his head against the wall in defeat.

Fucking squirrels, man.

MORTIMUS

D ora clung to Terrance as a dark room spun around them. She tried to contain the feeling of sickness as the room materialized and finally stopped spinning.

Where the hell has he teleported us to this time?

She waited for her vision to clear and for her stomach to stop churning before glancing at the walls and breathing a sigh of relief when they didn't cause bile to rise in her throat.

They appeared to be in some kind of wooden cabin. Thick logs for walls and wooden floorboards made up the interior. The room would have been cozy if not for the effects of time.

Thick dust lined every surface, and stringy cobwebs hung from every corner. The curtains were torn and faded, and the windows behind them were shattered shards of glass. Time had made the place creepy, dark and unwelcoming.

"Where are we?" She glanced around at Terrance.

He walked over to the broken couch and slumped

down on it. "This was my weekend getaway." He peered around the room with sadness in his eyes. "I guess the caretaker died while I was away."

"Looks like—gah!" She yelped when she walked over to him and face-first into a massive cobweb.

She panicked and repeatedly rubbed her face until all the webbing was gone. Goosebumps popped up on her arms at the thought of a million spiders crawling all over her.

"Let's get out of here."

"And go where?" He stared down at his hands. "Banished by my own kind, what place can I call home?"

She rolled her eyes.

Here we go.

"Lost, lost in an abyss of darkness with only my memories to keep me warm. I am a dark soul in the harsh, bright world. Why would my kind abandon me so? Such betrayal in this new world, such heartache—"

She slapped him across the face several times, interrupting him before he got going.

"Snap out of it."

"Why? Why should I?" A red handprint blushed his cheek.

He stared at her with angry eyes. "We've got time. No one is chasing us anymore. If I want to mope, then mope I shall."

"And what good will moping do you?"

"I'll probably create a great sonnet from my woe or perhaps an anthology."

She shook her head. "Fine, I need an hour out of insanity anyway, but like hell I'm listening to your sonnet of woe. I'll be looking for something to eat instead." She left

151

him in the main room and wandered over to a doorway that led to a small kitchen.

"You'll appreciate my deeper meaning when you're older." He called behind her.

"I doubt it," she muttered as she swung open the doors to a large, antique dresser.

The interior of the dining cabinet was shadowed, so she leaned closer and stared into the darkness. It smelled musty and old.

Her eyes eventually adjusted to the inky interior of the cabinet, noticing a dark lump on the top shelf. She studied it closely.

It moved, and she jumped back with a yelp.

A green eye popped open and stared at her.

She screamed and fell backwards onto the cracked, tiled floor, landing on her ass and staring up at the monstrous beast in the cupboard.

A fat-bodied, three-foot-wide spider glared at her from the shelf. It had short, patterned fur all over it, and a gray beard of fuzz hung from its chin. Its tiny, pointed fangs glinted in the light as it hissed at her.

She watched in horror as its thick, hairy legs tensed in preparation to pounce.

She tried to scream, but her throat seemed to have closed up in terror. She could barely breathe. Her pulse raced, and her heart pounded.

Terrance dashed into the room and peered down at her. "What is it?"

She pointed at the eight-legged monster that was staring at her. "S-s-s-spi—spid ..." She tried to speak.

Terrance glanced inside the dresser, and then back to

her. He seemed to freeze, and his eyes narrowed in anger before he spun around to face the cabinet.

"Mortimus! What the hell are you doing?"

The spider blinked and stared at Terrance.

Dora frowned. If she wasn't mistaken, the spider looked apologetic.

What the hell?

"Massssster! I thought you were dead," Mortimus said.

"So in honor of my memory, you let the place fall apart?" Terrance raised an angry eyebrow. "Some caretaker you are!"

"It wasn't my fault, ssssir." Mortimus peered at his spider-feet.

Dora watched the conversation between Terrance and Mortimus in silent awe.

His caretaker is a talking spider.

"I'm greatly disappointed, Mortimus." Terrance shook his head. "There is no reason for this kind of mess." He gestured to the cabin around them.

"It wasn't my fault, sir. I swear it! When you didn't return, I continued my duties, but then bad things happened. More spiders came here. I fought against them, but they neutered me."

Dora noticed the giant spider was kicking what looked suspiciously like a joint behind him.

"I am powerless in this new world, my master," Mortimus cried.

Dora and Terrance spun around when the back door opened, and three giant spiders wandered in. One was pulling a crate of beer behind him.

"Hey Morty! You shoulda come to the store. Dude

nearly crapped his pants when we ..." The orange-spotted spider trailed off when he saw Dora and Terrance.

"Shit," Mortimus muttered.

"This is what has you neutered?" Terrance shouted. "Decadence and laziness!"

"Dude, chil—" The orange spider began as he cracked open a beer with his tiny fangs.

"Chill?" Terrance roared. "You've spun my weekend retreat into a speakeasy!"

"Who are these idio—" The orange spider paused when Mortimus violently shook his head at them.

Terrance turned to face Mortimus with his hands on his hips. "What treachery is this?" he hissed, flashing his fangs at Morty.

Mortimus shook his head. "It's just my cousins, sir. They'll be gone by the morning. I promise!"

Dora picked herself up off the floor. "So, um, the webs are part of partying?"

"Babe, you have no idea how much fun it is to shoot a web out of your ass." The orange spider turned and winked at her.

"No one will be shooting anything out of their ass in my cabin," Terrance cried.

"Killjoy," the blue spider muttered while pulling the crate of beer up to the refrigerator.

"Sir, if you'll just leave for a day or so, I promise to restore the cabin to its former beauty." Mortimus respectfully bowed towards his master.

Terrance held two fingers up to Mortimus. "Two days. That is all you have," he said while gripping Dora's arm. "Two days, or I shall withdraw my gift."

"Understood." Mortimus nodded.

"What gift?" Dora asked as Terrance dragged her towards the exit.

"Dude, what about the kegger?" the orange spider whined.

"No more kegging!" Mortimus snapped. "Pick up that cloth and start cleaning."

Dora could hear the other spiders grumbling until Terrance pulled her out of the cabin, and the door closed behind them. It was nice to smell fresh air again.

They were deep in the forest, standing in a small clearing with vast pine trees towering above them.

"Aww, come on. That was actually fun. Why didn't you tell me you had a talking spider?" She stared back at the cabin in awe.

"He's just a familiar." Terrance shrugged.

"What gift did you give him?" she asked again, but he remained silent as he scanned to forest.

"We cannot stay out in the open," he said. "Do you have anywhere we can stay for a couple of days?"

She considered the question. With the vampires chasing them, not to mention the Black Bishop, it seemed the obvious choice was the werewolves.

"I think we should visit the werewolves. They know things we don't, and they'll probably help us."

He narrowed his eyes. "Not a chance in hell."

"Come on. They're not that bad. They won't hurt you if you're with me."

"No." His face reddened with stubborn fury.

"Well, the only other place you could go is to my parent's church, but I can't come with you," she said, hoping that the idea of a church would sway him towards the werewolves.

She still needed to find Kieron, and the wolves were her best bet.

"I'll go to your church then," he said.

"Are you kidding?" She spun to face him with wide eyes. That was the last place she expected him to choose.

"No. What shall I say to your parents?" he asked.

"Touchy-feely bullshit, and never mention you're a vampire," she said jokingly while shaking her head.

"Okay, then I shall see you here in two days, fair Dora." He faded into mist as he teleported away, leaving her standing alone in the forest.

"No, Terrance, shit!" She stared at the space he had once occupied.

"Idiot." She glanced around the forest and considered her options. She couldn't go after him. She knew the second she set foot in the church that she'd be captured again.

Either Terrance is going to be okay, or I'm going to need supernatural help to get him out.

She stared into the dark forest.

"Werewolves here I come," she muttered.

20
GUESS WHO'S COMING TO DINNER

A s Terrance peered up at the looming church, which had once been Dora's home, a shiver of fear trembled down his spine.

He stared up at the large cross that was engraved into the stone above the doors.

Am I going to turn to dust if I go in there?

In all his years of being a vampire, he had never set foot inside a church. He had heard far too many stories about what would happen to him if he did.

He shook his head.

No. This is insane. I should go somewhere else.

He turned towards the alley across the street, freezing when he heard footsteps skittering down it.

Beads of sweat popped up on his brow.

Are the other vampires following me?

He felt a bubble of panic in the back of his throat. He had no choice. The church was the only sanctuary he had. The vampires had overrun his mansion house and seemed to have eyes watching him all over town.

Locking his jaw, he swung open the rusty iron gate and strode up the garden path towards the daunting wooden doors.

He quickly knocked on the door before he lost his nerve. The knock echoed through the church, and he shivered at the sound.

His eyes traveled up to the cross above him again. Would God punish him for entering his house of worship?

No, surely he won't. I've been a good vampire.

Loud footsteps echoed through the inside of the church, growing louder as they approached the doors.

He nearly squealed in terror at the sound. He was almost tempted to teleport himself to Honolulu and escape this drab and dismal place, but the memory of the hot sun of the islands kept him frozen to the spot.

He winced as the door swung open with a loud creak, but was pleasantly surprised when a drunkard in a dirty undershirt opened the door.

"What?" The drunkard narrowed his eyes at him.

"Ah, I see the pastor is helping the unfortunate. Might I speak with him?" Terrance asked.

"What?" The drunkard rubbed his weeks' growth of stubble, making a loud scratching noise. His bushy eyebrows knitted together into a frown.

"The er ..." Terrance trailed off. What the hell was Dora's full name? He heard a skittering noise behind him again and felt panic setting in. "Reverend, the reverend of this church. Please, I need to see him."

The drunkard eyed him for a moment. "What for?"

Why is it so hard to get into a church? Perhaps God

doesn't want me to go inside.

The skittering noise seemed to draw closer as it became louder.

"Sanctuary ..." Terrance gasped. "I need sanctuary from evil." He didn't dare glance behind him for fear of what would be there.

The drunkard sighed. He opened the door wide and stepped back as if to invite him in.

Terrance paused, knowing he couldn't walk in without an invitation.

The drunkard shot him an incredulous look. "Come on then. Get in here."

He nodded while thanking God and all his saints for their forgiveness. He lifted his foot to step over the threshold, pausing for a moment in fear.

What if this was some kind of trick? What if once he stepped on hallowed ground, he burnt to a crisp? He stared down at the intricate mosaic tiles that decorated the threshold of the church.

"What are you fucking doing? Get in here if you want sanctuary."

Terrance considered his options. Hiding in a sweaty hole in Honolulu to avoid the sunshine wasn't particularly appealing, but neither was staying out here with skittering vampires following him or risking burning in holy fire inside a church. None of his options were very appealing, but if God allowed this drunken imbecile in his church, why wouldn't he allow someone as nice as Terrance into it?

He gritted his teeth and set his foot on the tiled floor before stepping into the church.

He waited for the wrath of God to strike him down,

but it didn't. He breathed a sigh of relief as he walked into the church foyer and turned to face the drunkard.

As the man closed the church doors, Terrance spotted a vampire hovering in the alleyway outside. He was hard to see as he clung to the shadows, but his mouth appeared to be wide open with surprise.

Terrance didn't want the vampires knowing it was safe here, so he imitated an expression of pure agony and mimed himself writhing in pain while the drunkard's back was turned as he closed the door.

Once the door was shut and they were free from prying eyes, Terrance resumed a calm stance and waited to be taken to the reverend.

The other man turned to face him and appeared to waiting for him to do something.

"What?" Terrance asked.

"Don't just stand there. Go into the church and start praying," the drunkard said.

"What about the Reverend?" He would prefer to become acquainted with the man before he defiled his church. "I'd prefer to meet him before I pray in his church."

"You have done," the drunkard said, pulling on the black vestments of a priest. "Now, go and pray for your soul."

"You're the pastor?" He widened his eyes with shock as he studied the man. His white hair was overgrown and sticking out at crazy angles. There appeared to be mustard stains on his white collar and a telltale flask of alcohol poking out of his left pocket.

Given that Terrance's vampire nostrils were getting drunk from just being near the man, he was pretty certain that he was a drunken preacher.

"Of course I am! Who else would be stuck in this place?" The reverend scowled at him.

Terrance felt it was unwise to mention Dora, but decided to use the information he had to get a straight answer.

"You live here alone?"

"What's it to you?" The Reverend narrowed his eyes.

"Oh, I remember seeing a television show about this church once." He lied. "I'm sure it was about a family who lived here."

The reverend lowered his head. "There was once." There was a croak in his voice and sadness in his eyes.

So, this is Dora's father.

Terrance found that what he saw and what he'd heard about the man didn't match up. Something had happened to him.

"What happened to them?" he asked with as much compassion as he could muster.

"God took them both." The Reverend flashed him a bitter smile while reaching for his flask.

Terrance reached out and rested his hand on the flask before the reverend could lift it to his lips.

"The answer to our problems can never be found in oblivion. Trust me on this. I wasted many years in oblivion, only to discover that when you come back out of it, the problems have become worse. You have offered me sanctuary. Let me repay you for that."

The reverend stared at him for a few moments before eventually relinquishing the flask. "If an angel can't save me, what do you think you can do?" he asked.

161

"Only the fallen can understand the fallen, Reverend," Terrance said with a smile.

"Call me Theodore." He smiled and gestured inside the church. "Would you care for some dinner?"

"That sounds lovely."

"So, she left you for a Greek? That's appalling," Terrance said.

"I know! She told me that she couldn't take it anymore when Dora died. That she needed a break, but who flies off to Greece during their daughter's funeral? Anyway, a few weeks later I hear about *Giorgio*." Theodore spat out the name.

"Next thing I know, she sends me divorce papers and a YouTube link to her smashing plates in a Greek restaurant."

"I can see why you hit the bottle after that," Terrance said. "But then women are a confusing gender. When Carissa went through her feminist phase, it was quite a challenge to communicate with her. She already had the right to vote. What more could she want? I just wanted my dinner on the table on time. A simple request for all that I provided in return. But noooo, she wanted to explore her gifts." He shook his head while recalling some strong words he'd had with Carissa during the Victorian era. And some strong slaps he'd received for them.

"That reminds me of when Josie decided she wanted to be a painter." Theodore nodded with enthusiasm.

"I tried to be supportive, but when a woman paints like a five year old, and you can't even tell what she's trying to paint, what can you do?"

"You should hire a tutor. I realize she's past her childbearing years now, but a lady should always be well versed in painting, dancing and singing." Terrance nodded in agreement of his own advice.

"Well, she's a good dancer if there is a pole nearby," Theodore muttered.

"So, she's quite accomplished then?" Terrance asked while wondering what kind of pole Theodore was referring to.

A Maypole perhaps?

"I guess so." Theodore laughed. "You know, Terrance, it's been a real pleasure having you here. If you're in trouble, you're welcome to stay as long as you like."

"Thank you, Theodore. Your hospitality is greatly appreciated. I'd be happy to stay here with you. Perhaps we can help each other resolve our problems in this little sanctuary?"

"You have a deal, my friend." Theodore shook his hand.

"On that note, I think I shall retire for the night. Take your pick of the guest rooms. We have several." He smiled one last time before he left the room.

Terrance glanced around the dining room. It was a mess of dirty dishes and unwashed clothes.

"I'll stay up a while longer." He called out to Theodore as he left the room.

Terrance walked into the kitchen and stood over the sink. It was overflowing with dirty crockery. He hummed as he pulled on some yellow rubber gloves that had little marigolds imprinted on them, and he began washing the dishes.

With his vampire speed, this place would be a clean sanctuary in no time. However, with his caretaker around, it would be done in a few hours.

He made a telepathic connection with his caretaker.

"Mortimus, stop working on the cabin. I need your assistance here, instead.'

A Witch's Kiss

D ora rested against an old oak tree and stared into the dark forest with a sigh. She had been searching for the werewolves for hours now and hadn't seen a hint of anyone.

She peered up into the dark sky. The full moon shone brightly amongst a dark blanket of stars. It was a werewolf paradise, but then maybe this wasn't the kind of full moon they came out for.

A cold breeze rustled through the trees, and she shivered. It was late, and she was getting tired. If she couldn't find them soon, her only option was to return to Terrance's cabin and sleep with the spiders.

She glanced behind her.

If I can find my way back to his cabin.

She frowned. The forest seemed unfamiliar in every direction. She had no idea which direction Terrance's cabin was in.

Oh great, I'm lost!

A loud cackle echoed in the distance, and she shivered again.

What the hell is that?

She listened closely, and her pulse raced with fear when she heard a twig snap to her left.

Is someone here?

She spun around to face the thick bushes next to her, studying them with narrowed eyes. The leaves waved a little, but it could have just been from the breeze.

"Hello?" She took a tentative step towards the dense brush and peered into it. "Is anyone there?"

Something let out a deep growl behind her. She spun around to face a large, snarling wolf. Its nose wrinkled up in a fierce snarl, and its dark gray fur was standing up on its back because of its raised hackles.

Its body shook as it prepared to launch at her. Saliva dripped from its yellowing fangs that seemed massive when it peeled back its lips in anger.

Oh, shit!

"I don't suppose we can talk about it?" she asked while backing away towards the bushes.

The wolf growled again, stalking towards her.

Her heart hammered, and she stumbled back against something solid in fear.

Arms grabbed her from behind.

She screamed, nearly swallowing her own tongue in fear as she spun around to face her attacker. She paused as she met Carob's big brown eyes.

After taking a few seconds to let her heart rate calm down, she punched him in the face.

"You scared the fucking crap out of me!"

Carob let her go and rubbed his chin with a laugh. "Yeah, but it was funny."

"It was not funny!" She smacked him in the chest. "I could have died from a coronary."

She spun around to check her ass wasn't about to be bitten off by an angry wolf and found a teenage boy standing behind her. He had messy black hair and wore glasses.

"You were so scared of me." He sniggered.

She walked towards him and stood as close to him as possible without touching him.

"You have doggy breath," she said.

He scowled at her, and she heard Carob laugh behind her.

"What are you doing out in the forest, again?" Carob asked.

"Actually, I was looking for you. I might need your help."

"Help with what?"

"Vampires."

He frowned. "What kind of help?"

She considered her answer. She didn't want to make the vampire wars worse, but she needed the werewolves assistance.

"I need sanctuary. They're trying to kill me."

After a moment of silence, he nodded. "We'll help you, but you need to prove that you are not a spy, and you'll have to meet with the den mother."

"How do I prove I'm not a spy?" She tried to think of what she could use as proof. "You could ask the spirit ride guy."

"He only speaks to you, everyone else is—"

"Mind-fucked?" She interrupted.

"What?" Carob's frown deepened.

"Oh, nothing," she muttered. Bloody supernatural beings and their stupid rituals. It was worse than the church!

"Okay, so how do I prove er, my loyalty or whatever?"

"She should run with the pack," the younger wolf said.

"Not tonight, cub." Carob shook his head. "The trees are alive with wicked intent."

"The what?" Dora asked.

"Can't you feel it? This forest is dangerous tonight. That's why we're out here, rounding up the pack." He pointed into the dark forest as a small light shimmered past a tree. "That is not natural. There is something else here tonight."

She stared at the misty lights that were shimmering through the trees. How had she not noticed them before?

"What is it?"

"Magic," he said. "And not the good kind."

"What kind is it?" She inhaled at the word 'magic'. This was what she'd always wanted, to find real magic in the world. She didn't care if it was good or bad, she just wanted to learn it.

"Witches," he said. "They are casting a ritual to the moon, one that we want no part of. It is not safe to be in this unholy place tonight."

"Unholy?" she asked. "What exactly are the witches doing?"

"They are sacrificing an angelic being to their master." He shook his head in disgust. "It is not safe for you to—"

Kieron!

She was already rushing towards the lights.

"What are you doing? Dora, come back. It's not safe!"

"I'll come and find you later." She called back to Carob as she raced through the woods.

"I'll meet you at the caves." She sprinted towards the lights without a care.

It's Kieron. It just has to be!

She glanced back to see that Carob and his friend had gone.

She faced forward and followed the misty trail of colorful lights that were dotted through the forest. Branches whipped against her skin when she plowed through the trees as fast as possible. Her heart was pounding. She didn't care how many cuts she got from the dense forest. She needed to save Kieron.

The lights seemed to be growing and amassing in a copse of trees ahead of her.

She lowered her head and pumped her arms and legs to reach it faster. She glanced down at the gauntlet on her hand. The toothpick was loaded and ready to fire.

Bring it on witches. You won't get your wicked hands on my boyfriend.

She broke through the trees with a roar. Then she paused and frowned.

She was in a clearing that had one ancient oak tree at the center of it. There was an angel bound to the tree with thick chains. His hands were tied above his head, and his wings were folded in submission.

She couldn't see his face, but recognized his thick blond hair and tawny muscled body. It was Kieron.

The reason she couldn't see his face was because it was mashed against the face of a red-haired witch, who was busy snogging him.

Dora coolly eyed the witch. She wore a simple white dress that fell to her ankles, and she was entangled around Kieron's body.

A part of her heart sank to near her feet and suffered a slow painful death.

Is he kissing her back? Was he even looking for me at all?

She glanced around the clearing. There were several other women wearing similar dresses, all seated around a pond. She assumed they were also witches as they turned to stare at her.

Sitting on a rocky incline above them was a man in a cape, who was wearing leather pants and eating an apple. He twirled a blade in his hand while idly watching her with curiosity.

She glanced back towards Kieron.

He wasn't struggling very much, but he seemed awake. She gritted her teeth.

I'll kick his ass later. First, these witches are going down.

"What the fuck do you think you're doing?" She shouted out to the red-haired witch.

The witch paused and glanced up at her. "This is a private event, child. I suggest you turn around and walk away."

Dora narrowed her eyes while anger boiled in her belly. The kind of anger she hadn't experienced since Hell.

She became vaguely aware of red smoke billowing around her as she raised her hand and aimed at the witch's backside.

The man on the hill raised his eyebrows and dropped

his apple in surprise as Dora shot a toothpick into the ass of the witch who was mauling her boyfriend.

The witch yelped and jumped off Kieron while rubbing her ass.

She turned to face Dora with a scowl on her face, but her expression froze when she saw her.

"Oh, fuck. I-I didn't mean it," she said while backing away from Dora and Kieron.

Dora frowned.

I didn't think it'd be that easy.

She glanced at the coven of witches. They were all standing and backing away from her, moving away from the pond with fear in their eyes.

A brunette one glanced up at the man on the incline. "Help us, master," she cried.

Dora glanced up at the man on the hill.

"Screw this," he muttered, vanishing before her eyes.

The witches screamed in terror as she walked towards them. Then they turned and fled into the forest.

What the hell?

She shook her head and walked over to Kieron. He was staring at her with wide eyes.

"This is *so* not my fault," he cried.

She raised an eyebrow at him.

"Really! I was looking for you, and they captured me."

She began untying his chains while shaking her head in disbelief.

"Dora-minx, please look at me."

She sighed, dropping the final chain on the forest floor. She peered up into his clear blue eyes. He was staring at her with an intensity that made her pulse race.

171

"I'm so glad I found you." His voice sounded throaty.

That was all it took, one look into his eyes, and the red smoke around her evaporated. This was Kieron. He didn't lie and cheat. Okay, he did get into the most ridiculous situations in the universe, but he would never hurt her.

He's really here!

"I've been looking for you too." She hugged him against her. She felt a lump in her throat. It had been horrible not knowing if he was okay.

She felt his warm arms wrap tightly around her as he spun her in the air.

"I was so scared I'd lost you," he said. "But I shouldn't have worried, huh?" He laughed.

She frowned. "What?"

"Well, nothing on this Earth can hurt you now."

Her frown deepened. She pulled back and stared at him. "What?"

"Well, because of this." He waved his hand in front of her body.

"What?" She was beginning to get annoyed about having to ask the same question so many times.

"Your demon form," he said.

"My what?" She felt her head and gasped when she found horns poking out of the top of her skull.

"SHIT!"

"Didn't you know?" he asked. He grinned while stroking her face. "It looks very sexy on you."

Demon form, how the fuck can I have demon form?

She brushed his hands away from her.

"No. How could this happen?"

She ran to the small pond and stared down at her

reflection.

"No, no, no!"

Her skin was blood-red, and her teeth had elongated to fangs. She still looked a bit like herself, but there were big black horns poking out of the top of her head and veiny red wings poking out of her back behind her.

Shit, do I have a tail?

She spun around to check, breathing a sigh of relief when she didn't find a forked tail behind her.

She solemnly stared down at the demonic version of herself in the pond.

What the hell am I?

She saw Kieron appear in the reflection behind her. He glowed with angelic light, his white wings stretching out behind them as he put his arm around her waist and hugged her against his bare chest.

She hung her head in sadness.

This relationship is never going to work.

"What's wrong? You look beautiful, and it means you will be safe. Nothing can harm a demon." He squeezed her tightly against him. "Whereas, angels appear to be bitch bait for any psycho in this world."

She rested her head back against his chest in defeat. She felt drained and weak.

She glanced down at her hands as the skin turned from red to pink.

At least it wears off.

22

SOMETHING STINKS

Dora frowned, trying to come to terms with her gift from Hell. Becoming a demon was not something she wanted.

How can I be a demon? Don't you need to be dead first?

"This sucks." She turned to face Kieron, and he rested his hands on her hips.

"That wasn't what I expected you to say to me when we were reunited." He frowned.

"No, not this." She pointed to him.

"This!" She pointed to herself. "How can I be a fucking demon?"

"I'll swap you." He glanced back at his white wings. "You try having a white fluffy glow and getting raped by witches."

She hadn't really thought about it that way.

"You try getting hunted by the Vatican and a bunch of vamp—"

"I was shot by them." He interrupted before she could finish.

"I was buried alive!"

"I was buried in a statue in Vatican City!"

"Shit, really? Was Pooey with you?"

"No, I haven't seen him. I thought he was with you."

She shook her head. "I looked for you both, but he could be anywhere."

Kieron hugged her. "Don't worry, we'll find him ... and Carissa too."

She frowned.

Who?

"Who's Carissa?"

He slowly rubbed his hand up and down her back. "This wolf girl I'm traveling with. People keep thinking she's you. It's kinda weird, but she is good and kind."

She scowled and pushed him away from her. All this time, he'd been with another girl!

"Oh, well if she's a perfect version of me, then I'm sure you'll end up much happier with her."

His brow knotted into a frown. "There is no perfect version of you."

He tried to grab her hand, but she stepped away from him.

"Wonderful. I'm so messed up that I'll never be perfect."

"No! That's not what I meant. I meant you are unique and can't be copied. You are the perfect Dora."

"Perfect demon more like," she muttered as she turned to walk into the forest.

"Yes!" he said as he followed her. He caught her in his

arms and hugged her. "My perfect demon."

She pushed him away. She didn't want to be a demon. She carried on walking into the forest.

"Dora where are you going?" He followed her.

"To see the werewolves, maybe your wolf girl is there." She ground out the words.

"How do you know where the werewolves are?"

She smiled as she felt a moment of satisfaction when she answered. "I've met a wolf boy called Carob when he was half naked in the forest one night."

She heard a growl behind her before she felt Kieron grab her arm. He spun her to face him.

"I don't want you seeing him ever again!"

"You don't get to tell me who I can see."

"Yes I do. You are *my* Dora!"

"You're fucking delusional! What about you and wolf girl, you're allowed to see her, but I'm not allowed to see Carob?" She wasn't really bothered about seeing Carob again. She was more bothered by Kieron and this girl.

"You can take your archaic double standards and shove them up your as—"

She didn't finish as he cupped the back of her head, pulled her towards him and pressed his lips against hers in an angry kiss.

She wanted to fight him, but for some reason the battle turned into a passionate embrace.

Her anger faded away in the rush of desire that flooded through her body when his hands tightly gripped her, locking her against him.

She clawed his back and pressed her body against his as he took her breath away with deep kisses from his persistent lips.

She gasped when he lifted her into his arms as they frantically touched each other. She hooked her legs around his waist, clinging to him and leaning over him while kissing him and gripping his broad shoulders.

He slammed her back against one of the trees, pinning her to it with his body as he cupped the back her head, pulling her closer.

Her skin heated up with bursts of pleasure, and she could barely breathe from excitement. The warmth of his large hand as it traveled up her thigh was sweet torture that caused her to arch in anticipation.

"FUUUUUCCCK!" A voice cried out above them.

They broke apart and glanced up in unison, both panting.

She frowned at the murky shape in the sky above them as it fell towards the Earth.

Shooting a sideways glance at Kieron, she found him staring at her with intense eyes.

"This isn't over," he muttered in a throaty voice.

She nodded as he released her legs, and she slid down his body until she was standing on her own feet.

She fought through the clouds of desire that were fogging her mind as her pulse slowed to a speed of fast, rather than insane.

They both peered up to see a dark shape falling from the sky. She frowned. It appeared to have several legs.

They moved to the side as the shape neared the ground and landed with such force beside them that it plowed a crater in the forest floor.

"Fuck!" it muttered.

She peered into the hole to find a man on horseback slumped in it. The man was the same one from the hill earlier. He was flattened against his steed, which was spread eagle beneath him on the bottom of the crater.

She studied the creature. Amazingly, it appeared to be alive.

The man groaned and then slapped the creature on the ass.

Dora widened her eyes when the mount stumbled onto its feet, rising in the crater.

Is that a fucking unicorn?

It was hard to tell if it was a unicorn or not. It was a dirty brown-color with a bent horn and flies buzzing around it. If there were such things as flea-bitten mongrel unicorns, this creature was the queen of them.

She covered her nose with her hand when it cantered before jumping out of the crater and standing before them.

Both rider and steed stood proudly in front of Dora and Kieron.

Her eyes watered at the smell coming from the unicorn that was beyond rank.

She glanced at the man's hand as something tiny in it squeaked. She frowned as she noticed that he held a tiny person in his hands and was shaking her over the unicorn's back.

Is that a fairy?

"Come on, you useless fucking thing." He shook the fairy, and she squealed.

"What the hell are you doing?" Dora asked.

"Fuelling my ride," he muttered while still shaking the fairy. "But it looks like she's out of dust."

He shrugged and threw the fairy behind him into the trees. The little pink being let out a 'Wheeeee' sound as she flew into the distance and flopped into some shrubs behind him.

"Peggy, you're going to the fucking glue factory," the man muttered as he climbed off the unicorn's back.

Peggy must have not liked that comment because she neighed and tossed her head, sending some flies and mold flying off her mane.

"Send her to the car wash first," Dora said.

"She's been in storage for a long time." The dark-eyed man protested. He brushed his hood back to reveal an attractive, rugged face.

"YOU!" Kieron roared.

"Well, I've been called worse." The man shrugged. "Please, carry on being defiled. I love watching angels fall." He gestured to Kieron.

"I'm not an angel!" Kieron cried.

"Well, you won't be if you're fucking a hot, demon girl. You may continue." The man rested an arm across his trusty steed, and it stumbled sideways before righting its stance.

Kieron growled and launched himself at the man with his fists raised, knocking him to the ground. They rolled across the ground in a flurry of fists until they became a blur of white wings and a dark cape.

"Will you two cut it out!" Dora cried. "Kieron stop it," she added as he gripped the man's throat.

The man punched Kieron in the ribs before pushing him off him and rolling onto his feet.

"Back up kid, or I'll burn your ass," he said while

conjuring a ball of dark energy in his hands.

Kieron rolled over holding his side and scowled at the man. "Careful you don't fall over," he muttered as the man stumbled over a rock.

The man narrowed his eyes, and his nostrils flared in anger. "The ground moves!"

"Does it move for your falling horse too?" Kieron taunted.

"Peggy can fly," he snapped. "She just requires some magical assistance."

"I wonder why that is?" Kieron said as he got to his feet and then flapped his wings until he rose off the ground.

"Being a wet angel is nothing to be proud of." The man lowered his arms and shook his head.

"Who the hell are you?" Dora asked.

The man turned to her and smiled. "Oh, how rude of me, I am Lucian, the Fallen One." He bowed. "And you are?"

"I'm Dora. What are you?" She eyed the knife at his hip and his dark flowing cape. "A demon superhero?"

He waved his hands in the air in a dramatic gesture, and lightning cracked in the sky behind him. A dark cloud amassed above them, and a purple-tinged mist surrounded him.

"I am the darkest entity on this planet. I control th—" He stumbled backwards and waved his hands in the air to stop himself from falling. "Motherfucking Earth, stop moving!"

Kieron sniggered.

Lucian scowled at him. "Don't mess with me, boy."

"So, why did you tie Kieron to a tree? And, what's with

the witches?" She interrupted before they started fighting again.

"It gets boring when you've been on Earth forever." Lucian shrugged. "If an angel pops by, just asking to be fucked with, why shouldn't I?"

"I'm not a fucking angel." Kieron scowled and folded his arms.

"Yeah, keep telling yourself that," Lucian muttered.

Dora grabbed Kieron's arm and held him back as he tried to run at Lucian again. "And the witches?" she asked.

"If you could have a harem of stupid women tending to your every whim, wouldn't you? Although, in retrospect, maybe I should have become the king of vampires or something instead. Master warlocks have to listen to far too much whining. If I have to hear one more word about hair extensions, I'll rip my own fucking ears off."

"You can just choose to rule anything you want, then?" She shook her head in disbelief.

"I can, you can't." He nodded at Kieron. "And that angelic dumbass certainly can't."

Kieron narrowed his eyes, and she felt his muscles tense under her hand. She tightened her grip on him to keep him from flying at the man again.

"What makes you so special?"

Lucian flashed an enigmatic smile and said nothing.

"Fine, don't tell me." She shrugged. "We're going to be leaving now, and you're not going near my boyfriend again."

"What if I followed your hot, demon ass? Maybe I want to go where you're going?"

Kieron growled and tried to run at him again, but she

held him back with all her strength.

"Ooh, he's such a jealous little angel. That's a sin you know?" Lucian shook his head. "They sure don't make angels like they used to. Oh, and you do have a nice ass." He winked at her with a wicked grin on his face.

"Let's leave my ass out of it. If you follow us, I'll set a pack of werewolves on you."

"Fantastic! I always wanted a dog," he said as he picked up the reins of his unicorn and walked towards them.

"He's not coming with us," Kieron said, shaking her hand off his arm.

"I don't think we have a choice," she muttered. "Let's just find Carob, and he can help us find Pooey."

"Great. What's a Pooey?" Lucian asked.

"I don't want to find Carob." Kieron narrowed his eyes at her.

"Come on! I need to sort this all out, so I can save Terrance from my father."

"Who the fuck is Terrance?" Kieron widened his eyes.

"Demon girls are always hard work." Lucian interrupted with a shake of his head.

"He's just a vampire I know. It's nothing to worry about." She winced when she imagined Kieron's reaction to Terrance's flowery way of speaking to her.

"We need to find Pooey, right? They can help us."

"I'm not helping. I'm just here because I'm bored," Lucian said.

Kieron snorted. "Wonderful. Fine, but we need to find Carissa too."

She narrowed her eyes. "Fine," she muttered as she led them both into the forest with the smell of moldy unicorn wafting past her nose.

23

WEREWOLF FARM

Dora followed Carob through the woods with an angry Kieron marching beside her, and the smell of unicorn feces following them.

She glanced at Kieron. His chin was set in determination, and his eyes were narrowed while staring at Carob's muscled back.

She shook her head. Ever since she had found Carob, Kieron had been quiet and moody.

I probably shouldn't have wound him up about Carob being hot.

Finding Carob oiling his naked chest near a waterfall probably hadn't helped the situation either.

"Are we there yet?" Lucian asked for the hundredth time.

She rolled her eyes. Having Lucian's commentary following them certainly wasn't helping the situation.

"It's just ahead," Carob said, pointing to a farm in the distance.

She squinted at the old farmhouse as they left the forest and walked through long grasses towards the farm. "You live on a farm?"

"An organic farm." Carob nodded.

"Oh, hell no! It'll be full of hairy-legged feminists," Lucian cried.

"What?" She spun around to confront him. "That's the stupidest thing I've ev—"

"Happy-clapping, eco-friendly, psycho-vegan, bean-munching, hairy-legged feminists," Lucian said.

"That's just ridiculou—" She began.

"Actually, some of the girls there do have hairy legs." Carob turned back with a grimace on his face.

"Sexy," Kieron said, and everyone turned to stare at him in shock.

"What?" he asked. "There's nothing hotter than a succubae with cloven feet and soft fur on her shapely legs."

Dora grinned as Lucian's mouth dropped open in silent awe.

"Are we going to the farm or not?" Kieron asked as he folded his arms.

Carob and Lucian froze on the spot and stared at Kieron with wide eyes.

"Come on. We need to get out of the open," Dora said while turning to face the farm.

Carob turned with a shake of his head and continued walking towards the farmhouse.

She hooked her arm through Kieron's and smiled up at him. He was just great, sometimes.

He shot her a moody glance. "Why are you smiling at me?"

"I'm just happy," she said.

"You are not jealous of me for fantasizing about the hairy-legged girls we are about to meet in the werewolf farm?" He appeared upset.

"Oh yes, very jealous." She smiled at him.

He frowned. "You do not appear jealous."

She scowled for him. "Is that better?"

"Yes. Now, I am happy." He smiled.

She couldn't help grinning up at him. He was so cute sometimes.

"I'm going to be sick if you two don't stop it. What the hell is a demon girl doing pleasing an angel, anyway?" Lucian's voice interrupted her serenity.

"I'm not a demon, and he's not an angel," she said.

"What the fuck are you then?" he asked.

She stared at the farmhouse as they drew closer to it. She didn't know what she was. Maybe she would find out here.

She studied the house. It had solar panels on the roof and was a massive structure that was painted white. It had an abundance of herbs and flowers littered around it. Pots of lavender and mint dotted the windowsills, and a giant apple tree grew next to the house. Roses climbed up the wooden trellis surrounding the garden.

It appeared to be a nice, eco-friendly place in the country.

After a moment, she shook her head. "I don't know what I am, but I'm not a demon."

"You look like a demon," Lucian muttered.

"You look like a warrior, but you're actually a pain in my ass …" She began, but trailed off when the front door of the farmhouse opened, and a giant wolf stood in the doorway.

He was gray around the snout and ears with thick brown fur covering the rest of his body. He bared his teeth and raised his hackles as they approached the front gate.

Carob waved a greeting to the wolf.

The wolf raised his head and sniffed the air before coughing.

I guess he just smelled Peggy.

She widened her eyes as the wolf morphed into a man in his forties with short brown hair and a scar running across his muscled chest.

"Gah!" Lucian cried.

She turned to see him cover his eyes.

"Dude! Put some fucking pants on."

She turned back to look at the wolf-man, but was blinded as Kieron's hand covered her eyes.

"Oh, come on!" she cried. "It's not as if I was going to look."

She struggled against him, but felt Kieron's chest pressing against her back and his arm around her waist while his other hand covered her eyes.

"Oops, my bad." She heard an unfamiliar male voice say, followed by the sound of footsteps rushing away.

"Kieron stop it." She wriggled in his grip.

He released her, and she rubbed her eyes. "It's not like I haven't seen a naked guy before," she muttered as she glanced at the doorway to see it was empty.

"Ohh, how many naked men have you seen?" Kieron asked as he put his hands on his hips.

She defiantly raised her head and turned to face him,

about to reply until Lucian butted in.

"Yes, you dirty little slut, how many naked men have you seen?" Lucian flashed a grin in her direction.

She narrowed her eyes at both of them. "You two are far too similar for my liking."

Kieron widened his eyes. "I'm nothing like that hack warlock!" he cried.

"You think I'm like Angel-boy! Are you shitting me?" Lucian cried.

She smirked at them both and then turned her back to them.

The door to the farmhouse opened again to reveal the same man, who was now wearing pants and a chequered shirt.

"Hey Carob, what is er, this?" The man called out while gesturing at the group.

"Hi Rodney, these are beings in need of sanctuary from the vampires," Carob said. "I need to speak with mother about it."

Rodney eyed up the group with a doubtful expression on his face. When he noticed Peggy, his eyes widened.

"What the fuck is that?"

"*She* is a unicorn," Lucian said while glancing under his hood at Rodney with menace in his eyes.

"For real? Because I've seen flea-bitten mongrels with more class," Rodney said.

"How dare you compare a benevolent creature to a mongrel!" Lucian cried.

He turned to his trusty steed. "Cover your ears Peggy. The man is an imbecile."

Dora sighed. "Can we come in? I need your help," she

asked Rodney.

Rodney studied her for a moment.

"Okay, but that thing is going into the stables." He pointed to Peggy.

"The stables better be clean," Lucian said as he opened the gate and walked into the farm.

Rodney widened his eyes. "Like she'd fucking notice the difference."

"I'm pretending I didn't hear that since I only came here to pick up a dog," Lucian said.

Rodney growled and bared his teeth.

Dora groaned. This was going to be a nightmare.

She glanced at Kieron and Carob who both shrugged in unison.

She scowled and decided that now was the time to test out her demon powers on Lucian's ass. The last thing she needed was the Fallen One causing trouble and getting them kicked out of here. She didn't want the werewolves hunting them too.

She inhaled a deep breath and closed her eyes to summon whatever powers she had inside her. The world felt hazy, and a sudden attack of dizziness hit her.

She opened her eyes and glanced at Kieron, his face seemed to swirl around her. He was shouting something at her, but she couldn't hear it.

The world spun, and she felt herself falling.

She felt Kieron's arms wrap around her and catch her before she hit the ground. His worried face hovering in front of her was the last thing she saw before darkness claimed her, and she passed out.

24

THE PRICE OF POWER

Voices filtered into Dora's thoughts. She frowned, trying to recognize them and then winced as spikes of pain shot across her brow.

"Don't hover over her like that, you giant lummox," Lucian said.

"I'm checking she's okay." She recognized Kieron's deep voice.

She smiled when she heard him, inhaling so she could smell his familiar scent. She always felt safe near him.

Her smile wilted when she smelt rank unicorn instead.

"Because you're such an expert at healing people," Lucian muttered.

"Don't even start that again," Kieron grumbled.

"A fucking angel who doesn't know how to heal!" She felt someone move away from her, and she opened her eyes to see Kieron walking towards Lucian, who was still talking.

"In all my long years of existence, I have never encountered such dumb ass, lame—Oh, hey look. She's awake."

"Dora!" Kieron spun around and rushed to her side, dropping to his knees beside her.

"Are you okay?" He looked down at her with worry knotting his brow.

She braced her hands at her sides to push herself up and frowned when she felt straw beneath them.

"Yeah, I …" She sat up and glanced down at a handful of straw. "Where the fuck are we?"

He scowled at Lucian. "After you passed out, the Fallen *Dick* decided to blame Rodney and started a fight. As a result of that, we aren't allowed in the farmhouse until the den mother has seen us, but Carob let us stay here." He stroked her shoulder and stared into her eyes. "I was so worried. How do you feel?"

"Hey! I do have a name you know, several actually," Lucian said.

"I feel okay, Kieron." She smiled at him to reassure him. She felt a bit weak, but her headache was going off, and there was no pain anywhere else.

She glanced at Lucian. "Oh yeah, is it fucking moron by any chance?"

Kieron laughed, causing Lucian to scowl.

"You can call me, Lucian-imma-bout-to-kick-some-lame-angel-ass, if you prefer," the warlock said.

Kieron narrowed his eyes at him and let out a low growl.

She shook her head at the warlock, then she touched Kieron's arm, so he looked back at her.

"I'm okay." She reassured him.

"You went all red and then fell over." There was an

edge of panic in his voice. "Then you wouldn't wake up."
He grabbed her in a tight hug, and she melted against his
warm chest.

"You can't do that to me," he mumbled into her hair.
"You're never allowed to get ill. Promise me, you never
will."

"Oh for fucksake. She's not ill, you idiot," Lucian
muttered.

She frowned into Kieron's chest before pulling her head
back and glancing at Lucian.

"What caused it then? I never pass out."

"There was a dark energy around you when it
happened. Normally, I'd guess that you pissed off a demon,
but since you are one ..." Lucian shrugged.

"Oh, because you sensed some dark energy." Kieron
turned to face him. "How very fucking psychic of you."

"I may not be a demon, but I know my Hell magic,
Angela—yes I'm calling you that because only girls whine
like you do. I know enough about it to sense when it's being
invoked." He pulled a cigar out of his pocket, popped it in
his mouth and lit it.

He took a drag and then slowly let it out. "That was
Hell magic surrounding you." He nodded at her.

She frowned while Kieron helped her to her feet. She
glanced into his clear blue eyes. "Do you think it was a curse
from Hell?"

His expression darkened. "My fucking parents!"

"Whoa, hold on there, Angela. Your parents are in
Hell?" Lucian asked.

Kieron spun around and waved his fist at Lucian.
"Don't fucking call me Angela!"

"Fine, whatever, little lady. Keep your panties on," Lucian replied with a grin.

Kieron launched himself at Lucian and knocked him to the hay covered ground.

Dora sighed and glanced around the barn while the two rolled around in the hay, kicking and punching each other.

The barn was a massive wooden structure with stables. Mounds of hay carpeted the floor, and she spotted more bales packed up in the thick wooden rafters above.

"Will you two behave?" She eventually snapped. "Hey, guys. Remember me, the poor little, fainting girl?"

The flurry of fists paused.

Lucian rolled off Kieron, who jumped up and dabbed a split lip with edge of his hand.

She shook her head at them, and they both peered at their feet in unison.

"What the hell is wrong with you two? You act like … like." She couldn't think of a way to describe it, so she just shook her head again.

"He started it," Kieron said.

"Oh, very mature." Lucian rolled his eyes.

"Enough!" she said. "Tell me about this dark energy," she asked Lucian.

He frowned. "It's not a curse. I cast curses all the time. They don't feel like that, but I have seen it before."

"Where?" she asked.

"You won't like the answer."

"Just fucking tell me."

"Okay." He held up his hands. I've been around a long time and seen my share of demons before. That energy is what comes about when they are about to cast something."

192

"Do they pass out too?" Kieron asked.

"No, dumbass! Demons feed on Hell for their power. They have a direct link to the magic of Hell—it's unending. Even the ancient Greeks knew that."

"You were in ancient Greece?" she asked.

"Kinda where I landed," Lucian muttered.

"Landed, on Peggy?" Kieron smirked.

Lucian scowled.

Dora quickly spoke up before they ended up fighting again. "But I don't have a link to Hell. I'm human."

Lucian studied her for a moment and then frowned.

"What?" she asked.

"Well, no. It's just a theory."

"What is?"

He scratched his jaw. "You were in Hell, yes?"

"Yes, Kieron and I both were thrown out of there." She nodded.

"And you were imbued with demonic powers as a human?"

"Yes." She ground out, wishing he would get to the point.

"Then you came back to Earth?"

"We were ejected from Hell," Kieron said. "Banished."

Lucian laughed. "And they made you into an angel?"

"No, he already was one. Well, he was half one," she said.

"Epic! An angel and demon got it on, huh? I told them demon chicks were hot," Lucian said while wiggling his eyebrows.

"Them who?" she asked.

Lucian waved away the question. "Oh, no one

important. Anyway, we were talking about you. You wanna hear my theory or not?"

She bit back her curiosity and nodded. The guy was an ass, but he did seem to know a lot.

"You're back on Earth with demon powers, but with no links to Hell. I think the demon powers are using something else as a source of power." Lucian eyed her with curiosity.

"What?" she asked.

"I think they're using your life force. So every time you invoke your inner demon, you die a little bit. It makes sense really. By doing so, your demon powers are trying to send you back to Hell. Right now, they are in limbo."

She frowned. It did make sense. Without a link to Hell, her powers were draining her life force.

"What do you know about limbo?" Kieron asked.

"Oh, I know a lot about it." Lucian narrowed his eyes. "I had to crawl my ass out of that dull fucking waiting room."

"I think he might be right, Kieron." She interrupted.

Kieron shook his head. He peered at her with a worried expression. "Okay. No more using your powers, not for anything," he said. "You'll be okay."

Lucian let out a loud sigh.

"What is it now?" Kieron scowled at the warlock.

"If only it was that easy. Take it from someone who's older than time, you will eventually use them."

"No, she won't," Kieron said. "I won't let her."

Lucian rolled his eyes. "Good luck with that."

She held up her hands. "Okay, hang on guys. I'm not dying right now, so we can deal with this later. First things first, where is Carob?"

Kieron shrugged. "He ran off. I was busy tending to you."

"He said he had to go feed some shit," Lucian said.

"What?" She widened her eyes while trying to reorganize the words in her mind so that they made sense.

"That's what he said." Lucian shrugged. "His exact words were, 'gotta go feed poo'. I think that was it, or was it ploppy?"

Dora and Kieron stared at each other with wide eyes. A sinking realization of what Lucian was saying appeared to hit them both at the same time.

"Pooey!" They shouted in unison.

"Yeah, that mighta been it." Lucian scratched his nose.

PRETTY IN PINK PRISONERS

"Which way did Carob go?" Dora asked, staring at the open stable doors and preparing to run towards them.

"Down," Lucian said as he put out his cigar on a metal bucket and dropped the remains into it.

"Huh?" She blinked at him.

Lucian kicked some hay aside and pointed to a trap door in the floor.

She studied the door in the ground. It was unusual in a barn because it was made of shiny metal and appeared to be brand new.

"What is it?" Kieron appeared at her side.

She glanced at him. He also stared down at the door.

"Something odd," she said as she tugged on the shiny chrome handle of the door and pulled it open.

"Why odd?" Kieron frowned.

"People don't usually have secret basements in their barns with coded locking mechanisms on them." She pointed to the keypad on the top of the door, which was fortunately unlocked.

Lucian nodded in agreement, but Kieron appeared confused.

"So a basement is bad?" he asked.

"No. I ... oh, forget it," she mumbled as she dropped the open door onto the floor and stepped onto the rungs of the metal ladder below. The rungs were cold to touch and embedded into the wall of the dark tunnel.

"Come on," she said before climbing down into the dark underbelly of Werewolf Farm.

She ran her fingers over the cold, metal walls surrounding her.

What is this place?

She peered down and noticed a dim light several feet below her, reflecting off the shiny tiled floor.

She glanced up to see Kieron stepping onto the ladder above her as she continued climbing down.

"Seriously?" Lucian's voice echoed from above. "You want me to climb into some dark hole to find some shit. Are you fucking kidding?"

"Just get down here." She called out, wincing when her voice echoed down the tunnel.

She continued making her way down until she reached the bottom and stood in a wide corridor. She peered down the tunnel. It had a bluish glow from the halogen lights embedded in the ceiling.

Her boots made a clattering sound on the metal floor, and she could see her reflection in the chrome walls.

Air vents in the ceiling blasted cold air down the corridor, causing goosebumps to appear on her bare arms, and there was a low buzz coming from a nearby flickering bulb.

She spun around when she heard a thudding noise behind her, letting out a sigh when she realized it was just Kieron jumping off the ladder.

"Okay," he said, glancing around. "This isn't normal."

"No shit," Lucian muttered as he jumped off the ladder and joined them in the corridor.

"Let's just find Pooey and get out of here." She pointed down the tunnel to a door in the distance. "I think it's this way."

"Great, we're guessing our way through the creepy, sterile tunnels." Lucian rolled his eyes. "This is sure to end well."

"We'll get out of here faster if you don't speak," she said.

"We'll get out of here faster if we don't go down the long, freaky tunnel," Lucian replied.

She narrowed her eyes. "No one is stopping you leaving."

"What, and miss all the fun of watching angel-boy getting mauled by a dog? Not a chance." Lucian grinned.

Kieron growled but she grabbed his hand and pulled him down the tunnel with her before he could start fighting.

"Just, don't get in my way." She glanced over her shoulder at Lucian.

"I wouldn't dream of it."

She rushed down the corridor, wanting to get out of here as fast as possible. The eerie lighting and electronic buzzing sound frayed on her nerves.

When they reached the door at the end, they came to

a T-junction in the tunnel.

She tried the metal door and frowned when it opened with a click. She peeked into the room and widened her eyes.

There was a cage in the center of the room with a girl inside it. The girl was holding onto the bars and staring at the door with a sullen expression on her face.

"What the hell?" Dora pushed the door open wide and stepped into the room.

"Carissa!" Kieron gasped behind her.

Dora stared at the girl.

She glanced up with a hopeful expression when she saw Kieron.

Dora scowled, noticing she was very pretty. "So, this is Carissa?"

"Yes." Kieron nodded. "Although, I don't know why she is in a cage."

He turned to Carissa. "Is this a private moment or a punishment?"

"What? Eww! I'm a prisoner," Carissa said.

"Yes, but do you want to be?" Kieron asked. He appeared to be trying to understand the situation in a diplomatic manner.

"Get me out of this fucking cage!" she cried.

Dora bit back a grin as she walked towards the cage and examined the room for a key.

On the wall, she found a hook with a large key ring hanging from it. She picked it up and walked towards the cage.

"How did you end up in here?" she asked Carissa as she tried different keys in the lock of the barred door.

"My fucking mother," Carissa said. "I came back to help Kieron find Dora, which I assume is you?"

Dora nodded. "Yep."

"But it seems my mother is even more insane than I remember. She had me thrown in here."

"Who is your mother?" Dora asked as one of the keys turned in the lock, and it clanked as she unlocked the door.

"They call her the Den Mother now, but she used to be the matriarch. The crazy bitch is trying to recreate my ex-boyfriend's blood. When I found that out, I might have acted a bit rashly."

Carissa pushed open the cell door and stepped out of it. "But, there was no need to lock me in a fucking cage!"

"You're her," Lucian cried.

Dora spun around to see Lucian staring at Carissa with wide eyes.

"Her, who?" Kieron asked.

"The hybrid child." Lucian grinned.

Kieron stared at him as if he was crazy, but Dora realized that everything the spirit wolf had told her was true.

"Wait. Who's your ex-boyfriend?"

"It doesn't matter." Carissa sighed. "He died a long time ago. He was murdered by my mother."

"No, it really does matter. What was his name?" She had a feeling that she already knew the answer.

"Terrence. He was called Terrence, and he was a noble and honorable—"

"Plank who had a spider called Mortimus?" Dora interrupted.

"Well, I supposed he was a bit of a pla—wait, yes! He had a butler called Morty. How did you know that?" Carissa narrowed her eyes.

"Because I met him, he's not dead. Well, he's undead. You know he's a vampire, right?"

"Yes, but she staked him. I saw it happen!" Carissa frowned and shook her head. "It was so long ago, but I remember it like it was yesterday. He fell to the ground and wasn't moving."

"Er, that's not what happens to staked vampires. They usually turn to dust," Lucian said.

"But I buried him." Tears shone in Carissa's eyes.

"Yeah, he probably just went to sleep for a long time then," Lucian said.

"Well, he's not asleep now. He's at my place," Dora said. "So, let's get Pooey and then reunite you guys."

"Pooey? I've heard of him. My mother's obsessed with him. He's in her pet room, I think."

"Do you know where that is?" Kieron asked.

"Yeah, come on." Carissa led them from the room. She glanced back at Dora. "Thank you."

Dora shrugged. "You're welcome."

As she gripped Kieron's hand and followed Carissa, she decided that she didn't hate her. She'd like her even more once she was reunited with Terrence though.

They followed Carissa out into the T-junction and down the left tunnel, past several closed doors.

"It's just at the end of this corridor." Carissa pointed to the end of the tunnel.

Dora squinted to see a brightly-lit open doorway with bars on it ahead of them. As they rushed down the hall, she could see beige fluffy furniture and giant, cat toys inside the room.

They paused at the doorway and stared inside it in silence as a three-foot-tall teddy bear wearing a pink ball gown wandered past the doorway. He was holding a bag of cheesy puffs in one hand and cramming handfuls of the orange snacks into his mouth with the other while staring down at his protruding belly.

"Pooey?" Dora gasped.

She heard Kieron snort with laughter behind her and glanced back to see him silently laughing with tears forming in his eyes.

The bear spun around to face them with wide eyes. "Dora!" he cried, spraying them all with semi-masticated corn.

"Nice dress, princess," Lucian said.

"Shut it, leather lord," Pooey retorted. "Or I'll chew off your puny ass."

Dora was still holding the key ring from Carissa's cage and decided now was the time to try her luck on Pooey's cell door. She began testing the keys while shaking her head at Kieron, who was bent over laughing.

"Yeah, if you can reach it, short ass," Lucian muttered.

"Don't fuck with me, you inbred fool. I'm an ancient demon who is three times bigger and stronger on this plane of existence." Pooey ripped off his pink dress and pushed out his cute, little chest.

"So, you're only a foot tall in other planes of existence?" Lucian grinned.

Kieron and Dora glanced at each other and nodded. It was true. He was three times taller here, but he was only the size of a toddler.

Pooey narrowed his eyes and flew at the bars with a

cute, bearlike roar.

The cell door shook, and Dora dropped the keys.

"Come on, Pooey. Let me get you out of here before you rip Lucian's face off, okay?" she asked, reaching down to pick up the key ring.

"Lucy? His name is Lucy? What is he? A tranny, rom-com star. Hey, Lucy is your husband home yet?" Pooey called through the bars.

"Don't mess with me, you fugly carebear." Lucian scowled at him.

"What's a fucking carebear?" Pooey asked, still hanging from the bars on the door.

"It's like a magical bear," Dora mumbled, avoiding the real answer as she tried another key in the door and sighed when it finally worked.

She pulled open the door with Pooey still hanging from it and scooped him into her arms.

"Come on, let's get out of here." She gave Pooey a quick hug, relieved to have found him.

"It's a lame ass, tedd——" Lucian began. He paused as squeaking sounds echoed down the hall.

"What the hell is that?" Kieron asked.

"Squirrel guards," Carissa said. "It must be her guards."

"Oh, no. Not those fucking things again." Kieron peered in the direction of the noise.

"You're scared of a squirrel?" Lucian shook his head. "Do fluffy bunnies frighten you too?"

"Enough!" Dora said. "Unless you all want to be wearing a princess gown and stuck in a cage, escape now and fight later."

"The Den Mother doesn't scare me," Lucian muttered.

"Fine. You stay here to see if she makes a real woman out of you, and we'll go on our merry way."

Dora didn't wait for a reply as she rushed down the hall with Pooey in her arms.

She glanced back to see Kieron and Carissa following her, and a reluctant Lucian shake his head before following them.

They ran down the tunnel, back to the ladder.

She put Pooey on the ladder first, watching him scale up it with amazing speed. Carissa went next, glancing back when the squeaking noise became louder.

"Keep going," Dora said, urging her up the ladder before staring into the distance to see hundreds of moving shapes flying down the tunnel towards them.

"Flying squirrels?" Lucian asked with wide eyes.

"Get up the ladder," she said, bracing herself for an attack.

"No," Kieron said. "Dora goes next. She can't use her powers."

She frowned. He was right, but she wasn't used to being helpless, and she didn't like it at all.

"Go on!" he said, pushing her towards the ladder.

"Okay, okay. Just be careful." She hurriedly climbed up the ladder, glancing back to ensure that Kieron was following. She saw a fanged ball of fur fly at him, and he batted it away with one of his wings.

There was a loud bang below, and a dark mist filled the corridor below her.

"Kieron!" She called in panic as her pulse raced.

She began to climb back down, but paused when Kieron's face appeared out of the mist.

"It's okay. Lucian blew them up. Keep going."

She quickly climbed up the ladder, pulling herself out of the basement. She got to her feet and stared down at the hole in the ground, sighing when Kieron's head appeared.

He climbed out of the tunnel, followed by a grumpy-looking Lucian.

Once everyone was clear of the tunnel, they slammed the door shut and pulled a heavy cabinet onto it to keep it closed.

"Now what?" Pooey asked, glancing at the open barn door and the group of werewolves in the field outside of it.

"Oh shit," Dora muttered.

"We fly," Lucian said, pointing to Peggy.

"No fucking way." Kieron shook his head. "That thing can't fly, let alone hold three people and a bear."

"Peggy can hold any weight, and you can help her fly," Lucian said.

"It might work," Dora said.

"This is going to suck," Kieron muttered.

"Care for a ride, ladies?" Lucian gestured towards his skanky unicorn.

Dora sighed and climbed onto Peggy's back. Carissa climbed up in front of her, glancing back while holding her hand to her nose.

"It smells like shit," Pooey grumbled as Kieron passed him to Dora.

Lucian boosted himself onto the steed behind Dora and pressed himself against her back. "Who knew I'd get a Dora sandwich."

She scowled back at him, and he grinned.

Kieron flashed his wings and narrowed his eyes at

Lucian. "Get this thing moving," he snapped.

Lucian winked, and then picked up the reins before Peggy cantered out of the stall.

Dora glanced back, past Lucian to see Kieron running after them with his wings flexed out behind him.

As the unicorn picked up speed, he matched it. Both of them ran out of the barn in synchronization. There was a jolt as Kieron pushed against Peggy's rear end and launched them all into the sky.

Dora gasped when she looked down to see the farm disappearing below them. The air was cold as they rocketed into the sky at high speed.

She gripped the horse with her thighs as she peered back to try to see Kieron, but he was below her line of vision.

"Kieron, are you okay?"

"It's disgusting. I've got dirty unicorn ass in my face,' he cried. "Eww!"

WOODLAND RETREAT

"Carissa, how do you feel about warlocks?" Dora heard Lucian ask behind her.

She rolled her eyes, suspecting it was going to lead to more bickering.

"I don't think about them at all." Carissa gripped the unicorn's mane, turning back to face him and Dora

"Really? You don't fancy one as your master then?" Lucian said.

Dora gripped the unicorn with her thighs before turning and shooting him a warning glance.

"What? I need a dog, and we just picked up a stray from a farm. She looks cute and adorable. Why shouldn't I give her a good home?"

"What did you just fucking say?" Carissa lunged across the unicorn's back to try to gouge out Lucian's eyes, judging by her clawed hands.

Dora tried to fend off the angry wolf-girl and keep her balance as the steed dropped in the sky and turned sideways.

"Fuck! I can't hold it," Kieron cried beneath them as the unicorn slanted sideways in a downward spiral towards the forest.

"Shit!" Dora yelped, holding onto the mangy mane of the creature, so she didn't fall off.

"Lucian, you prick!" She managed before they crashed through the trees. Sharp branches scratched across her skin, and the unicorn let out a whining sound as it neared the ground.

"Oh this is just great," Pooey said, clinging to Dora's back with sharp, little bear claws. "I'm going to die on something that smells worse than a rotting corpse."

"No one's going to di—oof!" Kieron's words abruptly cut off.

Dora spun around on the horse to see Kieron several feet behind them, crushed behind a thick branch. He must have flown straight into it.

"Kieron!" she cried, but the words became lost as the unicorn crashed into the forest floor.

She jolted upon impact and was thrown off the steed before being catapulted into a thorny bush.

"Ohh, that hurt," she muttered as she untangled her arms and legs from the viciously sharp shrub. She scrambled out of it and rolled onto the leafy forest floor.

"You think that hurt. Try this bullshit." Pooey's muffled voice came from above her.

She glanced up to see Pooey hanging by one arm from a branch ten feet above her. He appeared to have a beehive on his head.

"Oh crap! Are there bees in there?" She shouted up at him.

"Not anymore." He shouted back.

"Let go, and I'll catch you."

"How far down is it?" The beehive moved as if trying to look down.

"A couple of feet." She lied, knowing he wouldn't let go if he knew how far the drop was.

"Okay then." He released the branch and dropped down towards her.

She moved to catch him, never taking her eyes off him. He fell safely into her arms, knocking her over with the force of his weight when he landed.

She fell onto her back and peered up to find Pooey sitting on her chest.

Pooey pulled the beehive off his head and tossed it into the forest. Then he glanced up. "A couple of fucking feet?"

"You had a soft landing," she muttered as she pushed him off her and sat up.

"Yeah, only if I'd landed on your head," he grumbled.

"Hey!" Kieron's voice came from far away.

She glanced in the direction he had been and saw he was still pinned behind a thick branch. One of his wings was caught up in a tangle of branches.

"We're coming!" She jumped to her feet and raced over to Kieron.

She climbed the tree to where he was pinned and ripped away at the branches trapping his wing.

"You need any help?" Pooey asked.

"No, help Carissa and Lucian," she said without turning around.

"What about the stinky unicorn?" he asked.

"What about it?" She turned back to see him standing

209

beside the unicorn.

The mount was wedged into a hole in the forest floor, face-first with its ass sticking in the air. By the looks of it, Peggy had tried to use her face to stop herself and created a ravine in the mud with it instead.

"Er, is she alive?"

He lifted the unicorn's head. She snorted in his face, making his fur ruffle.

"Yeah, I think she's just resting."

"Okay, then find Lucian and Carissa."

She turned back to Kieron and removed the remaining branches around his peppered wings.

She helped him down out of the tree and eyed the scratches on his tawny chest. "We really need to get you a shirt."

He raised an eyebrow at her, shooting her a devilish grin. "Do we?"

She bit the inside of her cheek as his words caused her pulse to race. "It depends on how many things you plan to crash into."

He reached out to pull a leaf out of her hair. "Will I be crashing into them with you?"

She took a step towards him, staring into his aqua eyes. "It could happe—"

"Hey, angel-defiler, you wanna help a guy out here?" Lucian's voice interrupted.

She turned left to see Lucian hanging upside down from some thick vines. The tree he was hanging against was particularly leafy, and the leaves were covering most of his face.

He blew sideways and some of the leaves rustled out of

his eyes before twanging back into his line of vision.

She put her hands on her hips and scowled up at him.

"Come on! All the blood is rushing to my head, and not the good one." Lucian wriggled to try to free his feet from the vines, but he remained tangled up in them.

"Much as I'd enjoy dropping you on your head, how exactly am I supposed to get up there?" She pointed to where his feet were tangled twenty-feet above her.

"I'll do it," Kieron said cheerfully. Then he quickly launched into the sky and flew up to Lucian's ankles. With a knowing smile on his face, he ripped off the vines and dropped Lucian on his head.

"Oww, you son of bitch." Lucian growled as he rolled onto his back, rubbing his head.

"What? You asked for it." Kieron grinned.

"You're asking for it." The warlock narrowed his eyes.

"Help!" A faint female voice cried in the distance.

Dora turned towards the voice and set off running. She heard the sound of running water as she dashed through the trees towards Carissa's voice.

Leaves crunched loudly behind her as Kieron and Lucian's footsteps crashed through the forest in her wake.

She came to an abrupt halt when the trees cleared to reveal a fifty-foot drop into a lake below.

She frowned at the rushing waterfall. Something was hanging from the top of it. She widened her eyes when she realized it was an arm.

She stared at the dark figure under the spray of water and gasped. It was Carissa.

"What?" Kieron asked as he caught up to her.

"Carissa." She pointed to the struggling figure hanging

from a waterfall.

"I'll get her." Dora's hair blew in her face as a rush of air swept up from behind her, and she saw Kieron launch into the air.

He spread his wings and glided over to Carissa, sweeping beneath her through the waterfall and scooping her up in his arms.

"My hero." Lucian mocked behind her.

Dora scowled, ignoring him and keeping her eyes on Kieron.

"That's the problem with angels. They save every girl they see."

She narrowed her eyes as Kieron glided over the lake towards them carrying Carissa. The petit werewolf fitted perfectly in his muscled arms.

Lucian's face appeared in her line of vision as he leaned over to look at her. "A demon like you can do better than that."

She turned away from him and folded her arms.

"Angels don't stay with demons, honey. Trust me, I know."

"I'm not a demon." She ground out the words.

"Yeah, sure you're not. That blush around your cheeks isn't hellfire. It's just embarrassment."

"Bite me."

"All you had to do was ask." He flashed his teeth.

"Fu—" She stopped when she was hit by a whoosh of air as Kieron landed beside them. He released a dripping Carissa from his grasp, and she staggered a little before standing up straight.

"Everything okay?" Kieron asked.

She nodded, but something in her expression must have given away her feelings because he frowned at Lucian before putting an arm around her waist and leading her back to the forest.

She glanced back at Lucian. He was grinning.

She wanted to slap the grin off his face, but a part of her realized he was right. What chance did a demon and an angel really have?

She shook her head as they walked back into the forest towards where they had left Pooey and Peggy.

The woods darkened as daylight faded from the sky. A howl echoed through the trees, and she shivered. The wolves could be anywhere, and this was their natural hunting ground.

"About bloody time," Pooey grumbled. He was sitting on Peggy's back and brushing mud off her mane. "Skanky and I were getting bored."

"What did you just call Peggy?" Lucian widened his eyes in horror.

"She likes Skanky more," Pooey said.

"She does not!"

"Skanky, take me to that tree," Pooey said to the unicorn while pointing at the old oak ahead of them.

The unicorn nodded her head and cantered towards the tree in front of her.

"Get your mangy mongrel off my unicorn." Lucian spun to face Dora with thunder in his eyes.

Dora shrugged and flashed him a grin. "I think Skanky should choose her own name."

"She's not calle—" A howl nearby silenced Lucian, and he glanced around the forest.

"We need to get out of the forest," Dora said.

"And go where?" Kieron asked.

She thought about it for a moment. The vampires were chasing her, so were the werewolves. She stared into the forest.

"Terrance's cabin." She nodded. Morty wouldn't mind visitors, and it was a safe place for them to figure out what to do next.

"Come on. It's this way." She rushed through the trees with the troop of strange beings following her.

The howling seemed to resonate from all around them as they raced through the trees. She hoped she was heading in the right direction and breathed a sigh when she recognized the clearing ahead of her as the large cabin came into view.

Another howl made her increase her speed as she neared the trees around the clearing.

We're going to make it!

She jolted to a halt when she saw headlights from a car outside of the cabin. She ducked behind a bush, waving for everyone to hide as she stared at Terrance's cabin.

It was swarming with men in suits. There were several cars parked outside. Men in dark suits and sunglasses wandered around the grounds, searching for something.

"What kind of dick wears sunglasses at night?" Lucian asked as he knelt beside her.

"What kind of dick wears a cone on his head?" Pooey asked on the other side of her.

She turned to face the front of the cabin and widened her eyes as a short man wearing a black papal crown and a dark suit left the cabin.

"It can't be," she muttered.

"The Black Bishop." Carissa confirmed in a dark tone, narrowing her eyes at him.

"What the hell is he doing here?" Kieron asked.

"I think he came to get me," Dora said as she slumped her shoulders.

Where are we going to go now?

Several howls echoed in the distance, and she frowned.

"Where the fuck do we go now?" Pooey asked.

She knew there was only one place left. She sighed and shook her head.

"My place," she said. "We need to go home.

REUNITED

S harp branches poked through Dora's sleeve as she crept through the thick forest away from Terrance's cabin.

She winced every time she heard a twig snap underfoot.

She glanced behind her at the group. Kieron was close behind, ducking under low branches. Carissa and Lucian followed him. Lucian held Peggy's reins while Pooey was perched on the unicorn's back, scanning the forest with narrowed eyes.

She glanced back at the cabin through the gaps in the trees.

Once we get back to the clearing, we'll be free and clear.

A loud howl from a wolf echoed in the distance.

She froze, trying to work out the direction it had come from.

Free and clear of PISS anyway.

Peggy snorted loudly, and Dora heard a yelp from

Pooey.

She spun around to see Pooey fall from the mount as she reared up onto her back legs.

Lucian fought with her reins, trying to silence her, but the unicorn was clearly spooked.

"Make her shut up," Dora hissed.

"Sure, have you got a horse-shaped gag on you?" Lucian snapped back as Peggy kicked her front legs in the air in front of him.

"They're going to hear us," Carissa whispered urgently.

"Too late," Pooey said, pointing through the trees.

Dora stared between the thick leaves towards the cabin. "Shit."

The agents of PISS were all staring in their direction.

A shiver of fear shot down her spine when she heard a deep growl behind her. She slowly turned towards the source and saw three wolves snarling at them a few feet away.

Fighting to control the panic that was bubbling in the back of her throat, she turned to her companions.

"Run!"

Kieron scooped up Pooey and grabbed her arm with his other hand as he set off running through the trees, pulling her after him.

Lucian and Carissa weren't far behind. Even Peggy seemed to understand the threat and galloped past them all at high speed, ripping her way through the thick trees.

Dora jumped when a loud bang filled the air.

Was that a gunshot?

She glanced back to see agents of PISS breaking through the barrier of trees behind them and being attacked by angry wolves.

Hopefully, they'll slow each other down.

She turned to face the forest and raced through the trees, trying to put as much distance between them.

"Do we even know where we're going?" She called out to Lucian, who had overtaken the group while trying to catch Peggy.

"Yeah." He glanced back. "I know these woods like the back of my hand."

Another howl echoed through the trees. It didn't seem very far away.

"I hope he knows the back of his hand better than he knows how to handle unicorns," Pooey muttered.

"I heard that," Lucian shouted.

"The werewolves heard that," Pooey said.

"Just shut up and run." Dora told them, feeling a moment of relief when she saw a clearing ahead that appeared to be leading out of the woods.

We're going to make it.

They raced into a suburban street near the edge of town.

She frowned. It seemed familiar.

Kieron tugged on her hand, but she froze on the spot.

"Come on. It's this way." Kieron turned to face her, pausing when he saw the expression on her face.

"What?"

"This street looks a lot like the one the vampire's live on," she muttered. She wasn't sure. This wasn't a part of town she'd visited much, but the houses all looked the same.

She glanced at the roofs and gasped when she saw the spires of the vampire castle a few streets away. "We can't go that way. It'll lead us straight to their lair."

"It's the only way back into town," Lucian said. "We have to go this way."

"It's worth the risk," Carissa said.

"I dunno. It's dange—" Dora didn't finish as there was a loud hiss behind her.

She spun around just in time to sidestep an angry vampire who launched at her with his fangs bared.

He flopped onto the sidewalk and knocked his head on the hard concrete

"Aww shit, is there anything not chasing us?" Pooey put his hands on his furry hips and shook his head.

"Run again?" Lucian asked.

"There's only one," Carissa said.

Dora glanced at her and noticed her eyes glowing yellow.

Another howl came from within the forest.

"Screw it. Run as fast as you can," Dora said.

Lucian walked over to the vampire and peered down at him. "Let's just silence fang-boy first, shall we?"

"How? He'll chew through a gag." Kieron frowned at the warlock.

Lucian scowled at Kieron. "Seriously, that's what you would silence someone with? Fucking angels, man, you're all so—"

"Don't even start." Dora interrupted. "Just tie him up or something, and then we can get out of here."

The vampire sprang to his feet and hunched low. His black leather coat hung open to reveal an argyle sweater concealed beneath it.

Lucian shook his head at the creature. "You know

someone should have staked you for crimes against fashion long ago."

The vampire scowled and launched at Lucian with clawed hands and bared fangs, but he never reached his target as Peggy neighed and butted into his body knocking him sideways several feet.

"There's my girl." Lucian patted Peggy on the back, and she neighed again.

The vampire scowled up from the road before he stood up, brushing gravel and dust off his leather coat.

He appeared to be sizing up the group for a moment before he grinned and pulled something out of his pocket.

Dora frowned at the device.

Is that a cell phone?

He flipped it open and began pressing buttons.

"Stop him," she cried, realizing that he was calling for back up.

A streak of lightning shot from the sky and hit the phone. The vampire's teeth chattered as volts of electricity shot through him, and his hair spiked out in all directions.

"This is not the time for sexting." Lucian muttered as purple smoke billowed around his hands.

The vampire dropped the phone, which was now a burnt crisp, and he shivered all over. He stared at the group for a moment while his burnt skin instantly healed.

With a roar, he launched at Dora again, this time taking her by surprise and wrapping one hand around her throat.

He dragged her backwards away from the group. "Stay back or I'll kill her." He snarled as he hauled her against him.

She struggled against the vampire, but his arm around her neck felt like an iron bar.

Kieron narrowed his eyes at the creature, his body tensed and ready to strike. "Let her go!"

"Nobody moves, or I'll rip out her throat." The vampire shielded himself with her body.

She felt his grip tighten around her throat, but tried to pull away from him anyway. It wasn't as if she needed the air.

He pushed her head sideways, and she felt his teeth graze her neck.

"Let her go." Kieron ground out as he slowly moved towards them, an inch at a time.

The vampire must have noticed because he sank his teeth into her neck.

Her pulse raced. She tried to fight her way out of his grip, but the vampire didn't budge. She glanced at Kieron.

He froze on the spot, staring at her with a helpless look in his eyes.

She breathed a sigh when she felt the vampire jump, and his fangs left her neck as his arm released her.

She ran into Kieron's arms while pressing her hand against her wounded neck.

She spun around when the vampire groaned, just in time to see the vampire fall forward, cupping his balls.

Behind him stood Pooey with his arm extended to the place where the vampire's balls had once resided. His eyes were narrowed in determination, and his fist was tightly clenched.

"Ooh, low blow." Lucian laughed. "But I do like your style."

Dora stepped forward, staring down at her attacker. The vampire knelt on the road, whimpering. He peered up at her, and she raised her foot and kicked him in the face with all her might.

His head knocked back, and he flipped over onto his back with his eyes closed. She nudged his head with her foot, but he didn't flinch.

"Let's dust him," Lucian said.

"Let's just get out of here." She shook her head.

"Are you sure?" Kieron wrapped his arms around her waist and gently touched her neck.

She felt a warm tingling and noticed his hand glowing with a golden light. When he removed his hand, the pain in her neck disappeared.

"Yeah, more vampires will mean more trouble, and we have enough trouble right now." She scooped up Pooey into her arms.

"Let's just get to the church as fast as we can."

"So, are you an angel now?" Pooey broke the silence and peered down at Kieron from Peggy's back.

"What? No, don't be stupid," Kieron said as they walked down the street towards the church.

"You healed Dora like one," Pooey said.

Dora touched her neck. There wasn't a scratch on it. It felt as if nothing had happened to her.

She glanced at Kieron.

Is he becoming more angelic now?

"Demons can heal too." Kieron shook his head, stubbornly refusing to accept his angelic side.

"If it looks like an angel and acts like one ..." Pooey

trailed off.

"If it looks like a teddy bear," Kieron muttered.

Pooey snarled, and his tiny fangs popped out.

"You're all screwed up," Lucian said. "It's like studying a band of supernatural rejects."

"Oh yeah, then what the hell are you?" Dora asked.

It was true that they were all a bit messed up. No one seemed happy with their new lives on Earth, but there had to be a way to fix it all.

"I'm whatever I want to be." Lucian beamed a self-satisfied smile.

"And you chose to be a master of bullshit, riding in on a skanky steed?" Pooey asked incredulously.

Lucian narrowed his eyes, and Dora giggled.

"You're going to make a great display in a toy store, fur-ball." Lucian scowled at Pooey.

"You're going to make a great character in World of Warcraft," Pooey said. "I can just see eight million noobs pwning your ass."

"No one can destroy me!" Lucian cried.

"Yeah? That's what the Lich King said, and now a couple of nubs on recruit-a-friend can one-shot him."

Lucian growled and narrowed his eyes at Pooey.

He opened his mouth as if to reply, but closed it when Kieron spoke up.

"Who's the Lich King?" Kieron asked.

"It's this world I discovered while I was held captive," Pooey replied. "I've got a level ninety warlock in full epics now."

Kieron looked around. "Where is he?"

"It's a game," Dora said.

"They keep innocent warlocks in games?" Kieron appeared distressed by the thought.

"No, they're fictional—" She stopped talking as the spires of the church appeared in the distance.

A shiver of fear shot up her spine. They appeared darker than she remembered.

She knew it was the only place they could go, but every essence of her being was screaming for her to turn around. It was the last place she wanted to go.

Especially now that I am a demon.

"Home sweet home," Lucian said as they crossed an empty street and walked towards the desolate-looking church.

It was situated on the edge of town with a few broken down buildings surrounding it. Behind it were fields of crops and farmlands stretching out for miles.

Dora glanced back at the busier part of town, wishing to return to the bustling streets that were full of life.

The church seemed so desolate and dark to her now. It brought back childhood memories, but along with them came the memories of her torture too. The bad outweighed the good, and she couldn't find anything good in this place.

She shook her head and tried to rationalize her feelings, but it all felt so dark. As they neared the front gate, she forced herself to keep walking.

We don't have a choice. There is nowhere else to go.

She pushed open the rickety iron gate and forced herself to step through it.

Was it always so broken here?

She tried to remember if the gate had been so rusted and old when she had lived here. For all her bad memories, the place seemed to have fallen apart in her absence.

She stopped, and the group stopped behind her.

"What?" Kieron asked.

"Something's wrong," she said.

"What do you mean?" he asked.

"Can't you feel it? This place wasn't this broken last time we were here." She stared up at the chipped stone and rotten wooden beams of the church exterior. "How long have we been gone?"

"It was only a few months in Earth time," Kieron said as he glanced around at the overgrown garden of weeds on either side of them.

She stared at her home. It didn't even feel like home anymore. Everything in it was rotten and broken.

She picked up a twisted lawn chair that she remembered had been new only a few months ago. It was rusted so badly that the seat had eroded away into nothing.

"How is this even possible?"

"Argh!" Lucian yelped behind them.

She spun around to see him pick up a moss-covered stone and prepare to launch it towards the ground floor window of the church.

"What the fuck are you doing?"

"Spider!" Lucian squealed like a six-year old girl.

"Are you kidding me? You're scared of a tiny spider?" She scowled at him and motioned for him to put the rock down.

"Tiny? It was the size of Pooey!" Lucian shook his head and continued brandishing the hefty stone.

"Wait!" Carissa cried. "Don't hurt him. It's Morty."

Dora turned towards the front door and saw Mortimus

skittering towards them. He wore a tea towel around him as a makeshift apron.

"I haven't seen a demonic arachnid that big in a long time," Kieron said in awe.

"Hi Mortimus, do you remember me?" Dora asked him as he drew near.

"Of course I do! I'm not a goldfish ma'am. I remember many things," he replied.

"What are you doing here?" she asked.

"Master called me to clean up the mess, but there's quite a lot to do. And …" Mortimus sighed.

"What?" She frowned.

"Miss Dora, I know this is your home, but there is something wrong here. When I clean something, it becomes dirty again. Master thinks I am not doing my duty, but there is something dark here. I swear it."

"Have you considered that it might be you?" Lucian asked, staring at Mortimus with a disgusted expression.

Carissa punched Lucian in the arm. "You leave Morty alone. He's wonderful."

Morty's eyes widened in surprise. "Miss Carissa! It is so good to see you again. Master will be so happy that you have returned, as am I."

"Hello Morty, it's great to see you again too. Don't worry about Terrence. I'll speak to him about the cleaning," Carissa said as she gave the large arachnid a hug.

After she released him, Morty's eyes settled on Peggy. He shook his head, staring at the unicorn with an expression of horror.

"Um, Morty," Dora said as she had an idea. "Why don't you clean Peggy for us? I'm sure she'll stay clean, unlike the church."

She wanted to see what state the church was in. The mention of darkness in it by Morty had confirmed her fears that there was something else happening here. Whatever it was, she didn't want it spreading to the unicorn.

"It would be a pleasure, Miss Dora. It would be a necessity," Mortimus said as he took the reins of the unicorn.

Lucian refused to let go of the reins. "I don't want a spider crawling all over my unicorn!"

"Sir, if you prefer, I could crawl all over your face," Mortimus said.

"Agh!" Lucian released the reins, and the spider gave him a short bow before he ambled off behind the church, leading Peggy behind him.

"You really think my unicorn needs a clean more than this decrepit church?" Lucian asked after he composed himself.

"No, but I think we need to find out what's happening inside the church without the evidence being cleaned away," Dora said.

She stared at the open doors of the church entrance. They were warped out of shape and covered in mold. A feeling of doom settled over her as she made her way down the gravel path towards the entrance.

Her instincts were on high alert. Something was very wrong here.

She glanced down as she climbed the steps up to the doors and noticed a red glow on her hands.

No, no, not now! This is the last place I want to look like a demon.

Her skin was tingling with goosebumps, and her body

tensed in fear. The demon part of her had gone on the defensive. It sensed danger, and it was coming out.

She heard loud footsteps echo down the hall of the church. The people around her faded away while she watched her father's dark robes swish around his legs as he came out of the shadows and walked towards her.

Memories of him burning her in Hell came flooding back, and fear consumed her.

She froze.

Demon!

The word echoed through her mind. The pain and suffering she had forgotten was a fresh wound, and the world swirled around her.

She stared down at her glowing red hands, feeling demonic power bursting to come out. She fought against it with all her will.

She glanced at her father's face in horror as his mouth formed words.

"D—" Everything went dark, and she felt herself falling.

Not again, please not again.

"…ora." She heard as she hit the hard stone of the church floor, and everything went black.

28

PARENTAL GUIDANCE

Dora groaned at the bright lights behind her eyes that were forcing consciousness upon her by waking her up. She felt exhausted and just wanted to sleep more. Every part of her body ached, and the brightness wouldn't go away, no matter how tightly she squeezed her eyes shut.

"She's waking up." A voice she recognized filtered through her thoughts. She knew the clipped tone of the voice. She tried to recall it, but her mind was a fuzzy white mess.

She unwillingly forced her eyes to open and waited for the face above her to come into focus. It took a moment for her to recognize the face above her.

"Dad?"

"Dora!" She felt her father's arms wrap around her in a tight hug. "You're okay. Thank God, you're okay."

She frowned in confusion, but hugged him back. She barely remembered the last time her father had hugged her like this.

"Are you okay?" she asked, wondering if this even was her father.

"I've seen the light," he said while hugging her so tightly, she felt as if he might crush her.

She peered over his shoulder to discover her old bedroom.

Standing in the room were Kieron, Pooey and Lucian. Kieron had his wings out, and he was peering at his feet. He glanced up at her with a sheepish grin on his face.

Her father finally released her and stood back from her bed.

She pushed herself up to sitting position and stared around her old room. There was something missing.

"Where's Mom?"

"Ah, she's on vacation." Her father looked away, refusing to meet her eyes.

"On vacation alone?" She frowned and narrowed her eyes at Theodore. He was lying to her. "Cut the crap. Where is she?"

"We'll talk about it later," he said.

"We'll talk about it now."

"Your mother and I were having some problems ..." He began before trailing off.

"Did she leave you?" She tried to process the information.

What the hell happened while I was away?

"We're on a break." Her father sighed. "Don't worry about it for now."

"A *break* is code for shagging a Greek god," Lucian added with a helpful smile.

Theodore shot Lucian a dirty look while Kieron slapped him on the back of his head.

"What? That's what I heard downstairs." Lucian rubbed the back of his head, pulling an innocent expression.

"She's in Greece?" Dora frowned. "With a God?"

"No, she's in Greece with a sleazy restaurant owner, but she'll come back." Theodore nodded.

"You okay?" she asked her father. He didn't look okay. His stubble was out of control, and he slouched and hung his head. He seemed nothing like the man she had known growing up.

He smiled at her and nodded. "Everything will be okay now that you're back."

She smiled.

He's definitely not okay.

"I must go help Terrance with dinner, but I'll be back later to check on you," he said before kissing her on the forehead and leaving the room.

"Something isn't right here," she said after he'd closed the door behind him.

She glanced around her room and frowned. Cobwebs hung from the ceiling, there were moth holes in her curtains, dust seemed to cover every surface and new books had old yellowed pages.

She jumped out of bed and scanned the room. Everything looked so old.

"Seriously, were we gone for a hundred years?" she asked as she picked up her 'Nightmare Before Christmas' plush doll. It was covered in mold and cobwebs.

"This was brand new," she said, shaking it at the other people in the room. Its head flopped off its rotted neck and

231

rolled across the floor.

They all watched the head roll in silence.

After a moment, Pooey spoke up. "Is it supposed to do that?"

"No!" She ground her teeth. "There's something wrong in this church."

"There's something wrong in all of us," Pooey said.

"What's that supposed to mean?" Kieron asked.

"Well, look at us. Dora's passing out in shock like a virgin at an orgy. You're getting more angelic every day, and me?" Pooey waved his fluffy arms around. "I'm a frikkin giant! You know how hard it is to be stealthy with these humongous feet?" He raised his stout little leg and wiggled a bear paw at them. "Earth sucks! The only person with demon form is Dora, and she can't use it when she's unconscious."

Kieron nodded. "And it's killing you." He turned to her with a sigh. "We need to set everything right again."

"How?" she asked, wondering if their alterations were affecting the world.

But that makes no sense. Only the church is messed up, not the world.

"We need to call Hell," Kieron said while peering at his feet.

"Oh yeah, you got the head of an angry boar and the blood of a demon in your pocket?" Pooey asked.

"What?" She glanced up, alarmed.

"We don't need to use old magic," Kieron said. "I've got my parents on speed dial."

"Speed dial to Hell?" Lucian raised an eyebrow.

Kieron shrugged and raised his arm.

232

A purple light shone from his fingers as he turned in a circle, creating a glowing purple circle around them. The thick beam was filled with symbols that turned around inside it on their own.

Dora stared in awe as the symbols spun around them faster and faster. She heard screams in the background as the walls of her room blurred with a purple hue.

"What the hell is this?" Pooey turned around inside the circle.

"I put it on speaker," Kieron said.

There was an urgent ringing in Dora's ears, which stopped abruptly with a ping.

"Greetings from Castle Lascher." She heard Lord Lascher's voice in her head. "Anika and I are not available right now. If your message is urgent, please press one."

Kieron frowned, and tapped three sigils in the circle of light around them.

Lord Lascher's recorded voice appeared in her head again. "We don't really care if it's urgent. Please call back when Hell freezes over." There was a loud clunk before the purple circle evaporated, and her room came back into view with startling clarity.

The disconnection from Hell seemed to dislodge the ground beneath her, and she fell onto the floor.

She shook her head, glancing around her to find that everyone else had hit the floor too.

"They put on the fucking answer machine!" Kieron cried.

"I guess that means you're disowned," Pooey said, pushing himself off the floor.

Lucian was suspiciously quiet, so Dora glanced at him.

233

He lay on his back, staring up at the ceiling with wide eyes and a pale face.

"What?" she asked.

Lucian didn't reply, so she nudged him with her foot. "Lucian, what's wrong with you?"

He jerked and quickly sat up. "What?"

"Is there something wrong?" she asked.

"Nope, nope, nothing wrong, it's all good." He rubbed his brow and then smiled brightly.

"How is that all good?" Kieron stared at him in disbelief. "We're totally screwed now."

"Dude, you look as white as a poltergeist," Pooey said as he wandered over to Lucian and poked his cheek.

Lucian stared blankly past Pooey at Kieron for a moment before shaking his head and focusing on the little brown bear.

He brushed Pooey's paws away from his face and stood up. "Because there is more than one power in this universe," he said. "I'll help you."

"How?" Dora asked.

"I'm not certain on the details yet, just gimme a bit of time." He refused to meet anyone's eyes. "I just need a moment."

They all jumped when there was a loud cry from downstairs.

"If only we could get a moment," she muttered as they all raced for the door. "What the hell is happening now?"

She raced down the stairs with the others close on her heels. The cries appeared to be begging, she realized, and they became clearer when they neared the kitchen.

She rushed down the corridor, past the organ pipes and

towards the back stairs.

"Who is that, your father?" Kieron gasped behind her as another wail came from the room below them.

"No, it—it sounds like Terrance," she said as she rushed down the stairs.

She burst through the kitchen door and then stared at the scene with wide eyes.

Carissa appeared to be holding Terrance by his earlobe. She was twisting it, which must have hurt because he was kneeling in front of her and begging her to let go.

Carissa glanced back and flicked her eyes over the group. Ignoring them, she turned back to face Terrance.

"Let's try this again," she said. "Why should we get married?"

Terrance appeared confused. He looked up at her with shining eyes. "Because you are my love, my precious gift and a gentle flower in need of my protection. I shall protect thee for all time, and you will make our home a place of love while I go out to work—OWWW!" he cried as she twisted his ear.

"Try again," she said.

"What are you doing?" Dora asked.

Carissa glanced back again. "Teaching Terrance about equality."

"I'm sure there are better ways," Dora said, peering at Terrance's twisted ear.

"No, trust me. This works." Carissa continued to twist his ear.

"My love, why do you hurt me so?" Terrance cried. "Should I not be your protector? Should I not shower you in gifts as I would a child—OWW!"

Dora shrugged. "It might take a while. Will his ear be okay?"

"Yeah, he heals pretty fast." Carissa nodded.

"Will his ego survive?" Lucian asked.

"It has so far." Carissa shrugged.

"Dora, tell her. Tell her how I am now a man of the modern age. I have dressed as a man of this new world, walked in his shoes," Terrance cried.

Dora eyed his white shoes, which appeared to be the tap dancing kind from the nineteen forties. "Where did you get those shoes from?"

"Stylish aren't they? I visited a store called 'Antique'. The good shopkeeper informed me that these were all the rage now. They are from a designer by the name of 'Retro'." Terrance gazed at his feet in awe.

"Yeah, if you want to look like Fred Astaire," she muttered. "All you need is a top hat."

"I'd very much like a top hat." Terrance nodded.

Carissa groaned. "It might take some time for him to adjust."

"No shit," Pooey said. "Let me know when he gets to the Gene Kelly stage. What? Don't look at me like that. You know you all love Singin' in the Rain."

"How do you even know about that? Do you get cable in Hell?" Dora asked.

Pooey and Kieron nodded in unison.

Lucian shook his head. "Forget the losers, dog-girl. Come stay with me. I've got the best kibble."

Carissa spun to face him, finally releasing Terrance's ear. Her eyes glowed yellow as she scowled at Lucian.

"Keep going with that, and you'll be next." She

growled.

"No thanks. I don't marry my pets," Lucian said.

"Stay away from Carissa," Terrance cried as his fangs elongated, and his eyes glowed red. "She's my pet!"

Carissa slapped Terrance across the back of his head. "I'm no one's pet! I'm the first hybrid, you fools."

Lucian grinned.

Dora slapped Lucian across the back of the head before staring at Carissa.

She remembered the spirit wolf's words.

"You can stop the war."

"What?" Carissa frowned.

"You're a hybrid child of the vampires and werewolves. You can bring peace and create harmony between the species," Dora said.

"Don't be stupid. Of course, I can't. They've been fighting for centuries."

"Yes, you can." Dora's mind was spinning. She knew that there was an answer to all of the problems on Earth if she could just connect all the dots.

Carissa frowned at her. "Who told you this?"

"The spirit w—" She jumped when there was a loud roar outside the church.

"What the fuck?"

"The spirit of what the fuck?" Carissa frowned at her.

"No, gawd, one sec," she said, waving Carissa away and turning towards the window.

"Something's going on outside." She dashed to the window and stared out into the fields behind the church. Her eyes widened in horror.

Marching towards the church were armies of

werewolves and vampires. In the distance, a massive beast marched behind them. It was a shadow of a giant.

"Aww shit," Carissa muttered behind her.

"What the fuck is that?" Lucian asked.

"Oh no, not again," Pooey cried.

"What?" Kieron peered through the window over Dora's shoulder.

"Is that who I think it is?" Terrance growled.

"WHO?" Dora shouted.

"It's my mother." Carissa sighed. "The matriarch."

29
UNHOLY SANCTUARY

"Oh shit." Dora stared at the armies of supernatural creatures heading towards the church.

She gasped when the shadow of the matriarch left the cover of the forest. Illuminated by the milky glow of the moon, the giant beast became visible. She was twice as tall as the other creatures and a mass of muscle and fur. Her fangs glinted as she moved slowly across the field behind her army of wolves, who were flanked on either side by vampires and witches.

Gunshots echoed across the field as agents of PISS darted through the trees on either side, shooting at the mass of supernatural creatures, but appearing to miss every single one of them.

Dora closed the window and locked it. "We need to lock the doors."

"We're fucked," Lucian said, peering over her shoulder.

"That's the spirit," Pooey said. "Roll over and play

dead."

"Oh, and what exactly would you suggest?" Lucian narrowed his eyes at the little bear.

"Barricade every entry point and use our collective powers to ward them off." Pooey frowned. "If they get in, then bend over and prepare for a total as—"

"Barricading sounds good." Dora interrupted. "Kieron, Pooey and Lucian, you come up with something that will keep them away. Carissa and Terrance, you're with me. We're going to seal all the exits."

Carissa and Terrance nodded, assisting her as she pushed a large dresser towards the kitchen window, blocking it off.

"What do you think?" Kieron asked Pooey. "A demon shield?"

Lucian shook his head and sighed loudly.

"What?" Kieron asked.

"You plan to use demonic power in a church, seriously?" Lucian asked.

"Why not?" Kieron frowned at him.

"You're on holy ground, dipshit. You're an angel standing on holy ground, and the best you can come up with is a frikkin demon shield?"

"I'm not an angel." Kieron cried.

"Clearly." Lucian shook his head. "But you'll do." He grinned.

"Why does that smile worry me," Pooey said.

"Don't worry. Fail-angel will be fine. We're going to use a holy ward. It'll protect the church by not allowing demonic creatures to enter it."

"What about the ones inside it?" Dora glanced up.

"They should be okay. I think it'll only fry the ones

outside of it." Lucian shrugged. "We won't know until we try it."

"What about the agents with guns?" Kieron asked.

"We can deal with them," Carissa said as her eyes glowed yellow, and she flipped over the heavy dining table, jamming it against the back door.

"This world is so uncivilized," Terrance said. "Why people can't discuss things over a cup of tea is beyond me."

Dora sighed. "Okay get the shield up. Come on." She waved to Terrance and Carissa. "Let's start barricading the upstairs and work our way down.

Kieron frowned as he watched Lucian carve a sigil into the front doors. "What's that for?"

Lucian shook his head before turning to face him. "We need to use the holy ground of the church to ward off the supernatural. These markings will create a protective shield around the church, so they need to be on all four sides of the building."

"They look like crap," Pooey said. "I've got tattoos on my ass that are more artistic."

Lucian narrowed his eyes at Pooey. "They're not for artistic interpretation."

"The sigils in Hell are nicer."

"Feel free to go back there—oh wait! You're not invited anymore, are you?" Lucian slid his knife back into its sheath at his hip.

"At least I managed to get in before, unlike a fail-warlock I can think of," Pooey said.

"I can ge—"

"Stop bickering! We need to do this now. What do I need to do?" Kieron asked.

"You need to feel the holy power inside the church and channel it. You let it expand inside you, and then send it out of you. Thinking about protective things will help you create the right aura. It should create a holy shield around the church if you do it right," Lucian said.

"So, I just think it? There's no spell?" Kieron frowned. It wasn't how Hell magic worked.

"You can chant a prayer if you want to."

Kieron realized that he didn't know any prayers, and a bubble of panic grew in his stomach. "Do I have to?"

"Not really. They're just for humans. Go on, try it."

Pooey shook his head and clambered onto one of the pews. "This is going to be an epic fail."

"Ye of little faith," Lucian muttered. "Well, you are little everywhere else. I guess it makes sense."

"The holy power of the church." Pooey waved his hands around the dingy room. "Have you seen this church? There's nothing good in it!"

Lucian glanced around the room, frowning. He walked over to the left wall and brushed moss and cobwebs away from it with his hand.

"There is something strange about this place." He admitted as he stared at the symbols engraved into an ancient-looking tablet that was embedded into the wall.

Kieron peered at the symbols. They made no sense to him. "What is it?"

Lucian was silent for a moment as he ran his fingers over the symbols. "Uh, what? Nothing," he eventually said.

"Nothing to worry about."

"You're not a very convincing liar, are you?" Pooey eyed him.

"Just forget about it. It can't be ... It's nothing." Lucian shook his head and walked away from the wall.

They all jumped when something heavy crashed against the front doors, and the fragile locks only just held them closed.

"Do it now." Lucian nodded at Kieron.

Kieron nodded and closed his eyes. He tried to feel the church's power, searching for something holy in it. He frowned when he instantly felt power flowing into him. It didn't feel holy, but it felt familiar to him.

That has to be it, right?

He inhaled deeply, drawing the power inside him. It seemed overwhelming as it filled every pore.

A murky darkness filled his mind while his eyes clouded over, and all he could see out of them was greenish mist.

Expand, he told it.

Even though it seemed to fill his body, he tried to make it bigger and more powerful. The power flooded into him at amazing speed, filling him to a point of bursting. "I can't—I can't take any more!" he cried.

"Let it out now." Lucian's voice filtered through the fog.

Kieron expelled his breath. He opened his eyes and stared up at the roof of the church, pushing the power out of his body while concentrating on protecting Dora.

A rush of pale green light clouded his eyes as he watched the power leave his body. A white beam shot up into the church above him and opened up like an umbrella around the room, spreading upwards to other floors of the building until it encompassed the entire structure.

"What the fuck?" Dora's voice loudly rang out behind him.

He spun around to see a soggy Dora scowling at him.

"What did you do?" she cried as she shook a green snotty substance off her arms. She was drenched from head to toe in green slime.

"Ugh, this stuff tastes like ass." She spat some out before picking up Pooey and wiping her lips on the top of his head.

"Hey, watch the fur." Pooey grumbled as he wriggled out of her grasp.

"Did I do it wrong?" Kieron asked.

"No, it was mostly right." Lucian replied. "I'm not sure what that is though," he said, pointing to Dora. "But the church is protected for now."

"What do you mean *for now*?" Pooey asked. "Isn't it supposed to last?"

"Well, it will do until Heckle and Jeckle start messing with it," Lucian said, peering out of the window.

Kieron rushed to the window and stared through the stained glass. Werewolves and vampires were fighting in the street outside. Howls and shrieks filled the air.

Witches were casting curses on the members of PISS while an army of squirrels were running into the barrier he had just created and bouncing off it.

Standing behind a group of holy agents were two priests. They were chanting over their prayer beads and focusing on the entrance of the church.

"What are they?"

"Exorcists," Lucian said. "Let's just hope they're stupid

ones, who don't know what they're doing."

Kieron stared at them. They were old, but their eyes were sharp, and they certainly looked as if they knew what they were doing.

He jumped back with a yelp as a rabid were-squirrel threw itself at the window, baring its sharp, little teeth.

It squealed at him as the barrier seemed to electrocute it, and it exploded on the window into red gooey clumps.

"Oh, that's just gross," he said as the bloody chunks slid down the glass.

"That's just gross?" He heard Dora ask incredulously behind him.

He turned to see her scowling at him, still covered from head to toe in slime.

He grinned as an idea came to him. "Let's get you cleaned up," he said wrapping his arm around her shoulders. "A nice shower should do the trick. Where is it?"

CHASTITY

Dora walked out of the downstairs bathroom while rubbing her hair with a towel. She found Kieron sitting on the stone pew outside it, frowning.

"What?"

"When I said we should take a shower, I didn't mean taking it in turns," he said.

"What?" She tried to fathom what he was talking about, but her mind was focused on the howling armies outside.

She walked over to the barricaded window and peered around the heavy armoire blocking it, looking out onto the lawn.

Unable to break through the barrier around the church, the armies of creatures surrounding the building had begun fighting with each other.

Groups of vampires and werewolves were fighting and clawing at each other. The witches were casting on anything that crossed their path. PISS appeared to have upgraded to machine guns and were clustered in a corner taking out anything that came near them.

"Are you my girlfriend?" Kieron asked.

"What?" The words barely registered as she frowned at the carnage outside, watching a werewolf writhe in agony as a vampire bit its leg.

"Hmph!"

She turned to face him with a frown. "This is bad. We need to do something about it."

"I know! I was trying to." He stood up and folded his arms across his chest.

"If it continues, it's going to be a bloodbath," she said.

"Well, I wouldn't go that far." He frowned. "It's just a case of communication."

"I don't think they're open to talking about it."

"They who? What are you talking about?"

"What are *you* talking about?" She stared at him, feeling confused.

"I'm talking about us!"

"Uh, what? There's nothing wrong with us." She frowned, forgetting about the howling monsters outside and seeing him as if for the first time since she'd found him. His lips were drawn into an angry tight line, and his muscles appeared tensed all over his body.

"I left Hell for you. I traveled across the Earth for you. Now we're finally together, you seem further away from me than ever!"

"I'm right here." She walked over to him. "What are you talking about?" Didn't he realize they were in a dangerous situation?

"It doesn't feel like it," he muttered.

She took his hands in hers and squeezed them.

"Everything is so messed up right now. I'm not trying to make it worse, but we can't get a minute where something bad isn't happening. I don't know when the crazy will settle down, but I'm here with you."

"So, you're my girlfriend?"

She'd never been anyone's girlfriend before. The concept was alien to her, but she nodded. She loved him. That was all that mattered. "Yes I am."

His muscles relaxed, and he wrapped his arms around her. "Okay then. That was all I wanted to know."

She snuggled into his broad chest and felt a moment of peace. It was the first time since she'd returned to Earth that she felt safe. The howls and gunshots from outside seemed to fade as she enjoyed the warmth of his embrace.

They both jumped when the old wooden door to the crypts opened behind them with a loud creak.

Her pulse raced as the door cracked open.

Did they get in through the crypt?

She stared at the door, certain she was about to have a panic attack. She sighed with relief when Mortimus skittered through the doorway, pulling the reins of a horse behind him.

She stared in awe as the horse came into view. It was an ebony mustang with pearl-colored hooves and a matching horn at the center of its forehead.

As it cantered through the doorway, its white mane brushed against the cobwebs.

Mortimus tutted before brushing them away with a long-handled, feather duster.

"Is that Peggy?" she asked, staring at the beauty of the flying unicorn.

Her black wings rested at her side. Her dark hide was glossy and smooth, and her white mane and tail shone with flecks of brushed silver.

Mortimus nodded. "Yes ma'am, but she keeps getting so dirty." He brushed her flank with a cloth, appearing to be polishing something that was already shining.

"She looks amazing," Kieron said, and the steed puffed out her chest and raised her head at his words.

"Thank you, sir. It took longer than we expected with all the ghouls in crypt, but we came through it, didn't we girl?" Mortimus patted Peggy.

Peggy snorted and neighed in reply.

"That's great, Morti—wait, ghouls in the crypt. What ghouls?" Dora stared through the open doorway.

It had been a long time since she'd been in the old crypts beneath the church, but there had never been anything supernatural down there.

"There were many down there, ma'am. They make such a mess that I had to clean Peggy several times." Mortimus shook his head. "So I thought it best to bring her up here."

A door burst open behind them with a loud crash as Lucian and Terrance tumbled through it and hit the floor.

"Both of you behave!" Carissa's voice followed them as she entered the room behind them.

"What the hell happened?" Dora spun around and peered at Lucian and Terrance, as they lay on the floor in a bloody mess.

Lucian sat up and dabbed his split lip while Terrance groaned and rolled onto his knees to stand up.

"They got bitch-slapped." Pooey's voice came from

behind Carissa as he wandered into the room.

"Trust me, they deserved it," Carissa said, peering at her feet.

"No violence in the house of God!" Dora's father's voice echoed down the hall.

"Great," Dora muttered as her father ran into the room.

"Is that Peggy?" Lucian jumped up and ran over to his steed. "What have you done to my horse!" he cried at Mortimus.

"She looks great, doesn't she?" Kieron said.

Lucian inspected the mount with a critical eye. "Is she okay? Peggy, what did that thing do to you?"

Peggy neighed and flashed her giant wings, causing a gust of wind in the chamber.

"An angel's steed!"

Dora turned to see her father fall to his knees before the horse.

Okay, that'll work.

"I'm very pleased with your work, Mortimus." Terrance told his familiar.

The giant arachnid smiled as he bowed to his master, almost glowing with pride.

"Dad, what's in the crypt?" she asked her father.

Theodore glanced up at her and tilted his head to the side. "The same things that have always been there, some catacombs, old headstones, and I think your mother might have stored some old furniture down there."

She nodded. It was just as she remembered, but something was wrong with the church. She needed to find out what it was, preferably without her father around.

"Lucian, why don't you take Peggy upstairs and feed

her? I'm sure my dad can help you find something for her to eat." She shot the warlock a look, hoping he would understand her meaning.

"What the hell for, she's a—oh, a—yes, okay. Show me the way padre." Lucian shook his head at her, wearing an expression that was full of unspoken questions.

"We'll talk about the plans later." She told him as he picked up the reins and followed her father out of the room. "We'll all be up for dinner soon. Thanks dad," she added.

Once they were out of sight, she turned to the rest of the group, who were staring at her as if she'd lost her marbles.

"Okay, we need to go into the crypt and find out what's down there. Mortimus, can you show us where the ghouls are?"

"Ghouls?" Terrance asked. "I don't like undead things."

Pooey shot him a look of disbelief. "You don't like yourself?"

"I am a complicated man." Terrance stood up, brushing dust off his waistcoat. "Often misunderstood by the world, especially the working class."

Carissa slapped him across the back of the head.

"Ow! Sorry, my dear. I mean, there are no classes anymore. We are all equal in this new world, except for wealth, etiquette, personal hygiene and blood lines—ow!" he cried as Carissa slapped him again.

"He's still learning," she said.

Dora stared at Terrance as something he said caused a flash of inspiration to pop into her mind.

"Are we going in the crypt then or just going to watch

you stare into space with your mouth hanging open?" Pooey asked her.

"What? Oh, no. Um, I just realized something important." She pointed to Terrance. "You just gave me an idea that might save us all."

"Really?" Terrance beamed with pleasure. "I have been known to be a great thinker of my time."

"Really, him?" Pooey stared at the vampire with a look of disbelief.

"Blood lines," she said. "You and Carissa can join the blood lines. Maybe it is more than just talking. What if it is actual bonding of some kind?"

"Like a blood pact?" Kieron asked.

"Yeah, they're the rightful heirs to the vampire and werewolf clans. What happens if they join together?" She considered it.

"Joining can mean many things," Pooey said.

"Well let's try blood first." Carissa extended her finger, and a sharp claw grew on the end of it.

She grabbed Terrance's hand and scratched a shallow cut into his palm. Next, she did the same to her own palm and pressed it against his.

They all waited for something to happen.

A small farting noise came from behind them.

They spun around to see Mortimus staring at his feet in shame. "Apologies, I appear to have wind."

Pooey rolled his eyes.

"What about sex?" Kieron asked.

Pooey rolled his eyes again.

"Now really isn't the time," Dora said.

"No, I mean them!" Kieron pointed to Terrance and

Carissa. "The joining of two souls comes from the act of love." He glanced at Dora. "But we will someday, in the not too distant future, right?"

She flashed him a look that silenced him before glancing back to Terrance and Carissa. "It could work."

"Well, we have been dating for over a century." Carissa appeared unsure of herself for the first time since Dora had met her. "I mean, if you want to." She refused to look Terrance in the eye.

"No, I'm not ready." Terrance widened his eyes. "It just can't happen."

Carissa raised her eyes to him, appearing hurt by the comment.

"No, I don't mean that. It's not that I don't want to, but like this. No, my love for you is deeper than the ocean. There should be poetry, sonnets of love. We shall rejoice in each other in a beautiful world."

"So, never then?" Carissa asked.

"Ye of little faith, my sweet angel." He cupped her face in his hands. "I shall show you the world my sweet girl, and we shall—" The was a loud clank as Carissa kicked him in the balls.

"What the fuck was that?" Pooey peered at Terrance's crotch.

"What?" Terrance pulled an innocent expression.

"In your pants. We all heard it." Pooey wandered over to him.

"I don't know what you mean," Terrance looked away from them all.

Carissa gasped. "Are you still wearing that thing?"

"What thing?" Kieron asked.

253

Terrance moaned. "Do not shame me, my love. I will die before I speak of it. I will take this unholy life and throw it into the wind. My soul shall weep for all time for those who absconded with my—ow!"

Carissa held his ear and frowned at him. "Is that why you won't get undressed in front of me?"

"What is it?" Kieron said. "What evil thing could possibly make a man keep his clothes on?"

"A chastity belt," Carissa said. "Something my mother had put on him when she found out we were dating."

Pooey snorted with laughter. "A virgin vampire! Ha ha!"

"You're a very cruel, little demon," Terrance said to Pooey.

"Why not just take it off?" Dora asked, staring at Terrance.

"I tried! It's made of silver and has some kind of spell cast upon it." He bowed his head. "Nothing works. The lock is unbreakable, and it really chafes."

"I know someone who can break into anything." She eyed Pooey.

"Oh, hell no!" Pooey backed up a step while shaking his head. "You've gotta be fucking kidding me. I'm not using my ninja skills to have undead junk in my face. Nu uh, I'm not doing it."

"You'll be saving us all." She cajoled, giving him her sweetest smile.

"I'm not doing it!" Pooey stamped his foot down on the floor.

"I feel violated," Pooey said as he walked out of the bathroom, carrying a silver chastity belt in his hands. "You owe me an entire planet for this!" He dropped the metal contraption onto the floor with a loud clank.

"I'll just make sure he's okay," Carissa said as she knocked on the door to the bathroom before entering it, then closed the door behind her.

"Check *he's* okay, what about me? I'm scarred for life!" Pooey stared at Dora with wide eyes.

"Now you know how I felt when you put me in your pit pocket." Kieron laughed.

"Sorry Pooey, but you did really well." Dora offered him a sympathetic smile.

"It better work," Pooey muttered.

They watched the bathroom door in silence, jumping in unison when there was a scream from within.

Carissa stormed out of the room, her face red with anger, and her eyes flashing yellow. Terrance followed her, looking humble until she slammed the door in his face.

"Is er, everything okay?" Dora asked.

"He won't do it!" Carissa said. "For how many years should I wait?" She pulled off her engagement ring and threw it in Terrance's face as he walked out of the bathroom. He caught it and stared at her with sadness in his eyes.

"What's wrong with you, man?" Kieron said. "She's gorgeous!"

Dora scowled at Kieron, who frowned back. "What? She is."

"We cannot do this until we are betrothed. My love, you are all that I think of. You consume me. But if we are not joined in the eyes of God, then we will never be truly joined." Terrance fell to his knees before Carissa and pleaded with her, holding the ring out to her. "Marry me, my love."

Pooey wiped a tear from his eye after rolling around on the floor laughing. "You're undead, and she's a were-thingy. You think God is watching over you?"

"Shut it," Dora said to Pooey out of the side of her mouth.

"My father can marry you." She told Carissa and Terrance. "And we are in a church ..."

Terrance smiled up at Carissa, who was biting her bottom lip as a smile seemed to grow on her face. "Can we really get married?"

"Of course you can," Dora said.

I'm going to Hell anyway. This can't hurt, right? I'll just tell dad they're holy beings.

Carissa took the offered ring from Terrance's hand and smiled. "Yes. I'll marry you," she said.

Terrance jumped up and crushed her in his arms, overjoyed by the news.

"Okay then, you guys go and tell the priest to get his wedding outfit on while we check out the crypt," Dora said.

The happy couple were both beaming with joy as they left the room.

That's gotta be a good thing, right?

She wasn't sure, but it felt like a good thing. She turned to Kieron, Pooey and Mortimus. "Let's find these ghouls, shall we?"

Dora yelped as she walked through a cobweb, and the clingy strings covered her face. She urgently brushed them off her, and goosebumps popped up all over her body. She shuddered as the thought of spiders crawling all over her filled her mind.

Kieron rushed to her side and brushed her back and shoulders. "It's okay."

"It's a bit lame," Pooey said. "Do you do the same thing when feathers brush past you?"

"It feels so creepy." She turned towards the little demon. "You try a face full of spiders, and see how you feel."

Pooey pointed to Mortimus, who was staring into his face. "Been there, done that."

"It wasn't me, ma'am." Mortimus' hollow voice echoed through the crypt.

She tried to shake off the feeling and continued through the crypt. It seemed so much darker than she remembered.

Mold grew up the walls, and the ancient stone was cracked in places she didn't recall it being cracked before. Dust and cobwebs covered every inch of the place, and it was much colder than she remembered.

Their footsteps echoed through the large chamber as they made their way through broken old furniture and ancient catacombs.

A sharp breeze howled through the room from an unknown source.

She turned her head to try to locate the source, but the gloomy darkness was only lit by the tiny windows dotted along the top of the room, showing moonlit grass.

She shivered and rubbed her bare arms. There was something dark here, a presence that seemed familiar and alien at the same time. She had played in these crypts as a child, and—although her mother called it morbid—she had never felt unsafe here before. It had been an adventure for her, a place where she could become lost amongst the ancient engravings.

"Just how old is this church?" Kieron asked as he brushed dust and cobwebs away from one of the many stones engraved into the wall.

"Dad said it was over a thousand years old, but I don't think anyone really knows. They had some archeologists down here once, but they couldn't understand the symbols." She pointed to the strange sigils on the engraving. "Some of it is Latin, but some of the other stuff isn't any known language."

"Maybe someone got bored with Latin down here." Pooey wandered over to the engraving and frowned at it.

"That one is ancient Greek," he said, pointing to one

of the symbols.

"Can you read what it says?" She was intrigued. She'd always wondered what these stones said.

"Nah, there's only one word in Greek. The rest is swirly bullshit if you ask me. Also, what kind of moron writes in ancient Greek and Latin on the same tablet?"

She stared at the tablet. It was the largest and oldest in the crypt. It was made of light limestone. Of all the things in the crypt, it appeared to be the only one that wasn't cracked or marred by time.

The stone went from roof to ceiling, making up a section of the wall, jutting out a little to create shallow alcoves on either side of it. It was covered in engravings of words she didn't understand that mingled with a few words she did.

She could read the words: holy, death and repentance. Out of hundreds of engravings on it, those were the only ones that made sense. But they were so far apart from each other the sentences could mean anything.

"What does the Greek word mean?" she asked.

At least I can add a new word to my collection.

"Gatekeeper," Pooey said in a dark voice.

They all jumped when there was a loud creak behind them. The sound was sharp, as if old metal was being ground against stone.

She spun around to see a pair of feet in sensible shoes dangling through an open window across the room from them.

"They must have broken the barrier." She gasped as she rushed around the old furniture to try to stop the person or creature entering to church.

"I'll stop them," Kieron cried as he vaulted over the furniture to try to reach the intruder before they got through the window.

Meanwhile, the pair of legs lowered into the room, stopping abruptly when the person's large ass became stuck in the narrow window frame.

"Damnation!" a familiar woman's voice cried as Kieron reached her feet.

"Wait!" Dora cried. She knew that voice.

"Mom?"

"Dora honey, is that you?" Her mother jiggled half in and half out of the window as if trying to turn around. "Are you a ghost?"

"No, I-I didn't die," she said.

"But we buried you!" her mother cried.

"I know."

Kieron glanced at Dora, shrugging in her direction as if waiting for instruction on what to do next.

"Help her get in here," she said.

"Her ass is never going to fit through that window." Pooey commented as he jumped onto one of her legs and used his weight to pull them down.

"This ass can get into anywhere it likes." Her mother wriggled in the tight space.

Dora rushed over, and she and Kieron tugged on her mother to try to get her through the window. Her legs were taut, and she appeared to stretch.

"Mom, are you okay?" she asked.

"Just keep going! Nearly there." Her mother gasped.

Dora pulled as hard as she could, and there was a loud popping sound as her mother's backside cleared the window.

They all fell into a heap on the hard stone floor.

Her mother rolled over and groaned, peering at Dora. She reached for her and held her face in her hands.

"My baby girl!" she cried before hugging Dora tightly against her.

Dora hugged her back before releasing her.

"Mom, what are you doing here? I thought you moved to Greece?"

"Don't be silly. I was only on vacation with some friends." Her mother brushed away the question and some cobwebs at the same time.

"We should close the window ma'am." Mortimus' hollow voice echoed from a few feet away from them.

"Gah!" Her mother yelped, jumping to her feet and brandishing her large tan handbag as if it were a sword. She pointed it at Mortimus.

"Out of my home, you vile monster!"

"Mom, it's okay. He's a good giant, talking spider." She glanced lamely at Kieron. There weren't many explanations she could come up with for Mortimus.

Kieron offered her a helpless shrug before reaching up to close the open window. It ground out a painful creek as he slid the bolt into place and locked it.

They all stared at Mortimus, who was dusting one of the catacombs with a feather duster.

"He's using my feather duster." Her mother narrowed her eyes at him.

"He likes to clean things." Dora shrugged.

"I don't like other people cleaning my house." Her mother growled. "Hey you, spider thing, stop that!"

Mortimus glanced up at Josie with innocent eyes. "But

it is dirty, ma'am."

"Are you calling my house dirty?"

Dora winced at the violence in her mother's voice. There was only one thing that brought out the beast in her mother, and that was someone implying that her house was dirty. "No, he doesn't mea—"

"Yes, ma'am. It's very dirty and moldy." Mortimus nodded, oblivious to the explosive vibes coming off her mother.

"Who gives a shit?" Pooey said as he untangled himself from Josie's legs and stood up.

Her mother glanced down at Pooey before turning back to Mortimus.

Her face paled as if the blood had drained completely out of it, and her eyes widened. She turned to face Pooey while stumbling backwards into an old gravestone. "What the hell?"

"It's okay, Mom. He's a—"

"Nice talking, teddy bear?" Her mother finished with widened eyes.

"Did someone drug me? Am I hallucinating?" She pressed herself against the stone and rubbed her eyes.

"A fucking teddy bear?" Pooey took a step towards Josie.

She scrambled back and tried to climb over the stone. "Keep it away! I hate LSD trips."

"Mom, it's okay, he—" Dora paused and frowned. "Wait a minute, when did you have an LSD trip?"

"Oh come on, everyone did in the eighties ..." She paused and turned to face Dora. "I mean what? It must be jet lag. That's what I meant, jet lag."

"I'm not a teddy bear." Pooey growled. "I'm a dem—
"

Wind howled around the room, making them all jump. Screams echoed around the chamber, and the gales forced them all back against the walls.

"What the hell is going on?" Dora cried as she tried to brush her ebony hair out of her eyes when it flew around her face in wild tendrils.

The wind slammed against them in harsh gusts.

She glanced at Kieron, who was straining his muscles to try to unpin himself from the wall.

"It's the ghouls," Mortimus said.

She glanced in the direction of his voice. He was flattened against her mother, who did not appear impressed.

"Ghouls don't look like that," Pooey said, staring ahead of him.

Dora glanced at the cloudy swirls in the center of the room. There were twisting gray shapes mingling in the chamber. They had a greenish tint to them as they swirled in the howling wind.

She frowned when agonized faces appeared in the smoke, distorting and stretching with each howl.

"What the fuck is that?" She shouted over the din.

"I don't know," Kieron cried as he pushed himself off the wall and staggered towards it. The swirling mist shrieked at him, sending him tumbling backwards a few feet. "But I'm getting rid of it." He growled and stood back up, every muscle in his body tensed.

With a determined glance at her, his wings shot out of his back and flashed across the large room. He reached into the swirling mass with his hands, as if trying to grab the ghouls inside it.

She stared in awe as the muscles in his bare back rippled, and a golden glow surrounded him. He ripped into the smoke and tore it apart with his bare hands.

Something shone bright white behind him. She frowned, staring at what looked like a doorway on the far wall. The ancient stone was still mounted on the wall, but there was a gap between it and the wall, as if it were ajar. A blinding glow shone through the tiny gap.

What the hell is that? It looks like a door!

Kieron roared as the smoke tried to smother him. He spread out his wings and arms with a force that shook the foundations.

The strange door ahead of him opened a tiny bit wider as the cloudy swirls exploded into mist and evaporated.

The howls disappeared, and the wind faded away.

She exhaled slowly and stared at Kieron, who had fallen to his knees.

She rushed over to him and knelt beside him.

"How did you do that? Are you okay?" She brushed her fingers through his short blond hair.

"I don't know, and I don't know." He smiled at her, and she tightly hugged him against her.

"I don't know what you are, but you have some powers now," she whispered in his ear.

"What was that?"

She glanced back to see her mother hugging both Mortimus and Pooey. Her hair stuck out in a crazy mess, and her eyes were wide with shock.

"Um, we're not sure, but it's gone now," Dora said. She was telling the truth for once. Whatever it had been, it wasn't in the crypt anymore. The place felt like it used to again—a dusty old playground that was full of history.

She rose to her feet and winced as her mother untangled herself from Pooey and Mortimus.

"Where's your father?" She was as white as a sheet and shaking all over.

"He's upstairs," Dora said, feeling sorry for her mother. "I'll take you to him."

"As long as I never get mommy hugs again, that's fine with me," Pooey grumbled, brushing dust and cobwebs off his brown fur.

"I quite liked them," Mortimus said.

Pooey shot him a disgusted look. "No shit! Is there an apron you haven't clung to yet?"

"You leave Mortimus alone," Josie said. "Bad bear!"

Pooey narrowed his eyes, but Dora spoke up before he could say what was on his mind. "Let's get out of here."

She guided everyone towards the stone stairs that led up to the ground floor of the church, glancing back at the stone tablet as they left.

It remained ajar with a bright light shining behind it.

When this is sorted out, I'm coming back and opening that door.

UNHOLY MATRIMONY

The church shook as if an earthquake had hit it when Dora entered the main chapel. She gripped onto the doorframe and glanced behind her to see her mother grab onto the stone banister of the stairwell for balance.

Mortimus collided into Pooey crushing him against the wall. Behind them, Kieron was bracing himself against both walls, his eyes wide as he looked up at her.

"What the hell?" She gasped as hairline cracks appeared in the wall beside her.

She heard shouts coming from the main chapel and instantly reacted, dashing into it and down the aisle towards the voices. The footsteps of the others following her pounded on the stone floor behind her.

She found Lucian, her father, Carissa and Terrance all standing at the front of the church, near the main doors.

Lucian stood at the window beside the doors, purple energy surrounding him as he shot blasts of it out of the window. Carissa and Terrance were trying to pull her father away from the doors.

"You can't open them!" Carissa cried.

"But the church is falling apart." Theodore struggled to reach the door handle.

"Block the doors!" Lucian cried as he shot another purple beam out of the open window, aiming it at something on the other side.

"What's going on?" Dora called out as she rushed towards them, followed by the others with Kieron now running at her side.

"Heckle and Jeckle are taking down the barriers," Lucian said as he shot another blast of purple at them through the window. "And that big bitch is gathering her armies outside the door."

"What can we do?" Kieron asked as he rushed to the window and peered out of it.

"Shoot at the priests before—" There was a loud bang, followed by the crackling of electricity in the air.

Dora glanced up to see the golden dome surrounding them cracking open and fading away.

"That happens," Lucian muttered. "Shit!"

"Theodore?" She heard her mother gasp behind her.

She glanced back to see her mother staring at her father as if she'd never seen him before. "What happened to you? You look so ... so rough."

Her father spun around, and his eyes widened.

"Josie!" For a moment, they stared at each other in silence. Then her mother blushed at Theodore before they rushed into each other's arms.

Dora turned her eyes back to the window when they started kissing.

Eww, parent snogging. Well, at least they're not fighting.

The church shook again. "Do something, warlock. Cast a stronger spell." Terrance shouted at Lucian.

"This is all I've got." Lucian scowled at him. He looked drained, and the purple light around him had faded.

Dora peered out of the window. The old priests were fast on their feet as they continued reading while dancing out of the way of Lucian's purple blasts. "What do we do if the barrier breaks down?"

"Get ready for war," Lucian said, shaking his head.

"Put up a new barrier then. What else are you good for if not that?" Terrance asked.

Lucian spun around to face Terrance with narrowed eyes. "Why don't you do us all a favor and go and get laid. Then you can start throwing around commands like a real man and stop whining like little a bitch."

"Why you damnable scoundrel!" Terrance cried raising his fists and taking on a boxing pose that hadn't been seen since 1901. "I challenge you to a duel."

"That's it!" Dora interrupted.

"A duel?" Lucian glanced at her with a look of disbelief passing over his face.

"What? No, don't be stupid. How are you two going to step outside? Marriage is the answer." She turned to face her father. "Dad, can you marry Terrance and Carissa?"

"Will that keep the barrier up?" Her father looked skeptical as he glanced up at the golden dome, which now had a gaping hole in the top of it.

"No, but, just trust me. It'll work. It has to." Dora pushed him towards Terrance and Carissa. "Quick, and very romantic—"

The golden dome cracked down the left side and the church shook. "But, a very quick ceremony, right now!"

"But don't we need to arrange the flowers and catering? I watched a show about wedding planning. Is it not customary to spend outrageous amounts of money and purchase lots of things that have nothing to do with marriage to make a wedding work in this era?"

Terrance glanced at Carissa. "And shouldn't she have a dress?" He folded his arms. "I will not do it, not unless my love has the perfect day!"

"Fuck," Dora muttered under her breath. "Lucian, how long will that barrier hold for?"

"You want it in minutes or seconds?" Lucian said.

"Fine, then we're going to invent a speed-wedding. Kieron, you're the best man."

"Why, thank you." He smiled, clearly misunderstanding her meaning.

Dora slapped herself in the forehead.

"Dad, can you take the groom and the best man to the altar while Mom and I get the bride ready?"

"Of course, my dear." Her father ushered Kieron and Terrance down the aisle.

"Morty, can you come with us?"

"Am I the maid of honor?" The giant spider excitedly jumped up and down while clapping his front legs together.

"Yeah, sure, why not." She glanced around at Carissa, who nodded while wiping a tear of joy from her eye.

"Lucian, are you okay dealing with Heckle and Jeckle?"

"Do I have a choice?"

"Pooey can help."

269

"What good is he going to be?"

"Er, hello. Planning battles and winning wars since 320BC." Pooey pointed to himself.

"Seriously?" Dora asked.

Pooey just stared at her with a disappointed expression.

"Okay, I'll take that as a yes."

"Fine, help me take out these fucking exorcists." Lucian turned to the window. He glanced back at Dora. "Do hurry the fuck up, or we're screwed."

She nodded and hurried her mother and Carissa into the choir room, followed by the skittering sound of Mortimus as his feet clattered on the stone tiles behind them.

They entered a room full of musical instruments and clutter.

Dora tried to focus on wedding things, but the constant, loud cracks of electricity distracted her as the dome fell apart around them.

What's going to happen if they get through the doors? Will any of us survive?

She forced herself to focus on joining the bloodlines. It was their only chance.

"Okay, a dress," she said to herself more than anyone else. She scanned the room, and a sliver of white lace caught her eye as it hung out of one of the wooden lockers at the end of the room.

She rushed over to it and pulled open the door. A white choir gown hung inside the locker. It was old with lacy sleeves and a lacy collar. It could pass for a white dress, or possibly a tent, but it was white and frilly.

Surely, we can make it look decent.

She picked up the hanger and showed the dress to

Carissa and Mortimus.

"Can we do something with this?"

Carissa scowled at the gown. "I'm not wearing that."

Mortimus pulled a tape measure out of his pocket and measured the length of the gown before eyeing Carissa. "Yes, I think we can."

"How long will it take?"

"Twenty minutes if you have a sewing machine."

"I have one in the spare room," Josie said.

"Excellent. Show us the way." Mortimus took the gown from Dora and guided Carissa towards Josie.

Dora followed them, listening to the sounds of the dome cracking around them. "Just hurry up."

I hope this fucking works.

"Do you Terrance, take Carissa to be your—"

"Hurry the fuck up!" Lucian shouted from the other end of the room as the dome loudly splintered and crackled.

Dora glanced up. The dome was no longer golden. It had become almost transparent and was barely holding back the raging armies outside of it.

"Really, it's a wedding. Have some respect," Josie said, shaking her head at Lucian, who promptly flipped her off when she turned her back to him.

Dora glanced at Terrance and Carissa. They looked like a beautiful Victorian couple. Terrance's suit was a sleek black one that fitted him like a glove.

Mortimus had done wonders with Carissa's gown. Brocade lace covered her from the neck to shoulders, trailing down to fitted white cloth that skimmed her waist and fell down over her hips into an elegant train behind her.

Pearls and jewels sparkled on the material, and her dark hair was curled up in an elegant twist. With the pewter tiara from her mother's jewelry box, she looked like a princess bride.

Dora's eyes traveled across to Kieron, who was standing beside Terrance and wearing one of her father's suits. It fitted him far better than it ever had fit her father.

When she met Kieron's eyes, she found he was gazing at her with a bright smile on his face.

Something about the sparkle in his eyes made her look away from him.

She nervously smoothed down her red silk dress. It had been an impulse buy that she'd never had the opportunity to wear, and the only thing she owned that was suitable for a bridesmaid.

She peeked back at Kieron and offered him what she could only assume was a dopey grin before snapping herself out of it.

Now is not the time for girly thoughts!

The dome shimmered. "We're not going to make it!" Pooey cried from the back of the room.

"Dad, hurry it up a bit," Dora said.

"Fine." Her father flipped through some pages in the bible he held. He slammed the book closed when a loud bang hit the front doors.

"Do you?" he asked Terrance.

"I do. For my love eternal, yes I take thee Carissa, my—"

"Do you?" Theodore asked Carissa, cutting off

Terrance's unending vows.

"I do." Carissa smiled, and she gripped Terrance's hand.

"Kiss!" Pooey shouted.

"I now pronounce you husband and wife. You may kiss the bride." Theodore rushed out as the front doors of the church burst open and an army of beasts flooded into the chapel.

The couple leaned closer and kissed each other, seeming oblivious to the dome cracking and disappearing around them while howls of werewolves filled the air.

33

INNER DEMONS

Dora turned towards the doors.

Why aren't they stopping?

She glanced back at Terrance and Carissa, who were still kissing. The newlyweds appeared oblivious to the carnage at the entrance of the church.

She shook her head and ran down the aisle when she saw Pooey knocked aside by a large werewolf claw and slammed into a wall.

She let out a growl as she charged at the mangy wolf, but someone grabbed her arm, yanking her back.

She stumbled back into a hard chest and turned to scowl at Kieron, who was gripping her arm.

He shook his head. "You can't. You'll die. Stay here!"

She frowned as he raced past her, ripping off his jacket and shirt. His giant wings flashed out of his back, spanning across the room as he flew into the fray. Blasts of white light shot from his hands as he pushed back the oncoming armies.

What? I'm supposed to just stand here? Kiss my ass!

But on some level, she knew that he was right. The second she used her powers, she'd just pass out like a limp rag anyway.

She sighed and watched the fight, itching to smash something every time she saw someone hurt her friends.

Lucian cast dark purple energy at a pack of werewolves, sending them flying back through the doorway. Meanwhile, Pooey had jumped up and launched himself at a nearby vampire.

"Why isn't the wedding working?" Pooey yelled from on top of a vampire. He paused to bite the creature's ear, making it howl in pain. "What the fuck is going on?"

"I don't know." She stared at her friends, and a feeling of helplessness washed over her. They were all fighting for their lives against a mass army of creatures, and she was just standing here.

What good am I to anyone if I can't fight?

"Screw this. I can still fight as a human," she muttered as she watched a werewolf making a beeline towards her mother.

Her mother stood in front of the pews with wide eyes, her hand hovering over her mouth. She stared in awe as a giant wolf bounded towards her.

Dora narrowed her eyes and hunched low as she charged at the wolf. She plowed into it with all her human strength, knocking it into a wall.

The wolf shook its head and blinked a few times before snarling and turning on her. Its yellowing teeth were dripping with saliva as it menacingly growled at her.

Her pulse raced, and she stumbled and fell back onto her ass.

A shiver of fear shuddered down her spine as it stalked towards her, emitting a low growl.

Its eyes seemed to bulge out as the church's sanctuary lamp crashed into the top of its gray furry head. Then the creature's face took on an almost comedy pose as its tongue lolled out of its mouth, and it slumped sideways onto the floor.

Dora glanced up to see her mother holding the heavy golden stand of the sanctuary lamp. She was watching the wolf with fury in her eyes as she bonked it on the head again.

"I think it's out cold, Mom." Dora glanced at the unconscious wolf in awe.

Great, even my mother is a better fighter than I am.

"Better safe than sorry," her mother said as she hit the wolf on the head once more.

"Shiii—t!" Pooey's cry echoed behind her and ended with a loud crash.

She jumped to her feet and spun around to see Pooey sliding down a wall with bits of broken vase and a heavy bronze donation plate falling with him. The plate bounced off his head and rolled across the floor, stopping with a loud clatter a few feet away from him.

"Mom, stay back here!" She called behind her before dashing towards Pooey, who lay in a crumpled heap on the floor.

As she raced across the room, something hard slammed into her side, knocking her off her feet.

She rolled onto her back to see a pair of vampire fangs descending towards her face. Her fingers brushed against the edge of the fallen donation plate.

She grabbed it, sliding it in front of her face like a shield.

There was a loud clank and the sound of teeth grinding on the other side of the bronze plate.

"Oww, you broke my fucking tooth!"

Her breath whooshed out of her as the vampire hovering over her landed heavily on top of her. She peeked over the plate to see Pooey mounted on his back.

"We're not finished yet, bitch." Pooey snarled at the undead as he smacked him on the top of the head with a clawed paw and dug his talons into the vampire's nostrils before pulling his head back.

The vampire yowled in agony, rolling sideways and taking Pooey with him.

She sat up and watched the tiny demon wriggle out from beneath the creature, who jumped to his feet and faced the little were-bear.

Pooey raced behind the vampire and bit him on the ass.

The vampire howled and ran for the doors with an angry Pooey attached to his backside by his teeth.

She was about to laugh, but it got stuck in her throat when the doors flew off the church. Shattered pieces of wood, brick and masonry exploded into the room as a massive beast with wolf-like features broke through the entrance.

The beast's vicious claws ripped their way through the vampires in her path to get to Pooey, who had released the vampire he was biting and appeared to be frozen on the spot.

Her fur was long and dark, her giant body a combination of rippling muscle and bulky fat.

The matriarch. Dora realized as wolves bowed to her when she passed them.

A loud cry made Dora look left to see her mother

pinned to a wall by a vampire.

Her father leapt onto the creature's back, knocking it down onto the floor. He pinned it down with his body and began slamming its head into the stone floor, knocking the undead unconscious with the assistance of her mother, who was still brandishing the sanctuary lamp.

A blinding flash of light lit the room.

Dora turned to face it, seeing Kieron glowing with pure golden light.

He turned to face the matriarch and strode towards her. His wings flapped, blowing gusts of sharp winds against her armies.

The wolves cowered back, but she stood and faced him with a sadistic smile on her face.

The Ancient One flew at her from the side with a roar, his sharp fangs glinting over his goatee.

The matriarch flicked him away like a bug with her massive paws, and he crashed into the right wall.

Kieron flew at the matriarch, his tanned skin glowing golden, and his muscles taut and tensed. He didn't get within two feet of her before she knocked him sideways.

Four wolves leapt onto him, tearing into his wings with their sharp teeth.

No!

Dora jumped to her feet and tried to dash towards Kieron, but a vice-like grip grabbed her wrists and pulled her backwards.

An arm wrapped around her throat, and she struggled to get free. Whatever was holding her was so much stronger than she was, and she helplessly watched as a pack of violent wolves tore into her angelic boyfriend.

She barely felt the teeth graze her neck as she watched Lucian throw himself into the pile up, trying to pull the wolves off Kieron.

Why isn't he using his powers?

It became clear that he couldn't when he tried to cast and only a purple fizzle shot from his fingers.

Pooey flew past her and slammed into the choir room door. She was pretty certain she heard tiny bear-bones crunching as he slid down the old oak door with his eyes closed.

Let me go you son of a bitch!

She fought against the hold on her, punching and kicking out into fresh air.

The creature behind her grunted in pain as she kicked back and connected with his kneecap.

He hissed, spinning her around and hoisting her up into the air by her throat.

She gasped and choked in his grip, staring down at the bloodied teeth of the vampire before he slammed her back down onto one of the pews, knocking the air out of her.

His cold fingers wrapped around her neck, pinning her down. She stared into his dark eyes that gleamed with a wicked glint as her vision blurred.

"Normally, I like it when they struggle." His sharp voice filtered through the fog that had settled over her mind.

He leaned over her, and she could feel his torrid breath on her cheek. "But now really isn't the time. I'm just here for some fast food." He opened his mouth and descended onto her neck with lightning speed before she felt his sharp fangs sink into her flesh.

She tried to ignore the grotesque gulping sounds as he

drank her blood. She struggled to try to get free of his grip, but he was too strong, and she was too weak.

All she could do was push against an iron-grip that wasn't going to move anytime soon and get increasingly angrier over her own pathetic humanity.

Fuck this. Better a demon than a vampire snack.

She fought against her frustration, closing her eyes to concentrate on summoning up all the power inside her and call forth her demon form.

Her skin heated up, and her blood seemed to boil inside her as something dark shuddered through her body. She used her lessons from Hell and directed all of her hate at the vampire that was sucking on her neck.

A dark ball of energy in grew her chest, expanding into every vein and pulsing power through her body.

The vampire coughed and pulled away from her, holding his throat as he choked. Black blood spilled over his lips as he fell to his knees before her, gagging.

As the black liquid rolled down his chin, it left burned skin and pustules behind. Like acid, the black liquid was eating away at his flesh.

She glanced down at her hands. They were glowing red with long black claws extended from each finger. She smiled. Even though she knew it might be her last fight, she felt powerful and strong.

She stood up and faced the vampire. "That's what you get for drinking demon, idiot." She told him as he keeled sideways, and the glint faded from his eyes.

She strode down the pews to the end of them, feeling power course through her veins as she turned to face the battle.

She focused on the matriarch as she headed towards the growing armies streaming through the doors. Wolves and vampires leapt at her, but she knocked them back with strength that she shouldn't possess.

She felt her body shifting into something else, something new. She raised her hand, expecting to see a tiny crossbow on it, but finding a heavy sword carved in black stone in her grip instead.

She twirled the sword in her hand with expertise that she didn't possess as she advanced upon the creatures.

She didn't stop to think about how she felt as she sliced her way through the supernatural beings and rushed at the matriarch.

"Get the hell out of my house." She roared, knocking wolves and vampires aside with ease.

The blood seemed to drain from the matriarch's face as she neared her.

Dora glanced at Kieron. The wolves had climbed off him to stop and stare at her. Kieron was staring at her too with concern in his bright blue eyes.

She shook her head. It didn't matter what happened to her as long as everyone was safe.

She swung her sword at the matriarch with all of her might, intent on clearing the church of every invader before she lost her demonic powers.

Rather than hitting the giant beast, the blade smashed into a million shards on impact, and the room froze.

Dora frowned, dropping the remains of the blade.

The hilt hovered in the air as if frozen in space.

She stared at it for a moment in shock.

What the fuck?

She glanced around the room. Everyone was frozen in place, and the room was silent.

Shit! What did I do this time?

She ran to Kieron's side. He was snarling with a dark look that she had never seen on his face before as he clawed the werewolf out of his way to try to get to where she had been standing. Both of them were frozen in time.

She reached out a hand to touch Kieron's face. It was ice cold.

"What the fuck is going on?" she cried, and her voice echoed around the silent chapel.

She spun around to stare at the frozen room, wincing and covering her eyes when a blinding white light exploded all around her.

34

WINNERS AND LOSERS

K ieron watched the matriarch fall backwards after Dora's blow.

He jumped to his feet and flew at the massive creature, intent on finishing her off.

He was knocked back before he reached her by a force of energy that exploded into the room and sent him, and everyone else, crashing into the walls as a flash of white light lit the room before it faded.

He shook his head to try to clear it as he watched the crowd of creatures in the entrance all do the same.

He winced as he pulled a wolf claw out of his side, pressing his hand over the open wound and ignoring the pain.

I guess someone is missing a claw.

Glancing beside him, he noticed Pooey slumped against the wall a few feet away.

"Hey." He reached across and shook the little demon. "Pooey?"

"Fuck off," the were-bear muttered as his eyes fluttered open.

"Are you okay?" he asked.

"Do I look okay?" Pooey ground out.

Kieron stared down at him. His fur was ripped off in places, and he had cuts and gashes all over his body.

"Er, no."

"Well spotted, dumbas—" Pooey's eyes widened as he stared ahead of him.

Kieron turned his head to face the armies ahead of him too. He frowned. They were all scrambling into a kneeling position and facing the altar with their heads bowed. Vampires and werewolves knelt beside each other in submissive poses.

He eyed the matriarch, who was not kneeling, but shrinking.

"Get up! Fight!" She shrieked in a girly voice as her fur fell from her body, and her muscles diminished before his eyes.

She was turning into a human. A short one with blonde ringlets, he realized as her body shrank, and her canine features disappeared.

"I command you to fight!" she cried, but none of the creatures acknowledged her existence.

"Did Dora do this?" he asked Pooey, and the little bear shrugged.

There was a rustle of curtains to the side of them.

He turned and peered past Pooey to see Terrance and Carissa slipping out of the confessional booth, holding hands. They both wore a satisfied smile while giggling and whispering in each other's ears.

"I think someone finally got laid, and did this." Pooey grinned.

The werewolves and vampires all bowed their heads as the couple approached them.

"Well hello, fellow supernatural beings," Terrance said. "Have you come to celebrate our joyous day?"

"What? The day you finally get laid?" Pooey asked.

"Our wedding day!" Terrance appeared appalled by Pooey's comment. "How dare you speak so rudely before my innocent bride?"

Carissa punched him in the ribs. "What?" She growled.

"I mean my beautiful wife." Terrance quickly amended his words while gasping in pain.

"Better," she muttered. Then she stared at the kneeling masses, and her eyes locked onto the matriarch.

"Mother?"

"I think it's the Queen Mother now." The small blonde ground out. "Can I at least get a frikkin shirt to put on?" She was crossing her arms over her naked body.

No one moved to assist her, so she rushed into the choir room and came out shortly afterwards wearing something that resembled a red tent.

"God, it's awful." She glanced down at the gown.

"You shall wear that in the dungeons until you have paid for your sins as a ..." Terrance trailed off under the glare of his new bride.

"Sorry dear, you were saying?" He turned to Carissa, offering an apologetic smile.

"You shall be banished back to Malton until I forgive you," Carissa said.

"Noooooooo!" her mother cried. "I hate that place. It's

creepy as hell!"

Carissa nodded at the army of creatures ahead of her. "Take her away. Then leave this church, and go back to your homes. This war is over."

Kieron watched in awe as the vampires and werewolves all stood and turned towards the doors.

Those near the matriarch restrained her, leading her, kicking and screaming, out of the church.

"This war is not over!" A red-haired witch cried as she stood up and began casting a murky gray ball of energy in her hands.

"Down bitch," Lucian muttered as he got to his feet and shot pale blue energy at the coven of witches.

Their glossy hair all spiked out in a frizzy mess, and hair extensions fell to the floor around them. Each witch screamed and put their hands on their heads.

"No master! Do not take away your gift," a brunette witch cried as her face sagged with instant age, and her two front teeth fell out onto the floor.

"Beauty is in the eye of the … ah, screw it. You're not twenty-four anymore, sweetheart. Get used to it, and get lost." Lucian shook his head as his coven ran from the room screaming, their bodies and faces all aging with each step.

Kieron's stomach flipped over as the one who had snogged him stumbled by, looking more like an old age pensioner than a hot witch.

He pushed himself up the wall until he was standing. He was relieved that the battle was over. Every muscle in his body ached, and he just wanted to sleep for a week.

"You are under arrest, demons!" The Black Bishop stepped forward, pointing a gun at Terrance.

"All of you, put your hands u—eeeeeeeee!" His command was cut short as Pooey raced forward and bit him on the balls.

"Dude, you're going to need mouthwash after this battle," Kieron said to the little bear, who nodded while still biting the bishop and making him shriek louder.

Agents of PISS ran forward with their guns all pointing at Pooey, but they stopped when Theodore rushed down the aisle, waving some kind of printout in his hands.

"Halt in the name of the Pope!" he cried.

Everyone turned to stare at Dora's father, who hurried towards them while gasping for air.

"I just got off Skype with the Pope." He panted for a moment before continuing. "Sidney Simkins, you have been relieved of your post as the Black Bishop and recalled to Rome." Theodore handed a piece of paper to the still yowling bishop before snatching the hat off his head and placing it on his own.

"And, I am honored to report that I am the new Black Bishop." He showed the printouts to the members of PISS, who all paused to read them.

"Where's the official seal?" One asked.

"The Pope said he'd send it via UPS, so it should be here by the end of the day." Theodore smiled at his new subordinate.

The man in the black suit saluted him. "What are your orders, sir?"

"Ah, orders, right." Theodore paused for a moment. "Okay, let's carefully detach the foul-mouthed bear from ex-bishop without harming either of them." He nodded at Pooey, who shrugged, released Sidney and walked over to stand beside Kieron.

"Okay, that's done. Right, I think you boys can take Sidney to Rome. The Pope is awaiting his arrival."

Theodore lowered his voice. "In handcuffs is probably for the best."

The suited men nodded as they holstered their guns. Two of the agents grabbed Sidney and led him towards the doors.

"Would you like some of us to stay here for your protection, sir?" One of the men gestured at the remaining supernatural creatures.

"Ah, no. I'm surrounded by my loving family and an angel." Theodore hugged Josie to his side and gestured to Kieron. "My duty is to work with these creatures, as now is yours. We are all God's creatures. If we are to bring peace and work together, then we must always keep that in mind." Theodore offered a serene smile.

The PISS agent nodded and saluted again. "Yes sir, a new world it is then." He turned on his heel and walked out of the church, and the other PISS agents followed him.

Kieron scanned the room for Dora, wondering how she would handle her father being the Black Bishop.

He frowned when he couldn't see her.

He tried to recall the last place he'd seen her. She had been fighting the matriarch near the doors.

He turned to face the entrance of the church, which was now a broken gaping hole in the front of the building.

A wisp of black fluttered on the top stone step of the entrance.

With a feeling of dread, he walked towards it, recognizing it as a black curl of hair as he drew closer to it.

He sped up and raced towards the doorway when he saw a mass of ebony curls draped over the steps. He fell to his knees as shock trembled through his body. He couldn't breathe and the world around him faded away as he stared down at her body lying on the hard stone.

Her skin was paler than usual. Her dark eyelashes and red lips a startling contrast to the pale skin surrounding it. She lay on her side with her knees bent and one arm stretched out behind her.

He touched her neck. Two bite marks marred her skin.

He felt for a pulse, but there was no beat. Her body was still and cold. No breath inhaled or exhaled.

He was silent, unable to scream. Inside his head, he was screaming, but outside he was trapped inside his body.

He hauled her into his arms and hugged her cold body close to his, rocking back and forth with his eyes closed in unbearable pain.

His body shuddered with locked up emotion. Tears escaped his clenched eyelids and slid down his cheek, falling onto her hair.

Pain wracked his body, and his muscles clenched in silent anguish.

She was dead. He couldn't feel her near him anymore.

Dora was dead.

35

HEAVEN'S DOOR

Kieron slammed his fist into the dresser in Dora's room, cracking the wooden surface with the blow and knocking a pile of books off the side of it. *Damn this world!*

He slowly exhaled, trying to control the rage that was building up inside him. It had taken them hours to make him let go of her body. Only after they had convinced him that he might be able to bring her back had he allowed them to take away her body.

A small sigh behind him reminded him that he wasn't alone.

He turned to look at Pooey, who was perched on her bed. His eyes were wide with sorrow as he looked up him.

"She can't die. She's a demon," Kieron muttered for the hundredth time.

"She wasn't a demon when she died," Pooey said.

"Why does it matter? She's somewhere right now. Maybe we can find her." Kieron couldn't face the idea of a world without Dora in it.

There has to be a way.

"She sacrificed herself. You know that will never get you into Hell." Pooey knelt to pick up the books that had fallen onto the floor.

"So? We'll go to Heaven then."

"Oh yeah, because that's so easy. How?" Pooey angrily waved a green book at him.

Kieron frowned, staring at the green tint on the grimoire in the little bear's hands.

"Where did you get my mother's cook book from?"

"Er, the floor, you dumba—"

"Holy shit!" Lucian gasped as he entered the room, his eyes locked onto the book.

"What?" Kieron clenched his fists. The warlock knew something, and it was about damn time he told them what it was.

"Oh, nothing." Lucian smiled and turned to leave.

Kieron launched at him, knocking him to the floor and pinning him down.

"Enough bullshit! Tell me what you're hiding before I beat it out of you." All Kieron could see was red as he stared at the warlock. Dora was dead, and this son of a bitch knew more than he was telling.

Lucian rolled over, scowled and shot Kieron off him with purple blasts of energy before he getting to his feet.

He rubbed his jaw and frowned at Kieron. "What the hell is wrong with you, boy?"

Kieron landed on Dora's bed and sank into it. He could still smell her scent on the pillow, so he buried his face into it.

"I need her." He managed to mumble into the pillow.

"Then stop acting like such a child, and go and get her then!" Lucian cried.

"Oh, know how to get into Heaven, do you?" Kieron heard Pooey's voice filter through the pillow.

"Actually, I do."

Kieron jumped off the bed and pulled the warlock into the room, shutting the door behind him.

"Tell me! Tell me everything. Please, help us bring her back."

Lucian sighed, shaking his head. "Look, I only know a few things. I don't know if you can get her back, but fine. Okay, I'll tell you what I know."

He snatched the book out of Pooey's hands and held it up. "This is your mother's. I recognize it. There is only one reason it would be here."

"How do you know my mother?" Kieron asked.

"I might have met her in limbo a long time ago." The warlock shifted his eyes to the dresser, refusing to look him in the eye.

"You're an angel!" Pooey cried.

"What?" Kieron asked.

"No. Not you, him." The were-bear pointed to Lucian with wide eyes. "I knew you smelt funny for a reason."

"I am not an angel." Lucian shook his head. "I was an angel once."

Pooey slapped his forehead. "The Fallen One. A fallen fucking angel! That's how you ended up in limbo."

Lucian narrowed his eyes and strode towards Pooey, looking as if he planned to strangle the little bear, but instead he flopped face-first onto the carpet halfway across the room, appearing to lose his balance on fresh air. "Oww."

"I thought it was because he fell over a lot." Kieron frowned at the fallen warlock.

Lucian rolled onto his back and stared up at them both.

"Fuck it. I fall over a lot because in Heaven the axis is different. When you come to Earth from Heaven, it's like walking sideways up a wall, difficult to master. But when you're dropped out of Heaven like a rock and fall, it's impossible to realign with the Earth's axis."

"So he's right? You were an angel." Kieron stared in awe, as events seemed to connect in his mind. "And you knew my mother, and I'm half angel, and …"

"Hold on there, sport. I didn't create any demon spawn if that's what you are asking."

"Then why are you here? Why did you stay with us all this time?" Kieron didn't believe him. "Are you my father?"

"Fuck." Lucian rubbed his brow. "I don't know. It was a long time ago. You know, a trip to limbo, a hot demon girl and a fallen angel get crazy on power in a stationary cupboard. You don't expect this to be the result." He pointed to Kieron. "But who did what and when is not really important right now, is it?"

"Not important?" Kieron roared. "You didn't even look for me!"

"I didn't know you fucking existed!"

"You tied me to a fucking tree!"

"I thought you were a regular angel, self-righteous mother-fuckers that they are."

"You called me Angela!"

"I always wanted a little girl, but I guess with all this whining, you'll do."

Kieron snarled and leapt towards Lucian, missing him by an inch as he rolled sideways into a standing position while Kieron landed hard on the ground, knocking the air out of his lungs.

"Is that anyway to greet your daddy?" Lucian's voice filtered down to him, making him even angrier.

He rolled over onto his back and stared up at the ex-angel, feeling hate and anger boiling through his veins. "You're not my father."

"Finally, something we both agree on," Lucian said. "So shall we carry on with saving Dora instead?"

Dora.

The name caused a wave of sorrow to pass over him, making his anger fade away as the pain inside his chest crushed his heart with a vice-like grip. "Can we save her?"

"I think so. Well, kinda. I wasn't sure until I saw this." Lucian picked up the green spell book and waved it at him.

"It's just a moldy book from Hell." Pooey frowned.

"No, it's not." Lucian shook his head. "I gave this book to your mother. Did you know that?" he asked Kieron.

Kieron shook his head. All he knew about the book was that his mother never left Castle Lascher without it.

"It's a special book. In fact, it's not even a book. Not really." Lucian flipped through the pages.

"What is it then, a fucking bicycle?" Pooey asked.

"It's an anchor. When I met Anika, we exchanged some gifts—spells to be exact. I gave this spell to her. If she ever wanted out of Hell, she could anchor herself to Earth with this book. Think of it as a passport from Hell." His eyes widened with realization. "That's why this church is such a shithole!"

"Huh?" Kieron frowned, feeling confused.

"The decay, the book will decay the place it is anchored to. It was meant to open a door, but not to leave it open for a long time. Your mother must have left the door to Hell open."

"So we can go back to Hell?" Kieron asked. "Dora might be there!"

Lucian shook his head. "She's not in Hell. I knew someone had died when the white energy flashed. That's a soul going to the gates of Heaven. She's up there, but the question is do you want to drag her back down here? You could just go home."

"The only place I belong is with Dora." Kieron scowled at the suggestion.

"Ditto." Pooey stamped his foot on the ground.

"Okay then." Lucian nodded. "There is something weird about this church. You can't anchor the book just anywhere. It's an angel spell. It takes real holy power to lock the anchor here."

"You guys can sneak into Hell whenever you want?" Pooey narrowed his eyes. "Isn't that cheating?"

"Trust me, you can't stay long, and it's punishment watching what you can't have," Lucian muttered.

"Why'd you fall out of Heaven anyway?" Pooey asked.

"That's not really important is it?" Lucian averted his eyes and then turned to stare out of the window. "Anyway, where was I? Oh yes, this church isn't just a church."

Kieron sat up and stared at Lucian's back. It was a lot to take in.

He can't be my father. Look at him! He's not that much older than me!

"What else is it then?"

"According to the plaque downstairs, it's a door. Heaven has more than one gate, more than one door. There are a few of them on Earth. I didn't know this was one until I saw the engravings."

"So we can go through the door into Heaven?" Kieron jumped to his feet.

"In theory," Lucian muttered.

"What does that mean?" Pooey narrowed his eyes at the warlock as he turned around.

"These gates haven't been used in millennia. They're like old sewer tunnels running underneath Heaven. Some are blocked, others forgotten. Angels rarely come to Earth anymore."

"So what? We go in one, and we try." Kieron jumped to his feet. "And we're taking Dora with us."

"Her corpse?" Pooey wrinkled up his nose. "Won't it start to smell?"

"I'm not leaving her behind."

"She'll get a new body in Heaven," Lucian said.

"I'm not leaving her!" Kieron snapped and slammed his way out of the room, heading towards the crypts.

Kieron sucked in his breath as he entered the crypts. Dora's family had laid her out on a stone altar with white lace draped over her from head to toe. Lit candles surrounded the altar, and there was a photograph of her at school resting near her feet.

He picked up the photograph and smiled at her

scowling expression. She hadn't been meant for school or a uniform, even back then. He narrowed his eyes.

She's not meant to die either.

"She was blessed to know you." Theodore's voice cracked as he spoke behind him.

"I was the one who was blessed." Kieron turned to face her grieving father. "She deserved more than she ever got."

Theodore nodded in agreement, and a stray tear rolled down his cheek. "She'll be safe in Heaven now, but God help me, I wish she was still here instead."

"We're going to bring her back." Kieron said before he placed the photograph back on the altar and clenched his jaw in determination.

"Isn't that a sin?" Theodore looked hopeful, regardless of the blasphemy.

"Not if I ask God himself."

"That's what I was looking for!" Lucian rushed down the stairs, staring in Kieron's direction. He dashed towards him and straight past him.

Kieron turned around and peered at the ex-angel.

He was running his fingers over the stone engravings in a plaque on the wall.

"Yes, this is the gate!" he cried. "Okay, angel-boy. Open it."

"Oh finally, we find it after looking through the whole frikkin church," Pooey muttered as he walked into the chamber, angrily brushing cobwebs off his fur.

"How?" Kieron asked, staring at the stone block. It was already slightly ajar.

He peered through the gap, only seeing darkness inside.

"Do your angel thing." Lucian nodded. "Then you can

all be on your merry way."

"But, you're coming with us, aren't you? We need a guide." Kieron had no idea how to open the door or how to get out of a Heavenly sewage system.

"No, what? You'll be fine. I believe in you, son." Lucian patted him on the shoulder.

"If you don't come with us and show us the way, then I'll make sure I tell every single angel about how their 'fallen one' landed on Earth instead of Hell where he belongs." Pooey said in a low voice "Fail-angel, you are going to take us through Heaven to find Dora."

Lucian narrowed his eyes. "This is going to suck. Fine, whatever, open the fucking door."

A sharp draft blew through the room, and the lacy voile over Dora's body blew off as a ghoulish howl echoed through the catacombs.

"Ah crap, the Hell door is going to be a problem. One sec," Lucian muttered as he cast a blue light upon Kieron's mother's grimoire. The book glowed turquoise, expanding and cracking in his hands.

"Say goodbye to going home boys," he said as it exploded into a thousand pieces and fell to the floor in a fiery mess, eventually burning up into cinder.

"Goodbye Hell." Pooey sadly mumbled, scuffing his feet on the stone floor.

The howling wind disappeared, and Kieron walked over to Dora's body. He leaned over and kissed her forehead.

"I'm going to bring you back," he whispered as he scooped her up into his arms. He stared at the door and flashed his wings while gripping her tightly against him.

He summoned every ounce of power inside him to get

through the gate.

A familiar golden glow surrounded him and Dora. For a moment, she felt warm in his arms.

The cracked door began to open, and the tunnel inside appear lined with silver and gold as it glowed at them while the door swung wide enough for them to enter.

"I don't know why you're bringing that. She's not in there." Lucian muttered, pointing to her body as he stepped into the tunnel.

"I don't know why we're bringing you, but shit happens." Kieron followed him, scowling.

"Good luck, and say hi to God for me." Theodore shouted after them.

"We'll get his autograph for you," Pooey muttered as he warily stepped into the tunnel. "And probably lightning bolts up our asses for breaking into Heaven," he added quietly.

They all spun around as the door slammed shut behind them with a loud crash.

Kieron caught a last glimpse of Earth, and the hopeful expression on Theodore's face as the door closed.

He sighed and turned to stare down the tunnel. It seemed to be an endless golden road with shiny silver walls.

"Which way?" he asked Lucian.

"This is a very clean sewer," Pooey said.

"Depends on your opinion of clean," Lucian muttered.

"What do you mean?" Pooey glanced at him.

"Angel piss comes out golden." Lucian pointed to the ground.

"Oh, gross!" Pooey stood on tiptoes. "You couldn't have got me some shoes before we came in here?"

"Which way?" Kieron shouted. There was no time for messing around. He needed to find Dora.

He glanced down at her body and gasped.

She was glowing golden.

"What's happening to her?"

"Aww shit." Lucian winced.

"What?" Dora's body was warm and glowed like the sun.

"Okay, don't freak out when—"

Kieron hugged her tightly.

It can't be this eas—

He froze as her body began to fade and disappear in his arms.

No, no!

No matter how tightly he tried to hold onto her, she evaporated into gold dust and disappeared.

"Where is she? What happened!" He turned on Lucian with fire burning through his veins.

"Fuck. Chill out. It's okay. She's just been processed, that's all." Lucian rolled his eyes. "Fucking admin, they never get it right."

"Processed?" Kieron asked.

"When a higher being enters Heaven, they are processed differently. Angels don't have to wait at the gates. They get their wings and get to work. It appears that Dora's demonic body has been mistaken for an angelic being, so she's probably being sent with her body to …" He trailed off with a look of shock on his face.

"Where has she been sent?" Kieron ground out the words, trying not to strangle Lucian.

Lucian winced. "Camp Angel."

"What the fuck is Camp Angel? Are they going to send my demon ass there?" Pooey gripped onto Kieron's leg.

"No, they probably only noticed Dora's body because she was dead and in need of healing. This whole place has sensors all over it, so watch your fucking tempers here too. And er, Camp Angel is really lame." Lucian narrowed his eyes.

"Well, at least we know where to look for her," Kieron said, determinedly striding down the tunnel.

"This is going to suck," Lucian muttered, following him.

"This sucks more!" Pooey cried, jumping after them barefoot, trying to avoid golden puddles.

36

CAMP ANGEL

Dora shifted uncomfortably on the hard plastic chair. She'd been waiting here for hours now. She glanced around the white room. It wasn't just white. Everything in it was white.

Talk about too much white space. She thought as she stared at the desks at the end of the long room. There were signs above them, which glowed golden with the words:

CHECK IN HERE

The people behind the desks were stamping people's arms as they queued to pass through the check-in area.

She considered making a run for one of the desks to ask them what the fuck was going on, but shook her head. Last time she tried that, she'd been flung back into her chair by an invisible force.

I need to get back to Kieron and the battle. What if they are in trouble?

"Takes a while, doesn't it, deary?" A croaky voice said to the left of her.

She turned around to face a blue-skinned old woman.

"I don't even know what I'm waiting for," she said.

The older woman patted her on the knee. "Ah, the impatience of youth, not to worry, my dear, you ended up in the right place, and in a far better state than that guy." She nodded to the other side of Dora.

Dora turned to face the person on the other side of her. It was a man in a business suit with a hoover end stuffed up his nose.

His nose was stretched to an impossible size to accommodate the hoover pole wedged into it, and blood dripped down his face onto his white shirt.

He nodded and smiled at her. "I wisch theysh hurry ish up," he gurgled.

She offered him a sympathetic smile and nodded before turning back to the old woman.

"Where are we?"

"Limbo, honey, we're outside the gates of Heaven. Oh lord!" She held her hand to her purple lips. "Don't you know?"

"Know what?"

"You died, sweetheart. You're going to Heaven."

Dora stared forward while she tried to process the information, but it just didn't compute.

How the fuck did I die? How the fuck did I get into Heaven?

"I think there's been a mistake," she said.

"Oh ho, looks like you're right." The lady nodded to a man in a white suit who was hurrying down the room

303

towards them while staring directly at Dora.

"They don't send anyone down for a soul. We just wait in the queue."

She listened to the man's white shoes clatter on the tiles as he rushed down the long room towards her.

Uh oh, busted.

He frowned when he reached her, then glanced down at the paper in his hands. After a moment, he shrugged. "You're in the wrong place."

"I know," she said. "I'm not supposed to be here."

"No you are not, but these things happen from time to time. Not to worry, we're sending you back."

"Oh, that's a relief." She smiled. She had been concerned about being stuck in Heaven. It was the last place she belonged.

"Are you ready to go home?" the man asked as he placed a hand on her forehead.

She nodded and closed her eyes, looking forward to seeing Kieron and Pooey again.

"Off you go then," he said.

A bright light flashed behind her eyes, making them snap open in shock.

Her body jerked backwards through the wall, passing straight through it as if she was a ghost.

She fell down into a glowing tunnel, crying out in panic as she fell into a shining white abyss. Her cry ended when she landed on a hard, wooden floor.

She groaned and shook her head for a moment.

"God, that fucking hurt!" she muttered.

A foot rested on her back and pressed down.

"Blasphemy! A million push-ups, recruit!"

She peered back over her shoulder to see a massive angel standing over her. He wore a white uniform with gold plating on it. His muscles bulged under the uniform as he cracked a golden whip against his hand.

"You've gotta be fucking shitting me." She gaped at him.

Where the hell am I?

He cracked the whip near her face. "You're a trainee warrior of the Lord, a recruit at Camp Angel. Act like it, you sniveling reptile!"

She stared ahead. Through the bunker door, she saw an army of angels marching by in formation with white explosions going off in the distance behind them.

"Shit!"

THE END

READ THE NEXT BOOK

Heaven just turned out to be worse than Hell!

After being killed, Dora Carridine was shipped off to Heaven, but she's not ready to give up her life just yet, especially not when it means spending eternity in Angel boot camp.

She does everything in her power to try to get home, but nothing works. Even if she manages to escape Camp Angel and survive the sadistic drill sergeant, she still doesn't know how to get her body back.

Powerless and alone, she decides that there is only one thing she can do. Dora has to find God, and hope he's not a sanctimonious dick.

CAN'T WAIT FOR CLAIRE CHILTON'S NEXT STORY?

Let her know by leaving stars and telling her what
you liked about

DECEASED DORA

in a review!

FREE BOOKS

Enjoy Claire Chilton's free books. Try out her
other series for free or read more of this series on
any device with **Free Reads**.

claire-chilton.com/free-books

WANT TO TALK TO OTHER FANS?

Visit *claire-chilton.com* and join the discussion.

AUTHOR

After completing her honors degree in English Literature, Claire Chilton was interviewed to work for MI5. Fortunately, for the sake of the United Kingdom, she did not get the job. Now a web designer and graphic designer with a passion for great stories, she writes about the adventures she'd like to have.

A prolific writer with wide-ranging interests, Claire specializes in romantic and speculative fiction, which includes genres such as mystery, science fiction, fantasy, horror, comedy and romance. Her mystery romance novel, *Hustle*, won Harlequin's *So You Think You Can Write* contest in 2013, and her previous books in *The Demon Diaries* won the *Most Read* award on Wattpad.

After exploring the world in her misspent youth, traveling across Europe, Africa, and the Caribbean, she now lives in an ancient Roman city in Yorkshire with her Californian husband and a fluffy kitten called Shadow, who is convinced she is a bigger cat than she is.

You can find Claire online at **claire-chilton.com**.

www.ingramcontent.com/pod-product-compliance
Lightning Source LLC
Chambersburg PA
CBHW031657170626
46808CB00005B/149